MY YOUTH ROMANTIC COMEDY IS WRONG, AS I EXPECTED
Wataru Watari
Illustration Ponkan⑧
3

Contents

MY YOUTH ROMANTIC COMEDY iS WRONG, AS I EXPECTED

Wataru Watari
Illustration Ponkan⑧

VOLUME
3

NEW YORK

MY YOUTH ROMANTIC COMEDY IS WRONG, AS I EXPECTED Vol. 3
WATARU WATARI
Illustration by Ponkan⑧

Translation by Jennifer Ward
Cover art by Ponkan⑧

YAHARI ORE NO SEISHUN LOVE COME WA MACHIGATTEIRU.
Vol. 3 by Wataru WATARI

Original Japanese edition published by SHOGAKUKAN.
English translation rights arranged with SHOGAKUKAN through Tuttle-Mori Agency, Inc., Tokyo.

Yen On
1290 Avenue of the Americas
New York, NY 10104

Visit us at yenpress.com
facebook.com/yenpress
twitter.com/yenpress
yenpress.tumblr.com
instagram.com/yenpress

First Yen On Edition: September 2017

Yen On is an imprint of Yen Press, LLC.
The Yen On name and logo are trademarks of Yen Press, LLC.

Library of Congress Cataloging-in-Publication Data
Names: Watari, Wataru, author. | Ponkan 8, illustrator.
Title: My youth romantic comedy is wrong, as I expected / Wataru Watari ; illustration by Ponkan 8.
Other titles: Yahari ore no seishun love come wa machigatteiru. English
Description: New York : Yen On, 2016–
Identifiers: LCCN 2016005816 | ISBN 9780316312295 (v. 1 : paperback) | ISBN 9780316396011 (v. 2 : paperback) | ISBN 9780316318068 (v. 3 : paperback)
Subjects: | CYAC: Optimism—Fiction. | School—Fiction.
Classification: LCC PZ7.1.W396 My 2016 | DDC [Fic]—dc23
LC record available at http://lccn.loc.gov/2016005816

ISBN: 978-0-316-31806-8

10 9 8 7 6 5 4 3 2 1

LSC-C

Printed in the United States of America

Cast of Characters

Hachiman Hikigaya........... The main character. High school second-year. Twisted personality.

Yukino Yukinoshita........... Captain of the Service Club. Perfectionist.

Yui Yuigahama.................. Hachiman's classmate. Tends to worry about what other people think.

Yoshiteru Zaimokuza......... Nerd. Dreams of becoming a light-novel author.

Saika Totsuka.................... Tennis club. Extremely cute. A boy, though.

Shizuka Hiratsuka............. Japanese teacher. Guidance counselor. Single.

Komachi Hikigaya............. Hachiman's little sister. In middle school.

Kamakura.......................... The Hikigaya family cat.

Sablé................................. The Yuigahama family dog.

MY YOUTH

Superlong titles are getting a bit stale.

Twin Blades Cross: Metempsychosis of the Inverted World

(abbreviated to "Twin Blades")

Coming up with the fan nickname before the book even comes out is so cringey. Just don't.

Protagonist: Yoshimitsu Ashikaga

I appreciate that you didn't just make this your own name.

The legitimate heir of Shogun Ashikaga's line. Reincarnation of Yoshiteru Ashikaga. Usually, he hides his powers, but in emergencies, he fights gallantly with his beloved blade, Kagedachi, in hand. He learned the sword from his grandfather, but when he was very young, his grandfather died protecting him from an enemy attack. Ever since then, he has chosen to fight alone in order to keep people connected to him from getting into danger. He is deliberately aloof, and though no one understands his stance of staying alone in order to protect others, he doesn't care. He's the greatest swordsman of the present day. It is said his strength surpasses that of the master swordsmen generals of old. His hidden blade, Nihil, has the power to end wars. It nullifies his opponents' moves, abilities, and techniques. His foes perish.

You M-2 syndrome types really like your nullification powers.

So then when did he learn to use a sword?

I appreciate the effort to make your name sound cool and English-y.

Rival: Bright "Swordian Master" Woodstock

Have you even Googled what homeomorph means?

Seventeen years old. Final boss. As the leader of the mirror world, he is the most skilled among them. Yoshimitsu's homeomorph. Though he was born in a mirror world that was created as a copy of the original world, he has doubts about his world and how fake it seems, and seeking meaning in his life, he heads into the other world alone to fight. His hidden blade, Thousand Blades of Mirage, instantly copies his opponent's moves, abilities, and techniques, so he can hit you a thousand times at high speed. If two people have exactly the same powers, then, inevitably, the stronger person will win, and that's what makes his powers the best. His foes perish.

You M-2 syndrome types really like your copy powers.

Familiar: Nakuharu

Small fry. Not only betrays you at the drop of a hat but is superweak. He's technically Bright's subordinate, but Bright basically only lets him hang around out of pity. He's trash. He's skinny and short, but he likes fancy clothing and has brown hair. He's a gossip and likes being a part of a group. He wears a headband. He has this habit of saying, "*Agh*, what a pain in the ass," and "Something here smells rank." Dies immediately.

This part seems oddly specific. This has got to be based on someone. Who? Someone in Class C? The darkness in your heart is deeper than I thought.

1

This is how **Shizuka Hiratsuka** kicks off a new competition.

I slapped a stack of crap thick enough to rival the Dead Sea Scrolls onto the table. "What the hell is this?"

I'd made the mistake of starting my day reading a manuscript that sent uncanny shivers down my spine. The source of my anxiety and déjà vu was, of course, the background material for Zaimokuza's sequel. *Finish the first book before you write the sequel, Zaimokuza.*

The draft was incoherent, no two ways about it. Even at the plotting stage, contradictions already abounded, and the whole thing was a mess. About the only thing the story had going for it was the aloof swordsman serving as its main character.

Solitude reigns supreme. Real heroes don't need friends.

To be unapproachable is to be strong. No connections means nothing cherished. "Something to protect" is just a euphemism for a chink in the armor. The Greek hero Achilles had his heel, and the powerful warrior monk Benkei Musashibou had his lord. If not for their weaknesses, history would have remembered them as winners.

Therefore, the strongest person is someone with no vulnerabilities, nothing to hold dear, and no connections with others. In other words, me.

The only realistic part of this dreck was the loneliness of its cheating, OP swordsman. The rest was garbage, so let's take a red pen to it. *G-A-R-B-A-G-E*… There we go.

I was basking in a job well done when my little sister, Komachi, finished making breakfast. Our parents both work and had already left the house, so it was only Komachi and me in the dining room. My sister sported an apron as she set out two places at the table. *Hey, wait, don't wear an apron with a tank top and short shorts. It makes it look like you're naked underneath.*

Before me was a golden-brown scone and some coffee. There were also a few jars of jam. The fragrance of the well-toasted scone and the aroma rising from the exquisitely pure coffee danced together in a harmonious *suite* before the colorful array of *sweet* jam. It was a *suite pretty cure* for my morning hunger.

"Thanks for making this," I said.

"Yep, eat it all up~. I'm gonna dig in, too!"

The two of us put our hands together, and then Komachi raised the scone to her mouth in a cutesy little motion. "Breakfast today is pretty fancy, huh? Kinda Englandish with the scones and everything."

"What the hell is *Englandish*? Your new power move?"

"No, it means 'super England-like.'"

"Are you serious? I think that's called 'British.'"

"Oh, Bro. 'Brit' isn't a country."

"Internationally, England is known as Great Britain or the United Kingdom. That's why if you want to say 'English-style,' you say 'British.' The more you know."

"I-I don't need your trivia! That's just one of those fake English words Japanese people made up! Like Great Gitayuu!"

I don't think Great Gitayuu is a pseudo-Anglicism. Ignoring Komachi's weak excuse, I pulled the condensed milk toward me. By the way, if you add condensed milk to regular coffee to make a MAX Coffee–style drink, it's called "Chibish" coffee. And a basketball anime set in the near future would be dubbed *Baskish*. Uh. I think. "But anyway, I thought English people drank black tea," I said.

"I know, but you like coffee better, Bro. So I think that's worth more Komachi points."

"Yeah, maybe you're right. I wish that kind of point system were real… Things would be so easy to understand," I answered. Life sure would be simpler if yeses and nos and affection ratings were clear and

open on a display. If someone gave you a firm "no" accompanied by numerical proof supporting the fact, then you wouldn't harbor any delusions they secretly like you, so you'd have no trouble giving up on them. That alone would be a saving grace to many poor boys out there.

As I slurped down my DIY MAX Coffee, Komachi dropped her scone with a splat. White as a sheet, she trembled like a leaf. "Y-you're acting weird, Bro..."

"What?"

"You're acting weird! Usually when I say stuff like that, you get all mean and cold and act like I'm annoying, but that's how I know you love me!"

"You're the odd one here." *Just how hypersensitive to these details are you?*

"Anyway, all jokes aside," Komachi began, but as I was unsure how much was actually a joke, it was kind of freaking me out. If my sister was the kind of depraved individual who liked guys who snubbed her, I had no idea how to approach her anymore. Maybe I'd just ignore her every day and rack up those Komachi points. What a twisted sibling relationship.

"You haven't been yourself lately, Bro. Kinda apathetic... Though you've never had much ambition anyway. Oh, and you've got this rotten look in your eyes... I guess they've been that way all along, too. Oh, I know! It's like your jokes are all half-assed...like they have been for a long time now. Mm... Something's just off!"

"Are you worried or insulting me? Pick one." I couldn't tell if she loved or hated me here. "Well, it's been humid out lately. It makes everything rot faster. Including eyes and personalities."

"Ohh, now, that was kind of witty!"

In the face of such sincere appreciation, I cheered up a bit, letting out a rather proud chortle. *Wait. Now that I think about it, wasn't that actually kind of backhanded?* "You know, though... June has too many damn insects. Why is there no debugging software for summer?"

"That one was bad."

"I-is that so..." Komachi's pun standards were surprisingly stringent. It was oddly crushing to watch my triumphantly delivered witticism get shot down. I understand a little how Miss Hiratsuka feels.

Thinking of Miss Hiratsuka reminded me that I had to get going to school. If I was late, she'd give me more punishment whacks. I washed down the rest of my breakfast with my Chibish coffee and called out to Komachi. "I'm about to leave."

"Oh! Coming!" She stuffed her cheeks to bursting with scone, like a chipmunk, and cheerfully began taking off her clothes. *Seriously, stop changing in here.*

"I'll head out first."

With Komachi's drawn-out "Okaaay!" at my back, I walked through the front door and into the distinctive humid air of the rainy season. I couldn't recall having seen a sky this blue since the day of the workplace tour.

X X X

The damp atmosphere hovered thick inside the school building. The entrance teemed with students in the morning rush, making the area increasingly suffocating and uncomfortable.

There is a tendency to imagine the loner ensconced in a dark corner, but in point of fact, as the resident loner of our class, I comported myself in a grand and stately manner. Thus, I was the eye of the hurricane, a single, isolated air pocket in the school.

People with lots of friends must have suffered in that crush of protein at thirty-six degrees Celsius in such humidity. Loners are unusually comfortable during the rainy season and the summer. They can lead well-ventilated lives at school.

I changed into my indoor shoes by the entrance and raised my head to see a familiar face.

"Oh..." Yuigahama was slipping on loafers with squished heels and avoiding my eyes with a lost expression.

I greeted her as I always did, without turning away. "'Sup."

"...Oh, hi." We didn't speak after that. She adjusted her bag on her shoulder, and then the decrescendo of a single person's departing footsteps rang out against the chilly linoleum floor. The noise faded into the rest of the din.

Even after the weekend had ended, things were still awkward

between Yuigahama and me, and this had been going on for the past week now. Before I knew it, it was Friday again. She didn't give me that obnoxious greeting in the morning or accompany me to the classroom, and I returned to my old, peaceful life.

Okay. Nice. I'd managed to completely reset our relationship.

A loner, by nature, burdens no one with their existence. By avoiding entanglements with others, they cause no harm. We are extremely ecologically friendly, clean, and environmentally aware creatures.

By returning our relationship to square one, I had reclaimed inner peace, Yuigahama had been relieved of her debt to me, and now she could go back to her old normie life. I didn't think it was the wrong decision. No, I was right. I mean, she had no reason to feel obligated just because I saved her dog. It was mere chance, a total coincidence. Like finding a wallet on the ground and taking it to the police, or giving a senior citizen your seat on the train—that level of charity. Plus, it was the kind of thing you could secretly brag to yourself about afterward, like, *Man, I just did such a good deed! Now I'm way different from all those shallow idiots out there. I'm a real man!* There was no need for her to agonize over simple happenstance, and even less for her to feel liable for the fact that I started high school as an outsider, since that was inevitable anyway.

That was why the matter was closed now. Our rapport had returned to its factory setting, and now we could both go back to normal. You can't reset your life, but you can reset relationships. Source: me. I haven't been in contact with a single person from my middle school cla—Wait, that's not resetting. That's deleting. Tee-hee.

X X X

The tedium of sixth period was over. I was a diligent student with integrity, so I didn't talk to anyone in class and passed the time in silence.

By the way, sixth period was oral communication, so I was practically forced into an English conversation with the girl next to me. Right when we were supposed to start, though, she began fiddling with her phone. I thought the patrolling teacher would catch us, but thanks to my class skill *Obfuscation*, I escaped detection. *Not bad, Hachiman.*

But, like…when would this status effect wear off? Even after the day-end homeroom class, the effects still persisted, and nobody noticed me at all as I quietly packed up my things. *What the hell? Am I a spy or something? Oh man. I might just get scouted by the CIA. But if AIC comes and recruits me by mistake, I'll be a good boy and make another* Tenchi Muyo! *OVA.*

As these thoughts crossed my mind, I could hear frivolous commotion unfolding at my back as if to tell me, *This is what high school is all about!* The kids in the sports clubs made their leisurely preparations for practice, abuzz with complaints about the senior club members or their advisors. The arts clubs chattered and exchanged smiles as they asked things like *What did you bring for your snack today?* And those in the just-going-home club droned about their plans to hang out after school.

One voice among the crowd was particularly loud and boisterous. "I'm so jealous of the soccer club guys. Their advisor is gone today." My gaze happened to follow the sound, and I saw Hayama chatting in a circle with seven boys and girls. The disgruntled remark had come from Ooka, the assimilating virgin from the baseball club.

The Yamato guy from the rugby team nodded his agreement, and the blond party guy, Tobe, took the idea and ran with it. "Man, it's hilarious. You guys still have club. Man. What're we gonna do? What're we even gonna do today?"

"I'm up for whatever." Miura left the planning to him, typing away at the phone in her right hand while *sproing*ing her drill-shaped curls with her left, as if utterly disinterested in what Tobe was saying. Flanked by Ebina and Yuigahama, the queen of the class reigned supreme as usual.

Tobe lit up with sudden fervor for the task. "Oh! Then why don't we go to Thirteen and One? Doesn't that sound good?"

Miura paused for a beat and then smacked her cell phone shut. "Huh? No."

…I thought you were up for whatever. I reflexively interrupted their conversation in my head. This is how loners polish their witty comebacks, day after day. My eyes flicked toward Miura and her clique. Yuigahama was among them, and that was when our eyes met. Though we acknowledged each other's existence, we did so wordlessly.

"……"

"……"

If I had to create an analogy, it was like when you're at the station near your house and you see someone from your middle school class waiting on the platform one train door over. When you notice him, you're like, *Whoa, it's Oofuna…* and he's like, *Oh… Who was that again? H…Hiki… Oh, whatever.* That sort of situation. *C'mon, man, don't give up trying to remember me.*

Oh, but, like…i-it's not like the other guy just couldn't recall who I was. My memory is just exceptional. I have a superior brain. Loners are surprisingly adept at remembering names. It's probably because we work ourselves into a lather thinking, *I wonder when they'll talk to me.*

Just how good is my memory? This one time, I called out to a girl by name even though I'd never spoken to her, and her face twisted in fear, like, *How does he know my name…? Scary…*

Well, enough about me. Basically, Yuigahama and I were a pair of first-class swordsmen visually assessing the distance between them. The energy in the air whispered, *In this match…whoever makes the first move will lose!*

Miura dispersed the peculiar tension. "Let's go bowling, actually," she suggested suddenly.

That prompted a nod from Ebina. "I get it! The pins are such seductive bottoms."

"Ebina, shut your face. And wipe your nose. Try to pretend to be normal," she sniped, exasperated, as she held out a tissue for the other girl.

Miura is surprisingly nice, I thought, *but you have to acknowledge that those tissues are advertising a telephone sex club, and that's a little weird.*

"Bowling… Man, that sounds really fun! I actually don't even know what else we'd do!" Tobe agreed.

"I know, right?" Miura smugly tugged at her curls.

But Hayama didn't seem so into it and adopted a thoughtful pose. "But we went last week… Why don't we play darts? It's been a while."

"If that's what you're into, Hayato, then let's do it! ♪" Miura immediately flip-flopped. *What is this, a game of* Concentration*?*

"Then, let's go. I'll teach anyone who doesn't know how, so let me know if you need help," Hayama offered, rising from his chair and striding away. Miura, Tobe, and Ebina fell into place after him, but Miura noticed that one member of the party was a beat behind. She turned and called out to her. "Yui! What're you doing? We're going!"

"...Huh? Oh...y-yeah! Coming!" Yuigahama, whose role in the exchange had been passive up until then, snatched up her bag in a panic. She leaped to her feet and skittered toward the doorway, but when she passed by me, her pace slowed for just a moment. She must have been conflicted. Follow Miura and her friends or attend the Service Club. Well, she was a nice person. No need for her to fret over us.

Though I say she didn't have to worry about it, when someone constantly lurks in your periphery, you start having qualms. *Bad Hachiman, bad.* Loners absolutely must not inflict trouble on other people. I should swiftly leave the premises. Hachiman Hikigaya withdraws coolly. How cool am I, you ask? Enough to record everything I see with a cassette player.

COOL! COOL! COOL!

I emphatically ignored Yuigahama and quietly left the classroom.

X X X

On the fourth floor of the special building, in the Service Club's room, Yukino Yukinoshita was situated in her usual spot at the back of the clubroom with her standard, frosty demeanor. The lone irregularity was that her reading material was not a paperback, but a fashion magazine. Curious. About the only other change was her summer uniform. Over Yukinoshita's blouse was not a blazer, but the designated summer vest. *Designated* sounds like a synonym for "lame," but on Yukinoshita, the uniform was like a breath of fresh air and oddly improved her appearance further.

"'Sup."

"...Oh. It's you."

Yukinoshita let out a short sigh and immediately dropped her gaze back to the glossy paper.

"Um, can you not act like that girl did when her seat ended up next to mine? That's actually legit hurtful." Major school events aren't the only fertile fields for distress. The seeds of trauma can also be planted on completely

random, normal days. In fact, the less special the incident is, the more sincere the emotions behind it and the nastier the memory. The monthly seat assignments are the ultimate example of this. "I didn't do anything wrong, so why did I end up feeling like the situation was my fault? We drew straws. She should curse her own poor luck for landing next to me."

"So you acknowledge that the seat next to yours is the worst one."

"I didn't say that. Now you're just projecting your own bias."

"I apologize. The subconscious is frightening, isn't it?" Yukinoshita remarked and smiled.

The fact that she did it instinctively was even more hurtful, though.

"That was just a slip of the tongue, so don't overthink it," she said. "I thought you were Yuigahama for a moment there."

"Oh, is that right?" It wasn't surprising Yukinoshita would make that assumption. Yuigahama hadn't shown her face in the clubroom for a few days. Yukinoshita had probably been wondering if the other girl would finally show up today.

"The day before yesterday, she had to take her pet to the vet, and yesterday, she had some errands to run for her parents…," Yukinoshita muttered quietly at the screen of her cell phone. There was probably some e-mail from Yuigahama on it. An e-mail that I was not party to.

Was Yuigahama even gonna come to club today? If she did, I figured she'd behave just like she had that morning. I knew quite well how things ended up once the atmosphere had gone in this direction. Both parties just somehow keep their distance, then somehow stop interacting at all, and then somehow never see each other again.

Source: me. This was how I lost touch with my classmates from elementary school, middle school, and everyone. The same thing would probably end up happening with Yuigahama, too.

The clubroom was quiet. The only break in the silence was the inconsequential rustle of the pages of Yukinoshita's magazine. Now that I thought about it, things had been pretty raucous here lately. At first, it had been just Yukinoshita and me in unremitting silence, interrupted only by the periodic exchange of quips. Though I'd barely been in the club for a month or two, the stillness already felt like a long-lost friend. While I stared off into the space near the door, as if she could divine my thoughts, Yukinoshita spoke.

"If you're thinking about Yuigahama, she's not coming today. She just e-mailed me."

"O-oh… I-it's not like I'm worried about Yuigahama or anything!"

"Why are you using that gross tone of voice?"

Relieved, I redirected my attention from the door to Yukinoshita instead.

Yukinoshita heaved a small, quiet sigh. "I wonder if Yuigahama intends to come back."

"Why don't you ask?" Yukinoshita was actually in touch with her, so if she probed, she should get an answer.

But Yukinoshita shook her head weakly. "There's no point in asking. If I do, she's sure to reply that she'll come. I think she would…even if she didn't want to."

"Yeah, I guess…"

That was the kind of girl Yuigahama was. She prioritized everything else over her own feelings. That's why she'd even talk to loners, and if Yukinoshita were to message her, she'd come back. But it was all just kindness and pity. Nothing more than an obligation to her. And that was more than enough for boys with low EXP to get the wrong idea, like, *W-wait…d-does she like me?* and that was a problem. I really wished girls like her would send more obvious signals, seriously. *There should just be an app that automatically converts e-mails from girls into stiff and formal Japanese. Then I could avoid getting my hopes up. Wait, that might really sell…*

As I fantasized about my get-rich-quick schemes, Yukinoshita sank into silence as she scrutinized me. The steadfast attention of such a flawless visage set my heart pounding…in fear. "Wh-what is it?"

"Did something happen between you and Yuigahama?"

"Nope, nothing," I replied, not missing a beat.

"I don't think Yuigahama would avoid club over nothing. Did you have a fight?" she pressed.

"No…I don't think so." I found myself at a loss for words. But I wasn't lying. More like, I just couldn't tell if it counted as a fight or not. We hadn't been close enough to clash in the first place. Loners are pacifists. We're not even nonresistance, we're non*contact*. In world history terms, we're über-Gandhi.

The only altercations with which I was familiar were those between brother and sister, and that was back when I was in elementary school. It always ended with Komachi summoning my dad and draining my life points to zero. I'd try dueling her when my dad wasn't around, but then my mom would appear on a trap card and I'd end up losing anyway. I'd endure a lecture, and then we'd sit down at the table for dinner together, and the sibling spat would end amicably.

As I silently reminisced, Yukinoshita opened her mouth once more as if she'd been waiting for the right moment. "Yuigahama is thoughtless and indiscreet, she brainlessly says whatever comes to mind, she presumptuously invades personal space, she always tries to avoid conflict with that awkward laugh, and she's kind of loud..."

"It sounds like you're the one fighting with her." If Yuigahama were to hear all that, she'd probably cry.

"Let me finish. She has many flaws, but...but she's not a bad girl."

After such a long list of flaws, I doubted it was even a question of her being bad or not. But when I saw Yukinoshita lower her lashes, blushing as she ended the sentence in a barely audible mumble, I understood this was her highest praise. If Yuigahama were to hear that, she'd probably cry...with joy.

"Oh, I get that. It's not like we're fighting, exactly. You have to be fairly close to someone for that level of conflict. So it was less a fight and more like a..." I grasped for the words, scratching my head.

Yukinoshita quietly put a hand to her chin and adopted a thoughtful pose. "A quarrel?"

"Yeah, sort of, but that's not quite right, I think. It's off the mark, but not that off, sorta."

"Then a war?"

"Still no. And getting colder."

"A massacre?"

"Did you hear what I just said? You're *way* off now." Why was she escalating the conflict? She thought eerily like Oda Nobunaga.

"Then...you're at cross-purposes."

"Yeah...something like that." That was exactly it. Our relationship was the transient passing of two individuals headed in opposite directions along the street. Like that thing you use to get the Masayuki Map.

I used StreetPass once back in middle school, and the whole class freaked out, like, *Who's this 8man guy?* I really wish they'd stop putting multiplayer communication into handheld games. I'm okay with online matches and all, but a game founded on the premise of interaction with nearby players is unquestionably a loner killer. Thanks to that trend, I couldn't evolve my Pokémon and finish my Pokédex.

"Oh? There's no helping that, then." Yukinoshita let out a small sigh and closed her magazine. Impassive though her words were, everything else about her reaction was resigned and fragile. She didn't ask any questions after that, and we managed to maintain the usual gulf between us.

I think Yukinoshita and I had something in common in the way we both kept our distance. We did engage in idle chat or discuss a given subject, but we rarely touched on our personal lives. We never asked each other questions like *How old are you?* or *Where do you live?* or *When's your birthday?* or *Do you have siblings?* or *What do your parents do?* I could hazard a few guesses as to why. Maybe it was just that neither of us had much interest in people to begin with, or maybe we were trying to avoid emotional land mines. And, well, loners are bad at asking questions. Making such random and sudden inquiries is really uncomfortable. Never trespassing, never taking that step, we were like two master swordsmen gauging the distance between ourselves.

"Well, it's like, you know...a once-in-a-lifetime thing. Where there are meetings, there are partings, as they say."

"I'm sure that was supposed to be an inspiring quote, but coming from you, I can only interpret it in a negative way." Yukinoshita sounded exasperated.

Really, though, *life* is a once-in-a-lifetime thing. Like that time in elementary school when we all promised to write letters to this kid who was transferring out, and I was the only one who never got a reply, and I never sent him a letter again. Kenta got a proper reply, though…

A wise man does not court danger. All who come to him are refused, and all who leave him are free to go. I think that's the only way to circumvent those risks.

"But…it's true that relationships are surprisingly fleeting phenomena. They break down readily for the most trivial reasons," Yukinoshita muttered, rather self-deprecatingly.

Out of nowhere, the door rattled open. "But people make connections for the most trivial reasons, too, Yukinoshita. It's not time to give up just yet." And who strode toward us, white coat fluttering behind her as she spouted her desultory declaration, but Miss Hiratsuka, who happened to be an expert on Hikigaya-centric offense.

"Miss Hiratsuka, could you knock?"

The teacher didn't seem to pay the slightest attention to Yukinoshita's exhortation as she scanned the clubroom. "Hmm. It's been a week since Yuigahama stopped coming here, huh? I thought by now you two would have been able to do something about it yourselves, but… I couldn't have imagined your condition was this acute. I underestimated you." Miss Hiratsuka's tone verged on admiration.

"Um, Miss Hiratsuka… Did you need something?"

"Oh yeah. Hikigaya, I told you before, didn't I? About the competition."

At the word *competition*, it all started coming back to me. That was the thing where Yukinoshita and I engage in a Robattle Fight! (not that *Robopon* thing) to determine who could serve others better. Not long ago, Miss Hiratsuka had said something about the rules of the game and "changing some of the specifications" à la a video game company. I figured this time she was going to explain these revisions in more detail.

"I came to announce the new rules." Miss Hiratsuka crossed her arms and adopted an imposing stance. Yukinoshita and I both stood up a little straighter and tried to seem more attentive. The teacher looked from me to Yukinoshita and back again, building up the suspense. The measured, deliberate gesture only made me more anxious. It was so quiet I heard myself swallow.

Then Miss Hiratsuka broke the silence flooding the room.

"You will fight each other to the death!"

"...*That* one's old."

You don't even see that movie on *Friday Roadshow* anymore. Also, *Roadshow* does *Laputa* every year, and it's getting to be too much. I have the DVD. You can stop now. Do *Earthsea*, man—*Earthsea*. I haven't bought that one.

But, like...I guess high school kids these days don't know these movies. As I ruminated, I looked at Yukinoshita to see she'd fixed Miss Hiratsuka with her frigid disdain. She was regarding the teacher the way one might a piece of roadside trash.

Unfaltering under that withering contempt (if nothing else), Miss Hiratsuka cleared her throat, blatantly disregarding my remark. "Hem. Ahem. A-anyway! Simply put, this means I'm applying battle royale rules. Three-way brawls are a staple of long-running action manga. Basically, it's like the Kaguya arc in *Yaiba*."

"There's another blast from the past."

"This is a three-way fight, so you're allowed to cooperate, of course. You have to learn not only how to oppose each other but also how to work in tandem."

It's true. Ganging up to destroy someone who initially caused you trouble is a staple of battle royales.

"Then that means Hikigaya will always be fighting at a disadvantage."

"Yeah."

I didn't even bother fabricating any protests or counterarguments. I just accepted my fate. It was clear this would end up being two-on-one, with me as the one.

But in contrast to my enlightened attitude, Miss Hiratsuka let slip a bold smile. "Relax. This time we'll go out and win over new members. Oh, but you'll be doing the recruiting, of course. In other words, you can get more friends by yourselves! Gotta catch 'em all! Go for all 151!"

Miss Hiratsuka brimmed with confidence as she said this, but her suggested number revealed her true age. *There's almost five hundred these days, you know.*

She said "get more friends" like it's so easy, though.

"Be that as it may, those rules still put Hikigaya at a disadvantage. He's not suited for recruitment, either," said Yukinoshita.

"I don't want to hear that from *you*."

"Well, you've already snagged yourself one person," pointed out Miss Hiratsuka. "No need to agonize over this."

Well, now that she mentioned it, we certainly had. But even if your heart is true, courage will not necessarily pull you through. And you teach me, Miss Hiratsuka, so I'll teach you…that in reality, though things had supposedly gone so well with Yuigahama, she was nowhere to be seen.

Perhaps Miss Hiratsuka realized that, because her expression clouded over. "But it seems that Yuigahama isn't coming anymore… This is a good chance for you. It's another reason I think you should go out and find some new members, to compensate for the one who's gone."

Yukinoshita raised her head in surprise. "Please wait. Yuigahama hasn't necessarily quit…"

"If she's not attending, it amounts to the same thing. I don't need a ghost club." Miss Hiratsuka's laid-back mien disappeared in favor of a powerfully chilling glare. "You kids haven't had some kind of misunderstanding, have you?" she asked, but it was less of a question than a reprimand. Though the sentence was interrogatory in form, she was implicitly accusing us of wrongdoing. When Yukinoshita and I fell silent, unable to reply, she turned it up a notch. "This isn't a club for you and your friends to goof off in. If you want to go act like teenagers, then do it elsewhere. Your assignment as Service Club members is personal development, not taking it easy and lying to yourselves."

"…"

Yukinoshita pressed her lips together and silently looked away.

"The Service Club is not for playing around. It's a fully fledged club at Soubu High. And as you know, coddling people with no initiative stops after middle school. You've chosen to be here, so those with no desire to do this can leave."

Initiative and desire, huh…? "U-um… I have no initiative or desire to do this, so can I leave?"

"Do you think a convict has that much freedom?" Miss Hiratsuka glared at me, cracking her knuckles.

"O-of course not." So I couldn't escape after all…

When she was done casually threatening me, Miss Hiratsuka turned back to Yukinoshita. While the girl was expressionless, her attitude made it clear she had various unspoken grievances. The teacher smiled at her as if at something of a loss. "But thanks to Yuigahama, I found out that an increase in members leads to an increase in activity. I suppose this means another member would balance this club out a little. So…you two have to come up with one more person with initiative and determination to fill up that empty spot…by Monday."

"Someone with initiative and determination by Monday? You have so many orders for us. Is this all just leading up to us being eaten by a wildcat?" I asked.

"You like Kenji Miyazawa, huh?" remarked Yukinoshita. Made sense. We're first and third place in Japanese, after all.

But if the deadline was Monday, that gave us only four days, including today and the due date. I thought having to come up with someone with enthusiasm for Service Club activities *and* a drive for self-improvement was a rather unreasonable demand. *Who the hell does Miss Hiratsuka think she is, Princess Kaguya? …Oh, maybe that's why she can't get married. Eventually, her family is gonna come pick her up, too.*

"Th-this is tyranny…" I made a perfunctory show of resistance.

But Miss Hiratsuka just smirked. "That's uncalled-for. I'm trying to be nice in my own way, you know."

"How is this in any way *nice*…?"

"If you don't understand, it's okay. Now then, that's it for club today. Come on, think of how you can get a hold of some new members," she said before chasing us out of the room. She tossed us, bags and all, into the hall and closed the door with a snap, locking it and then quickly striding away.

Yukinoshita called out to her back. "Miss Hiratsuka. To confirm: We're supposed to fill one position, is that right?"

"That's exactly right, Yukinoshita." And then she was gone, her words lingering in the air behind her. She did, however, smile faintly over her shoulder before she vanished.

Yukinoshita and I watched her go and then turned to each other. "Hey, how are we gonna get a third person?" I asked.

"Who knows? I've never invited anyone to join, so I have no idea. But I can think of one person who might agree."

"Who? Totsuka? Totsuka, huh? It's Totsuka, isn't it?" I couldn't imagine a single other person. And that was because I wasn't thinking of anyone besides Totsuka.

My barrage of *Totsukas* elicited some annoyance from Yukinoshita. "No. He might join, too, but…there's an even easier option, isn't there?" Yukinoshita prompted.

There was no one else we could ask, though. Raking a fine-toothed comb through every possibility, the most I could come up with was Hayama, the rare true normie. *Well, Hayama might help us if we asked.* But he probably wouldn't fulfill the "initiative and desire" requirements. I couldn't think of anyone else at all. *Huh? Zaimokuza? That's an unusual name. Who's that?*

Seeing me spinning my wheels, Yukinoshita sighed slightly. "You don't get it? I'm referring to Yuigahama."

"What? But…she quit," I said.

Yukinoshita swept her hair off her shoulders. The resignation in her eyes had been completely replaced with conviction.

"So what? We only have to get her to join again. Miss Hiratsuka's conditions stated we had to 'fill one position.'"

"Well, I guess, but…" She was right. If we found one person, then the issue would be solved. The bottleneck was the initiative problem. If we didn't get Yuigahama motivated, she wouldn't even swing by the clubroom in the first place.

Perhaps Yukinoshita herself realized this, as she softly put her hand to her chin in thought. "…Anyway, I'll come up with a way to get Yuigahama to come like she used to."

"You're brimming with initiative," I remarked.

Yukinoshita gave me a somewhat self-deprecating smile. "I know… I've only just noticed this recently, but in these last two months, I've grown fond of her, in my own way."

"..."

My mouth definitely fell open there. I couldn't believe Yukinoshita would say something like that.

Maybe my silence flustered Yukinoshita, if the red tint on her cheeks was any indication. "Wh-what? You're looking at me strangely."

"Oh, uh. Nothing. And I wasn't looking at you funny."

"Yes, you were."

"No, I wasn't."

"Correction. Present tense: You still look strange. See you," Yukinoshita said, and she walked away. Hers was not the downcast profile it had been just moments earlier, but rather her usual bold, confident expression.

2

Saika Totsuka's youth romantic comedy is right, as I expected.

Twenty minutes after the teacher had handed down her tyrannical decree, I was in the parking lot, totally confused.

Yukinoshita was right. It would probably be fastest just to somehow motivate Yuigahama to come to the Service Club again. I had no particular objections to her return, personally. I'd already reset our relationship and restored the distance between us to an appropriate level. As long as I maintained that, there shouldn't be any problems.

Okay then, so how were we going to make Yuigahama want to come back? We couldn't just be like, *Hey, bring 'er back!* drop a lasso around her neck, and drag her away, and if we begged her, *Please come back!* then things wouldn't be the same. *What to do?* I ruminated for a while.

But…I didn't know. *Should I apologize? I haven't really done anything wrong, though.*

When I used to fight with Komachi, it always ended when the guilty party was still kinda ambiguous… Maybe things would stay all nice and nebulous with this, too.

I was giving my head a vigorous scratch without much of an expression on my face when a voice caught me off guard.

"Hachiman? Oh, so it is you!" I turned around to see Saika Totsuka being his bashful self, standing against the shimmering halo of the setting sun. Just by standing there, he transformed dancing specks of dust into motes of light. He was seriously an angel.

His brilliance distracted me for a moment, but I decided to play it cool and composed. "'Sup."

"Yeah. 'Sup!" Totsuka raised a hand in greeting as if trying to copy me. I guess the curt gesture was rather embarrassing to him, as it was accompanied by a shy giggle. *Damn it, he is just too cute to handle.* "Are you heading home, Hachiman?"

"Yeah. You done with tennis practice already, Totsuka?"

Still in his gym clothes, Totsuka adjusted his racket bag on his back, paused for a moment, and then shook his head. "Practice isn't over yet, but I've got lessons at night…so I left a little early."

"Lessons?"

What kind of lessons? I guess someone as cute as Totsuka could study at the Okinawa Actors School or something and become a pop idol. Okay, I'll buy a hundred of his CDs! Then, once I get the ticket for a handshake, I'll sell them somewhere.

"Umm, it's tennis lessons. Since practice at the school club is only basic techniques."

"Huh… You're pretty serious about tennis, then."

"I-it's nothing that serious… It's just…love."

"Huh? Sorry, could you say that one more time?"

"Um…it's nothing that serious?"

"No, the part after that."

"…I-it's love?"

"Okay, I heard it that time." I pressed the X button in my heart and engraved his words into my soul. I sighed a blissful sigh.

"Hmm?" Baffled, Totsuka tilted his head.

My work was done for now. Mission complete. "Oh, sorry, Totsuka. You have lessons, right? So I guess you're heading out. See you, then." I gave him a light wave, threw my leg over my bicycle, and was about to start pedaling when I felt a tug at my back. I checked to see what it was, thinking my clothes must have gotten caught on something, and found Totsuka grabbing my shirt.

"U-um… My lesson…starts in the evening. So I've still got some time until then… It's near the station… It's really close on foot… Wait, no, what I mean is…do you want to go hang out for a bit?"

"Uh..."

"Well...if you've got the time..."

I don't think anyone could refuse a request phrased like that. If I'd had some part-time job to go to later, I probably would have skipped it. And then things would get awkward at work, and I would end up quitting. If this were an invitation from a girl, first I'd search around the area for the people who'd won the bet against her. Even if I couldn't find any, I'd refuse just in case, though.

But Totsuka's a guy.

...*He* is *a guy.*

Well, he was a guy, though. What an absolute relief. When it was Totsuka, no matter how nice he was to me, he couldn't be leading me on, I wouldn't get carried away and confess my love, and he wouldn't cruelly reject me and shatter my heart. Well, if I went around confessing my love or whatever to a guy, it'd shatter my reputation beyond repair.

Suffice to say, there was no reason to refuse. "I'll go. I have nothing to do but read at home, anyway." I really did have surprisingly little to do. It was like, I could read books, read manga, watch DVR'd anime, play video games, and when I got bored, study. It was all incredibly fun, too, which was troubling.

"Oh, great! So...so...then let's go to the station."

"Wanna ride the back?" I asked, lightly patting the luggage rack.

Two guys riding together isn't that rare a sight. It's actually fairly common. That's why even if Totsuka were to sit down on the rack, wrap his arms tight around my waist, and say, *Your back is so big, Hachiman*, I wouldn't find it the slightest bit unnatural.

But Totsuka shook his head. "I-it's okay. I'm heavy..."

You're obviously even lighter than a girl, though. Or so I was going to say, but I thought better of it and went with "Okay." Totsuka didn't really enjoy being treated like a girl.

"The station's a little far, but let's walk." Totsuka smiled shyly and started off one step ahead of me. I followed him, pushing my bicycle. As we walked, he occasionally turned back to look up at me. He'd take five steps and glance, eight steps and then glance again. ...*Come on, you don't have to worry like that. I'm behind you.*

We rounded the corner by the park near Saize in silence and ascended the ramp to the pedestrian overpass bridge. We kept furtively sneaking peeks at each other like a middle school couple on a date, and I could never find the right moment to speak. It was a bittersweet journey. I felt like I would die from heart palpitations.

The bridge over the highway was a two-tiered structure with the road for vehicles on top and a pedestrian walkway underneath. The wind gusted through, dispersing the exhaust from tailpipes and carrying a cool breeze into the shade.

"This feels nice, huh, Hachiman?" As if he had taken the wind as his signal, Totsuka stopped five steps above me and looked back. His beaming smile was so appropriate for the summer season that I wanted to snap a picture and save it as a jpeg.

"Yeah. This is perfect for napping."

"You sleep so much during breaks, Hachiman. Haven't you slept enough?" Totsuka asked, giggling.

It's not about fatigue, though. I just don't have anyone to talk to or anything to do during breaks, so I figure I'll just sleep. That's all. "They have a custom of napping in Spain called siestas, you know. They rest in the middle of the day to relieve sleepiness and exhaustion, increasing efficiency during the afternoon. Apparently, businesses just schedule it in like it's a normal thing."

"Wow...so you've put a lot of thought into why you're napping, huh?"

"Uh, well, I—I guess."

Of course, I hadn't at all, and I'd just rattled off something that sounded like I had. I couldn't believe he bought it so easily. It threw me off a bit... I couldn't quite tell if Totsuka trusted me or if he was just gullible. Probably the latter. I was worried one day a bad man would come along and con him. I had to protect Totsuka!

The pedestrian bridge let out right near the station. We proceeded straight down the road at our usual pace. Right about when the station came into view, Totsuka's pace slackened. He seemed undecided as to which way to go.

"So where are we going?" I asked.

"Um...somewhere we can decompress for a little while."

"...Are you stressed?" I wondered why I suddenly felt so guilty...

Oh yeah, there was that little incident around the time we first got the family cat. We gave him too much attention, and he started getting bald spots… Maybe that was why our cat still didn't like me. Pets and other cute companions get stressed out if you're overattentive. I'd have to be more careful with Totsuka.

"Uh, um, it's not for me…"

"I don't really know," I replied, "but maybe karaoke or an arcade or something."

"Which would you rather do?" Totsuka asked, unable to choose.

I considered for a moment. Karaoke and arcades are both pretty good for letting off steam. It's nice to silently input a string of songs alone and break into a light sweat as you sing your heart out. But once you've finished about five, both your throat and your spirit are worn out, and then when the staff brings your drink order, it's incredibly awkward. And then once that's over, you get assailed by the brutal sense of *What am I doing…?*

And then there's arcades. They're effective de-stressing spots. Well, except for how the regulars monopolize the fighting games, and if some peasant dares to join, the more experienced players just obliterate them. The quiz games are kinda fun. Recently, online play has become the default, so you can even do nationwide tournaments. It's really nice to mutter to yourself, *Heh, ignorant fools!* as you rise through the rankings. And then you lose yourself in a game of Shanghai and try to conquer the Great Wall of China, and before you know it, three hours have passed, and you've wasted your time in the best way possible. That same *What am I doing…?* feeling afterward is marvelous.

Problem is, whichever path you choose, you wind up asking yourself, *"What am I doing…?"*

In a dilemma reminiscent of *Dotch Cooking Show*, I was compelled to make a final decision: karaoke or the arcade. But this was Chiba, so as you would expect, there was a solution for times like these.

"Well, if we go to Mu Continent, they have both," I suggested. I guess you could call the Mu a sort of general amusement facility. Besides karaoke and arcade games, they also had bowling, billiards, and even a bar. But since it was always full of people, there were some skeevy types, too, so you had to watch out for yourself.

"Okay… Let's go to the Mu, then," Totsuka replied.

Thus invited, I pushed my bicycle through the station roundabout and parked it in the Mu bicycle racks. We took the elevator to the top and decided to wander around the arcade first. The moment we set foot in the hall, we were instantly inundated with the sounds of the new world unfurling before us: flashing lights, rising tobacco smoke, and laughter that refused to disappear into the din. In front of us was the crane game corner. I saw a couple screeching and squealing to each other as they manipulated the claw, and I instantly wanted to leave. *Damn it, where's a delinquent when you need one? Please come beat these guys up. And after that, all of you please get arrested and tear each other apart.*

The guy was apparently having a hard time, because he convinced the staff to move the stuffed animal he was aiming for. Lately, I hear they'll even catch it for you. Kids these days have it so easy… Totsuka and I slipped by them and headed to the video game corner.

"Oh, wow…" Totsuka gushed. I was used to this landscape, but apparently, it was new for him. In front of us were the fighting games, in the back were the table machines for puzzle games and mah-jongg, and in between them were the shooters. To the right was the arcade for collectible card games. Among all these options, the card machines seemed to have the biggest crowd. The fighting games and mah-jongg were somewhere in the middle, and the quiz machines were sparsely populated. The ones you had to watch out for were the shooters and the puzzle games. Sometimes some ghostlike guy would materialize out of the ether and hammer out some crazy high score and draw a loose crowd of onlookers.

"What do you usually play, Hachiman?"

"Me? Quiz games and Shanghai, I guess." Of course I didn't say strip mah-jongg. Anyway, quiz games were a safe choice if we wanted something to play together. My perennial favorite, *Magic Academy*, was right beside the fighting game enclave. "Over here, Totsuka!" It was loud in the arcade, so I waved, too.

Totsuka nodded, curled his fingers into the hem of my shirt, and followed me. *Um… It seems to be Totsuka's first time here, so I guess he just has to do that to avoid getting lost. Yeah, there's nothing abnormal about it. It's extremely natural. Super-natural.*

As we slid by the fighting game enclave, I caught sight of a familiar coat. Its owner had crossed his arms arrogantly, wrist weights peeking out of his sleeves, and his samurai-style topknot swayed with each contrived chuckle from his lips. He and a few others were watching someone playing a round, occasionally whispering to each other.

"Um, Hachiman… Is that Zaimo—?"

"Nope." I cut Totsuka off as he questioned me with a silent *Huh?*

The figure in the coat was indeed familiar. But he was no acquaintance of mine. The guy I knew couldn't pull off fun social interactions like that. I mean, he had no friends.

"You think? It seems like Zaimokuza to me, though…"

"Ah, no, Totsuka, don't say his name…"

"Oh-ho? I hear a voice calling me… U-u-u-unbelievable! 'Tis Hachiman!"

He noticed us.

Sensitivity to the sound of one's name is a special trait of loners. Because the loner does not often hear his name, he reacts dramatically in the rare event the word is uttered. Source: me. I get so startled my reaction is completely ridiculous, like *Y-yeeeks!* It's so bad that when I ride the Sobu line and the announcer says, "Next stop, Ichigaya," I have to stop myself from replying.

"To think we would meet in a place such as this! Why are you here? This place is a battlefield… Only those who have steeled themselves for battle might set foot here."

"Uh, Totsuka invited me, that's all." I did not play along with Zaimokuza's obnoxious little act. Or rather, I just ignored it.

Zaimokuza's face fell slightly. *You're not cute, okay?* "So, Hachiman, what quest brought you here?"

"Oh, we just came to hang out."

"What?! Wait. Master Totsuka is with you?" Zaimokuza's eyes flared in exaggerated surprise and landed on Totsuka.

Totsuka twitched and hid behind me. "Y-yeah…"

"Oh-ho. Wait one moment." Zaimokuza ran off at a trot, a questionable smirk on his face. Apparently, he was going to say good-bye to the people he'd been chatting with. In less than five minutes, he was back, chortling bizarrely. "Now then, let us sally forth."

"Uh, you're not invited… At all."

Zaimokuza had decided at some point that we were a trio and must have been too exhausted to hear my gentle protests. His shoulders heaved as he wiped his sweat with a sleeve.

"Hey, Zaimokuza, was that guy your friend?"

"Nay. He is an Arcanabro."

"No, I'm not asking for his nick."

"Hum? 'Tis no nickname. That would be 'Ash the Hound Dog.'"

"Lame…"

"It comes from this one time where after KO'ing his foe in *Tekken*, the loser freaked out at him, kicked and punched the machine, and flung an ashtray at him, but he made this great catch, which just made the guy hate him even more. And then he got beat up. He's a regular here at the Mu. I know not his real name because everyone calls him Ash."

"Oh, I see…" *Wow. That was probably the most useless piece of information I have ever learned. I can't think of a single instance where I would ever need to know the Origin of Ash.*

"Then what's an Arcanabro?" Totsuka asked the very question lurking in my mind.

And also, Zaimokuza, don't just assume that I understand your specialized vocabulary. I didn't really want to know everything about it, so I wasn't about to ask myself, though.

"Well, it means people who are into the same game," Zaimokuza replied. "You use it for both game titles and geographical regions. For example, among Arcanabros, the Chibabros in particular are garbage. Sorta like that."

The Chibabros are trash? But I love you, Chibabros. Mostly the Chiba part.

"Hmm, so are you friends?" I asked.

"Nay, we are Arcanabros."

"Does that not mean you're friends…?" Talking with Zaimokuza was draining. We were both Japanese, so why did he not seem to understand the words coming out of my mouth? And what language was *Arcanabro* from? I guess the *bro* part meant they were supposed to be like some kind of family? Well, I guess all that mattered was that the term referred to a group of people.

Zaimokuza contemplated my question for a bit. "Hmm, I know not. When we meet, we converse, and we commune via IM. We venture beyond the prefecture together on trips, but…I know not their real names or what they do, either, because we discuss naught but games and anime. H-hey, are Ash and I friends?"

"That's what I'm asking you… Did they never teach you in school not to answer a question with another question?"

"Ngh, it feels more right to say they are not friends, but rather fighting-game comrades. That is a more reliable term than *friend*, in my opinion."

"'Fighting-game comrades,' huh…? That makes sense. It's nice." I sort of like that expression. It removes all the ambiguity of the word *friends*. Quite often things make more sense if you describe them in terms of functions rather than definitions. For example, marriage makes more sense if you express it not in terms of love and romance but as a relationship of mutual benefit, or having an ATM or doing it for appearances or because you want kids. Wow, an ATM, though. That's harsh, man.

"Indeed. Basically, this means that you and I are gym class pairbros."

"Uh…I see." I didn't particularly care for that profoundly lame way of putting it. Basically, he was saying that among Soubu High bros, the gym class bros in particular were garbage. But the pronouncement clarified that Zaimokuza and I were not friends, at least, so that was good. If we were gym class pairbros, well, there you had it.

"Then, Hachiman," said Totsuka, "if I'm paired with you in gym class, then I'll be a gym class pairbro, too!"

"Huh? I—I see…" So I wasn't friends with Totsuka… *I'm shocked. But hold on a second here. If we're not friends, then there's still a chance that we're lovers. Great! No, wait, that's not great.*

"It's kind of amazing you can get to know more people through video games, though," Totsuka continued.

"Hmm. Y-you think?" Totsuka's comment startled Zaimokuza.

"Yeah, I agree, it's amazing," I said. "I thought gaming was a more solitary thing."

"Nay, 'tis not. With fighting games there is this national team tournament we call 'the Melee.' Things get quite intense. Once, a band of warriors fought together for their very ill comrade and emerged victorious. It was so touching, it sent the entire venue into an uproar. It even brought a tear to mine eye."

"That's almost like Koshien," I remarked. *Huh... Surprising as it is, Zaimokuza has his own brand of community.*

"Wow, that's so amazing..." Totsuka gushed and clapped his hands.

Then Zaimokuza really started to get carried away. Babbling on and on about your own area of expertise is a bad habit us loners have. "'Tis indeed so! Games are marvelous wonders, and not just fighting games. First, comrades unite to bring them into being, and then even more come to enjoy them, and then from that group of fans are born the creators of the next generation. Such a beautiful circle of gaming, is it not? I intend to one day be one of those creators."

"Huh?" said Totsuka. "Are you going to make video games, Zaimokuza? Wow!"

"Eh...ehum! Mwa-ha-ha-ha-ha-ha!"

Uhh...huh? "What happened to your dream of becoming a light-novel writer?"

"Oh, that. I gave up," he declared without missing a beat.

"Why the sudden change of heart?" I asked.

"Hmph, because a light-novel writer is self-employed, after all. There's no job security, and you know not how many years you can carry on. And most important, if you don't write, you cannot earn money. 'Tis rough. But employment at a game company is enough to receive a salary!"

"You're so pathetic, I'm actually impressed..."

"Feh! I don't want to hear that from you, Hachiman!"

Well, of course. His plan was one of a similar ilk as becoming a house-husband to escape work. "But you don't have the skills to make games."

"Hrrm. That is why I shall write the script. That way, I can well employ my ideas and literary talents. I'll have a stable income *and* make what I want, with the company's money!"

"I—I see... Good luck with that..." I really didn't care anymore. I was an idiot for taking his dreams for the future seriously, even for a moment.

"Anyway, Hachiman, you came to divert yourself here, right? This is my domain, so I shall show you about to your heart's content. Is there naught you're keen to play?" Apparently, Zaimokuza figured this was a good time to take the initiative, as he was brimming with gusto. There was no point in a tour, though. A quick look around was enough to see what was available, so the gesture was laughably unnecessary.

"Oh, I want to do the *purikura*." Totsuka, who had been scanning the arcade like me, was pointing to the little photo booths in the far back on the left. "Do you...want to take some pictures over there, Hachiman?"

"Why...? I mean, there's a sign that says the area is only for girls and couples." The photo booth corner was a no-boys-allowed area. Only groups of girls or couples were allowed in. *What discrimination. A modern-day apartheid. The UN needs to rectify this posthaste.*

So there we were, a group of three boys. We fulfilled exactly none of the requirements.

"Y-yeah, but...we could sneak in. Or...is that really bad?"

"Well, not exactly..." If he was gonna ask me like that, refusing might be harder than smuggling ourselves in.

"Mwa-ha-ha-ha-ha! Worry not, Hachiman. I told you, this is my territory. You shall pass, if you are with me."

"What? You can do that? Wow, you're amazing. I guess you're an old hand at this, so I'll just let you handle everything." Apparently, his regular haunting of this arcade had borne fruit. It was kind of cool that the staff all recognized him. I'd expected nothing less of the great Zaimokuza.

"Leave it to me and follow my lead," Zaimokuza declared, and with him at the vanguard, we proceeded toward the *purikura* corner. His grand and stately carriage overflowed with confidence, alleviating us of any lingering unease. He advanced with a dignity that warranted the term *majestic*. I'd expected nothing less of the great Zaimokuza.

We neared the counter in front of the photo booths.

"Hey, what are you kids doing? You can't go in with an all-boys group!"

"Ngrk! Uh, um. S-sorry..." As the nine-to-one odds had predicted, the oddly casual arcade staff member blocked us decisively. I'd expected nothing less of the great Zaimokuza.

"I knew it…"

"…Ah-ha-ha, oh well."

This outcome had been quite foreseeable, and so, not particularly surprised, Totsuka and I exchanged a glance.

But a moment later, a miracle occurred. "Sorry about that. It's okay, go on through." The arcade guy indifferently prodded Zaimokuza away from the booths and opened up the way for us. Zaimokuza was as docile as a cat picked up by the scruff of his neck as he was dragged away.

"…I—I wonder why?" Totsuka blinked his big eyes in confusion, but the reason for our admittance was unquestionably his appearance.

"…Who knows? Anyway, we're in, so let's go."

"Y-yeah…" Though Totsuka didn't look quite convinced, he followed me in.

Inside the photo booth area was a wide variety of machines. Frankly, every last one of them was covered in sparkles and hearts and words like *beauty*, *flower*, *butterfly*, or *style* and radiating a vibe like something out of Tokyo's red-light district. The curtains and the bodies of the units hosted photos, too, like sample images or something. All the subjects looked like models, and they all had exactly the same face. Seriously scary stuff. *Why do these teenyboppers all have the same facial structure? I can't tell them apart except by their hair or clothing. Is this like real-life same-face syndrome or what?*

"Whoa… They all look like hoes…" These images made even Miura seem modest and demure, never mind Yuigahama. I guess this was what they meant by *a world unknown to you*. Seriously scary stuff.

"Hmm, maybe this one? Are you okay with this one, Hachiman?"

"…Oh, sure." Suddenly, they all seemed perfect.

We entered the booth, and Totsuka turned his full attention to reading the instructions. "Um, 'kay. Choose a background… Yeah, looks like this will work," he said, and he pulled my hand, taking a few steps backward.

"H-huh? What, is it starting? What do we do now? Agh, I can't see!"

Suddenly, the flash went off. *Oh, so Tien Shinhan isn't the only one who can use Solar Flare. So both Goku and Purikura can use it, too?*

"One more time!" chimed the dopey electronic voice, and my retinas burned a few more times. *We're borrowing your move, Tien Shinhan!*

"Aaaall done! Go outside the booth and decorate your photos!"

"Decorating, huh...?" said Totsuka. "I wonder what we should draw." We pulled back the booth curtains and went over to the drawing station. A countdown on the screen ticked down the time we had left for embellishments. "'Confirm that this is your picture'... Okay..." Totsuka opened the photo, and it popped up onto the screen. "Wh-whoa! Is that a ghost in the photo?!" He was so surprised that he grabbed my arm.

Whoa, y-you startled me there. Calming my racing heart, I peered at this so-called ghost photo, and indeed there was part of a man's vengeful countenance in the frame.

Wait, that was Zaimokuza.

We drew back the curtains in search of him, and there he was crouching underneath.

"Oh, so it was you, Zaimokuza." Totsuka sighed in relief.

"What are you doing...?" I asked.

"Heh-hem. I infiltrated the premises on my hands and knees that I might not be noticed. And you seemed so intimate with Master Totsuka, I thought I'd ruin your pictures by photobombing them! How do you like that?! I have turned your beloved photos into nothing more than a disappointment!"

"Hey, doesn't saying that about yourself make you feel sad?"

"...Heh, I overcame that paltry level of sadness back during the photo sales from the class field trip. Girls cried just because I was in their pictures."

Whoa, he's got some serious emotional land mines... "Oh. Um, well. S-sorry, Zaimokuza."

"Oh, don't worry about it," Zaimokuza said, but he was quietly wiping tears from the corners of his eyes.

It wasn't his fault, though. Blame whoever decided to sell the photos in the first place. "That photo sale causes nothing but misery, anyway. They should cancel the whole system. Sometimes when you secretly buy a photo of a girl you like, everyone finds out, and then they treat you like a creep."

"...Th-that's creepy even to me," Zaimokuza remarked.

"H-Hachiman...w-we'll take lots of photos together from now on, okay? I'll try to be with you as much as I can." Totsuka swiftly swooped in to make me feel better.

I-is it that weird...? I thought it was fairly normal for a middle schooler, though...

Meanwhile, the drawing timer ran out, and the photos got printed.

"We look so pale..." said Totsuka.

"The filters really are impressive...," I replied.

"They are. But seeing you sparkle like that is fearsome indeed," commented Zaimokuza. "You're glittering so valiantly, and yet your eyes alone are polluted and foul..."

Well, the photo seemed to be a lesson in how excessive light would wash out a subject. The extreme flash turned even the photobombing Zaimokuza a fair white. Totsuka in particular looked like a prettier girl than any actual female could dream of becoming.

"Okay, here you go. This is yours, Hachiman." Totsuka deftly cut the photos apart and handed them to us. "And for you, too, Zaimokuza."

"F-fwaa? I—I can have these?"

"Hmm? Yeah." The smile on Totsuka's face sparkled even brighter than the photo booth flash.

Zaimokuza's response was a teary one. "Er-hem. Th-then I shall accept." He received the photos with the utmost care, gazing at them with pleasure.

I looked at the glossy little papers in my hands as well. Apparently, Totsuka had only barely squeaked in a few embellishments before the drawing time ran out, because only three of the photos had any writing on them. One of the photos read *Gym class pairbros* in Totsuka's slightly rounded characters. I guess he liked that title...

There was another one that said *Best friends!*

"Hmph. That description does not suit Hachiman and myself, though," said Zaimokuza.

"No, it doesn't," I agreed.

"Really?" Totsuka tilted his head quizzically. "It seems like it would."

"Actually, I'm really more of a *Ribbon* kind of guy," I said.

"Indeed. *Kodocha* is particularly superb," replied Zaimokuza.

"Yeah, the ending of the manga really gets you."

"What? The anime is clearly superior."

Zaimokuza and I both clicked our tongues and exchanged fiery glares.

"What'd you just say?" I demanded.

"You heard me."

While we were busy with our staring contest and preparing for imminent war, Totsuka giggled. "You really are best friends."

"Yeah, no..."

"Ba-humph! Agreed."

"Well, whatever. Totsuka's got this really cute smile on his face right now, so I'll forgive you. Listen, I'm bringing the manga on Monday, so you'd better read it and then write me an apology."

"Hmph. Then I shall bring the DVDs, too, so prepare thyself to write a report on that." Zaimokuza turned away with a snort and slipped the tiny photo in his hand into his wallet. "Ugh, if you hadn't caused such ado, Hachiman, we would have had the time to draw on the photos. We only got to do two. You'd better choose volleyball for gym next month in atonement for your sins. If you don't, I'll end up alone."

"Uh, I don't want to do running, and I planned to pick volleyball anyway. Wait...two?" *Was that right?* I was about to check when I sensed a tug at the cuff of my shirt.

I found Totsuka going "Shh!" with a finger to his lips. He quietly uncurled his fingers to reveal the last photo with writing on it. It said *Hachiman* and *Saika*. It was a little embarrassing. Actually, it was too much for me to handle. *Zaimokuza has got to be jealous over this right now.*

"Oh, it's late already. I have to get going," said Totsuka.

"Right, your lessons." Oh yeah. He came here to kill time before his lessons. I felt kinda bad, considering how this hadn't done much to cheer him up.

"Then I'm gonna head out. It looks like you're feeling better."

"Huh?"

"Because you've been down lately. I wanted to cheer you up."

"Totsuka..." Now that he mentioned it, I seemed to remember

BEST FRIENDS!

Komachi saying the same thing this morning. My little sister is weird in general, so I didn't really pay attention, but Totsuka has common sense, so if he was saying the same thing, it was cause for concern.

"I don't really know what happened, but...I like it best when you're your normal self, Hachiman." Totsuka checked the time on his cell phone, said, "Bye, let's hang out again later!" and dashed off. Right before he vanished from sight, he spun around and gave me a big wave. I raised my hand up high as well in reply.

"Hmph. Master Totsuka is so kind, even though there's no value in being nice to you."

"Huh? What was that? You were still there? And I don't want to hear that from you."

"Ba-humph. I would expect nothing less from my comrade Master Totsuka. He's worthy of admiration."

"...Do you think you and Totsuka are friends?"

"Huh? W-we're not...?"

"I don't know. Don't freak out just because I suggested it." *Zaimokuza's really been breaking character a lot lately. Is he okay?*

"Oh, hey! What're you doing? You can't be in there, you know!" came the informal and stupid-sounding call of the arcade guy.

"Ngh, alas, I must withdraw! Farewell! *Mon dieu!*"

"I don't think that means what you think it means..."

After that imbecilic exchange, Zaimokuza and I fled the scene. From the corner of my eye, I could see the staff hemming in Zaimokuza.

Totsuka was right. Brooding and stressing wasn't very like Hachiman Hikigaya. My style had always been to just give up on anything bad enough to stress over. Don't hesitate. Just act like nothing happened. Changing your attitude only when there's some incident is insincere and wrong.

Before I got on my bicycle, I slipped the glossy paper in my hand into my wallet. I'd buy a frame or something and set it out somewhere.

Huh? Where's this coming from? ...Oh, I-I'm having a great time! I—I never get bullied!

Regarding

Yukino Yukinoshita

I—I never get bullied!

Hmm... I guess a good analogy would be like a high-spec PC with great design and performance but no keyboard or mouse. Something like that.

Too complicated? A simpler way to put it would be like how the Keiyo Express Line gets to Tokyo Station pretty fast but is just too far from the other platforms once you get there.

The Sobu Express Line is pretty far, too. You have to go up all those stairs, and it's not even a subway.

Alrighty then, I wonder how my brother is doing at school? Let's find out!

Bro,
are you having a good time at school?

Oh, I don't mean it like when Mom asks that question. Don't worry. I shouldn't have put it that way. It's just you have Yukino and Yui, so I was thinking, "Man, your club seems fun," and I was wondering what you talk about with Yukino. What's she like? Do you get along?

Oh, okay. I think I get the idea. So, like, what do you think of Yukino, Bro?

Uh…what? I don't really use computers, so…

Oh, yeah, yeah. It's way too far.

And the regular Sobu Line train doesn't even go to Tokyo Station… Wait, what were we talking about?

3

Yukino Yukinoshita really does love cats.

Saturday is the mightiest day of the week. It's unshakably, overwhelmingly superior. Not only is it a day off of school, the following day is also a day off, like some kind of Super Saiyan bargain sale. I love Saturday so much, I think in the future I'd like my whole week to be like a bunch of Saturdays. On Sundays, you get depressed, thinking, *School again tomorrow, huh…*, so that day is no good.

Just out of bed and still feeling groggy, I blearily skimmed the morning newspaper. *Kobo* was amazing today. Actually, *Kobo* was the only thing I read. Once I was done catching up on the news, that is to say *Kobo*, I checked the coupon flyers as per usual. If I found something cheap, I'd circle it in red and hand it to Komachi, and then she'd note it on the shopping list, and either my mom or Komachi would go out to buy it.

But then the particularly sparkly lettering in the flyer caught my eye. Given the amount of light radiating from the page, I wouldn't have been surprised to learn this font had inspired the word *photon*.

"K-Komachi! Look, look at this! The Tokyo Cat and Dog Show is happening now!" I snatched it up and thrust it high above my head. It was like a scene from some lion-related musical, so I let out an appropriate roar. *U-Ra-Ra!* Wait, that's Beetlebomb.

"No way! Really? Yes! Nice work finding that, Bro!"

"Ha-ha-ha! Praise me, praise me more!"

"Eeek, you're so cool! You're amazing, Bro!"

"...Cram it, you two. You're too loud." Our mother crawled out from her bedroom like a golem and intoned a curse. She had bedhead, her glasses were sliding down her nose, and the bags under her eyes appeared to be permanent residents.

"S-sorry...," I apologized, and our mother gave a little nod before returning to her room. She was apparently going back to sleep for a while... *It must be rough being a career woman. When I find a wife to support me, I'll treat her with sympathy and kindness. That's what it means to be a superleech who transcends leechdom.*

She rested her hand on the door and then turned back to us. "Hey. You can go out, but be careful of cars. It's like a sauna out there, and drivers are grumpy, so there's bound to be more accidents. Don't ride your bicycle with Komachi on the back."

"I know. I won't let Komachi get into any danger." My parents' love for my sister is profound. It's partly because she's a girl, but she also does a lot of chores, she handles everything like a pro, and she's even cute to boot, so she's like their little treasure.

The eldest son of the family, on the other hand, was apparently not. Even then, my mother was sighing wearily at me. "Agh... You dummy. It's you I'm worried about."

"...Huh?" I found myself tearing up. I'd never imagined she would spare so much concern for my sake... *She doesn't wake me up in the morning, she only gives me a five-hundred-yen coin for lunch, and sometimes she buys me those weird-looking shirts they sell in the neighborhood, so I thought for sure she didn't love me. Still, why does she buy me such disappointing clothes? That's bordering on deliberate harassment.*

Still...the bond between mother and child is a wondrous thing. My eyes stung a little. "M-Mom..."

"I really do worry. If you get Komachi hurt, your father will kill you."

"D-Dad..." I found myself upset.

Speaking of Dad, he would still be deep in torpid slumber, lost in the world of dreams. In his eyes, I really was nothing. I knew quite well how much he loved Komachi, and to me he was practically hostile. All he ever said to me was useless stuff like *Watch out for badger games*, or *If a girl hits on you, she really just wants to make you buy paintings*, or *Futures trading is generally fraud*, or *Get a job and you lose*. That stuff was mostly based off his own experiences, so I couldn't ignore his rambling, making the whole thing especially excruciating.

When I left, I'd make sure to slam the door as hard as I could to disturb his sleep.

"We're taking the bus, don't worry. Oh, so I need money for it." Komachi trotted over toward our mom.

"Yeah, yeah. How much is a round trip again?" our mom asked.

"Um..." Komachi began counting on her fingers. *Hey, one way is one hundred and fifty yen, and a round trip is three hundred yen. What do you need to use your fingers for?*

"It's three hundred yen." I ended up replying before Komachi finished her calculations.

Our mother replied, "Okay," and pulled the change out of her wallet. "Here you go, then. Three hundred yen."

"Thanks!" Komachi chirped.

"U-um, Mom... I'm going, too..." I asked meekly, like I was Masuo talking to his mother-in-law.

"Oh, you need some, too?" Reacting like she'd only just realized, our mother took out some more coins.

"Oh, and I'm eating out for lunch, so I need money for food!" Komachi swooped in on the opportunity.

"Huh? I guess I have no choice, then..." As requested, our mother withdrew a couple of bills and handed them to her daughter.

Whoa, nice work, Komachi. But my normal lunch money is five hundred yen, so why does she get a thousand when she asks, Mom?

"Thanks! Let's go, Bro."

"Yeah."

"Okay, see you later." Our mother sleepily sent us off and disappeared back into the bedroom. *Good night, Mom.*

When I left the house, I rallied all the strength in my body and slammed the door with everything I had. *May this thunder reach you! Good morning, Dad!*

X X X

From our house, it took about fifteen minutes by bus to get to Makuhari Messe for the Tokyo Cat and Dog Show. Even though it's called the *Tokyo* Cat and Dog Show, it's actually held in Chiba, so watch out for that. You're bound to screw up and end up at the Tokyo Big Sight.

There was a modest horde at the venue, and some of them had brought their pets. It was packed, so Komachi and I reached out to each other to hold hands. We weren't having a lovey-dovey date or anything; we'd just gone out a lot together since we were kids, so it was an old habit. Komachi hummed and swung my arm back and forth. *Hey, you're gonna dislocate my shoulder.*

Maybe it was her clothes, but that day Komachi seemed sunnier and perkier than usual. She had paired a bordered tank top with an off-the-shoulder top made of pink jersey cloth, and she wore low-rise shorts that ended high on the thigh. Along with a carefree, bubbly, first-rate smile. I'm proud to be seen with her wherever we go. Not that anyone's allowed to look.

Anyway, the Tokyo Cat and Dog Show is basically an exhibition and market for cats, dogs, and other pets. They also have some rarer animals on display, so it can be fun. Admission is free, so it's an event to be reckoned with. Chiba really is the best.

The moment we set foot in the convention center, Komachi immediately started pointing and bouncing. "Wow, Bro! Penguins! There's a whole bunch of penguins walking around! They're so cute!"

"Yeah… That reminds me, the word *penguin* originates from Latin, and it apparently means 'obese.' If you think about it, it kinda looks like a bunch of paunchy salarymen are visiting for business."

"A-aww… Suddenly, they're not cute anymore…" Dejected, Komachi lowered her arm and admonished me with a look. "I didn't need to know that. Now every time I see penguins, the word *obese* will pop up in my head…," she muttered.

Complaining to me isn't gonna help, though. Go whine to the guy who first named penguins.

"Listen, Bro, you can't say that kind of thing when you're on a date. If a girl says, 'That's so cute!' you have to answer, 'Yeah, but you're cuter.'"

"...That's stupid." *You'd think all that hot air would be bad for an Antarctic native.*

"Whatever, man! I'm not really being serious. I just keep saying the word *cute* to emphasize how cute I am."

"Not a very cute ploy, though..." *This isn't a conversation we should be having in such a heartwarming place with all these dogs and cats and penguins around.*

"I'm just getting back at you for running your mouth! Anyway, c'mon, c'mon! Let's hurry up and look around," Komachi insisted, yanking my arm as she broke into a run.

"Hey, don't take off all of a sudden—you'll pull me over."

This area looked to be the bird zone, and an ostentatious polychrome world of parrots, cockatiels, and more unfurled before us. There was yellow and red and green... The plumage of every single bird was aggressively bedaubed in primary colors, gaudy and vibrant. When they spread their wings, feathers fluttered into the air, catching the light.

But within that flood of striking color, the most beguiling of all was the black of a girl's hair. She held a Tokyo Cat and Dog Show booklet in one hand, and every time she glanced about, her twin pigtails swayed.

"Is that...Yukino?" Apparently, Komachi had noticed, too.

Or rather, few people were as distinctive as she was, so she'd attracted considerable attention. She wore a long cream-colored cardigan unbuttoned over an airy and modest summer dress with a ribbon cinching it just under her bust. It made her look gentler than usual. With each step she took, the simple sandals on her bare feet tapped on the floor with a clear and light sound. She seemed completely oblivious to how many people were staring at her, though, as she was searching around for something with the same chilly expression she always wore in the club. She checked the hall display number and then dropped her gaze to her booklet. She looked around again, then back to the pamphlet, before letting out a short, resigned sigh.

What's with her? Is she lost?

Yukinoshita snapped the booklet shut, as if she'd made up her mind about something, and briskly marched straight toward a wall.

"Hey. There's nothing but a wall that way," I called out to her, unable to just watch.

Yukinoshita met my call with a glare of naked suspicion. *Scary!* But when she realized it was me, curiosity replaced skepticism, and she walked toward us. "Oh, what a rare animal."

"Don't greet me by calling me a *Homo sapiens*. You're trying to negate my personhood, aren't you?"

"But it's not incorrect to call you that, now is it?"

"Technically, but you can only take that so far..." The first words out of her mouth had identified me as order: primate, species: human. She couldn't be more correct, biologically speaking, but as a greeting it was of the lowest order. "Why are you heading toward a wall?" I asked.

"...I'm lost." Her eyes mourned her failure, and her tone suggested admitting that was agony and so she planned to commit ritual suicide right there. With no attempt to hide her annoyance, she studied the booklet she'd opened up once more.

"Uh, I don't think this place is big enough to get lost in, though..."

I wonder if she just has a poor sense of direction. Well, sometimes you can get lost even with a map. Especially when a building has a sort of samey-looking design everywhere, maps are kind of useless. Like at Comiket, or the Shinjuku subway station. And Umeda Station. That one's so bad you'll end up stranded if you don't carry a sheet of graph paper to map it all out.

"Yukino! Hello!"

"Oh, so Komachi is with you, huh? Hello."

"I didn't expect to see you here, though. Did you come to see something?"

"...Yes. Well, um, various things."

I bet it's cats... She even has a big red circle around where it says "Cat Corner."

Yukino detected my gaze and quietly folded the booklet as if

nothing had happened. "H-Hyeek… Ahem, Hikigaya, why are you here?" She tried to act calm, but she just stammered all over the place.

Withstanding the urge to mock her mercilessly, I pretended not to notice. 'Cause if I said something, she'd just return it to me fivefold. "I come here every year with my sister."

"And we got our cat here!" Komachi added.

As Komachi said, we originally got our cat, Kamakura, right here at this show. Though he is quite the feisty feline, he does have a certificate of pedigree. Komachi had said she wanted him, so her wish was instantly granted. I felt sorry for our dad coming all the way to Makuhari Messe just to pay for him.

Yukinoshita looked at Komachi and me and back again with a faint smile. That was the second time. She'd smiled like that once before. "You two seem as close as ever."

"Not really. This is more of an obligatory annual function," I replied.

"I see… Good-bye, then."

"Yeah, see you." We both avoided escalating the interaction and said our farewells.

"Hey! Wait, hold on, hold on! Yukino. I finally got the chance to see you again, so let's go check things out together!" Komachi caught Yukinoshita's sleeve as she started her escape and tugged her back. "When I'm with my brother, all he does is make these downer comments. I'd have more fun with you," Komachi urged as she continued pulling enthusiastically at Yukinoshita's sleeve.

"Y-you would?" Yukinoshita replied, taking a step back.

"I would, I would! Come on, come on!"

"Wouldn't it be a bother? …Hikigaya's presence, I mean."

She excluded me as if it was the obvious thing to do.

"You jerk," I said. "What're you talking about? When it comes to group activities, I usually just keep quiet. I won't be in the way at all."

"You give new meaning to the phrase *blending in with your surroundings*. It's an amazing talent, in a way…" The expression on Yukinoshita's face was one of neither astonishment nor exasperation. Well, actually, when there's some quiet guy in the group doing his own inconspicuous thing, everyone acts supercareful around him, though. "…All right. Let's go around together, then. Is there anything in particular you want to see? And…if there isn't…"

"Yeah… Since we're here, let's go check out something really unusual!" Komachi clapped her hands as if she'd struck gold.

"…I have no idea if you're perceptive or simply clueless," I said.

"Huh? What?" Komachi tilted her head, puzzled.

"…I'm fine with that. Haah…" Yukinoshita sighed in resignation.

Well, uh, you know. Sorry about my sister.

Though Komachi had said she wanted to check out something rare, space was obviously limited, so there wouldn't be anything big. That being the case, the bird zone was the best equipped. It was probably because birds were relatively uncommon and didn't take up much space.

We walked away from the colorful tropical-themed booth and emerged by a tremendously cool display. Beyond a dramatic metal railing were sharp beaks, sharp claws, and gallant silhouettes with sturdy wings and tails.

"L-look! Komachi! It's an eagle! A hawk! A falcon! Sweet… I want one…" *They're so cool…* I automatically stopped and leaned forward over the railing. If you've been plagued by M-2 syndrome even once, then you're bound to be drawn to their majesty. The American military probably has an especially acute case of this affliction.

But apparently, Komachi couldn't comprehend how cool they were and just whined. "What? They're not cute! You sound like an M-2 case."

"Hey, you idiot. What are you talking about? They're cute. See how they tilt their heads? C'mon." I turned around, attempting to persuade her, but Komachi was already halfway to the next area. Meanie.

"They're not cute…but I think they're majestic and beautiful." That reply came not from my stone-hearted sister but from Yukinoshita, surprisingly enough. It seemed she was telling the truth, too, as she touched the railing and moved beside me for a better angle.

"Whoa! So you get how cool they are? They appeal to your inner middle schooler, don't they?"

"…I cannot fathom what you're talking about."

Ngh, so a maiden cannot grasp their glory… Whoops, that was close. I almost turned into Zaimokuza.

M-2 syndrome is
a condition with no cure,
an illness of the mind.

(excess syllable)

A poem from Hachiman's soul. By the way, the seasonal word there is *M-2 syndrome*. This term evokes the verdant spring.

× × ×

We left the bird zone behind in favor of the small-animal area. This section included pets like hamsters, rabbits, and ferrets. This sort of place was right up Komachi's alley. In the petting corner, she fussed over the little critters, cooing and squeeing and *aww*ing with no indication she would ever leave.

And then there was Yukinoshita. She did try skritching and fluffing them, but after a little bit, her head tilted to a bemused angle. Apparently, the texture wasn't quite what she'd sought. *She's surprisingly picky about this stuff…*

By the way, when I approached the little bundles of fur, they all scurried away. *…I can't believe it. Even these guys hate me.* "Komachi, let's move on."

"Eeek! I could totally step on them! They're so cute! Huh? Oh, you can go on ahead. I'm gonna hang out here some more."

"Okay…" *That isn't a very cute reason to find something cute. Is she okay?* But Komachi had given me permission to move on, so I decided to do so. If memory served, the next area had the dogs, and after that would be the cat zone. "Okay, Yukinoshita. The section after the next one is the cats. Sorry, but you keep an eye on Komachi for me."

"I don't really mind, but Komachi isn't that young anymore. Don't you think such a measure would be excessive?"

"That's not what I meant—keep an eye on her so she doesn't smush anything."

"I'm not gonna smush them! Oh, Yukino, it's okay if you want to go check out the cats."

"R-really? Th-then, I might as well...," Yukinoshita said, already partway to her feet. *Just how badly do you want to see those cats?* "Well then, let's go." And then, without a glance to spare for me, she forged ahead to the next area, blind to everything around her. But the moment the letters reading DOG ZONE entered her field of vision, she twitched.

"Is something wrong?" I asked.

"No..." Yukinoshita casually decelerated and slid behind my back, making me walk in front of her.

Oh no, she's caught me from behind! She's gonna kill me! I thought, but she made no move to attack. *Oh, the dogs. She's kinda scared of them, isn't she?* "Just so you know, it's nothing but puppies here." This event was partly a commercial enterprise, so the sections for common pets like cats and dogs mostly had babies. It was sad, but that's business.

I didn't know if my words had any effect on Yukinoshita, but she avoided my eyes anyway. "I guess if it's puppies... J-just so you know, it's not like I'm frightened of dogs, you know. Um...I'm just...rather uncomfortable around them."

"That's generally called 'being scared of dogs.'"

"That interpretation is within the margin of error."

Is that so? Well, if she says she's okay, then whatever.

"Are you...a dog person, Hikigaya?"

"I'm a nothing person. I don't affiliate myself with any kind of label." The truly stalwart don't run with a group. Being alone is like standing against the whole world. Me versus the world. It's almost like I'm Steven Seagal. From a Seagal perspective, I'm super-Seagal.

But Yukinoshita refused to endorse my self-identification. "Maybe that's because no one wants to be affiliated with you."

"Yeah, you're right, more or less. And I'm fine with that, so let's go." She really was right, so I couldn't argue. All I'd get from a debate with

Yukinoshita was cuts and burns, so I neatly nipped that conversation in the bud.

When I began walking, I heard Yukinoshita mumble behind me, "I thought for sure you were a dog person, though…"

"What? Why?" I turned around to ask.

"…You were so desperate." Yukinoshita's reply was elusive.

When did Yukinoshita see me eager to do anything? I could only recall one time, so it was probably that. The tennis match over Totsuka. It was true—I had been burning to win, that time. I'd thrown my heart and soul into helping Totsuka. I mean, he was so cute. He had been trembling like a Chihuahua that day, indeed like a puppy. So I guess it would be correct to say that I'm a Totsuka person. I like Totsuka, you know.

Scratching my head, thinking, *I dunno*, I felt Yukinoshita nudge my shoulder.

"Could you walk faster?"

"Oh, 'kay." Thus impelled, I passed through a cheap gate bearing the words Dog Zone. Inside was an area crowded with a multitude of cages. It was like two or three pet shops fused into one. Dogs were indeed in high demand, and there were a lot of visitors. Aside from the popular small breeds like Chihuahuas, miniature dachshunds, *mameshiba* dogs, and corgis, a range of standard breeds like labs, retrievers, beagles, and bulldogs could be found. The dogs on display were all top pedigrees raised by breeders, with titles like Grand Champion or Festival Nominee or Monde Selection or Good Design, though how much weight the designations carried was difficult to tell with one glance.

From the moment we'd entered the dog zone, Yukinoshita had clammed up. She was so quiet, I began wondering if she was still breathing. The area around us bustled with so much activity that a single person's silence stood out as particularly troubling. Actually, everything else was just too boisterous. Particularly that woman squealing and snapping a stream of photos.

…Wait, that's Miss Hiratsuka. I'll pretend I didn't see her. C'mon, Miss H.… You finally got a day off, so go on a date or something… Well,

on the other side is the cat zone, so I guess we'll just head straight through, I thought.

But the moment I did, a tiny gasp escaped Yukinoshita. The apparent cause was an area labeled TRIMMING CORNER, spelled out in English.

"Huh? What? Are they editing photos?" I asked.

"No, it means they're maintaining the dogs' coats and grooming them to make their fur glossy. The English word *grooming* is also commonly used."

Grooming, huh…? Like *Jaja Uma Grooming Up*? Totally famous manga.

While my train of thought took a detour to the four sisters of the Watarai ranch, Yukinoshita continued her explanation with some impatience. "Basically, it's a dog beauty parlor."

"Huh? Is that a thing? Sounds fancy. Does Tsunayoshi have a hand in this, too?"

"And it seems there's not only grooming but obedience classes as well. Why don't you sign up?" She casually branded me as a dog as if it were the most natural thing in the world. Whatever, I was used to it.

As we exchanged our petty repartee, one particular long-haired miniature dachshund finished up its brushing session and trotted out, yawning. *Hey, where's its owner?*

"Hey, hey! Sablé! Wait, you've ruined your collar!"

The leashless mini dachshund acknowledged the yell and then insouciantly ignored it. And then it scampered toward the exit—that is to say, us—like a frightened rabbit. Though it was a dog.

"H-Hikigaya…th-that dog…," Yukinoshita stammered, rattled and bewildered. Her eyes darted around the room, her hands fidgeting and flailing in the air.

…This didn't happen every day. I was kind of getting a kick out of it, so I was tempted to just brush her off, but it'd be a pain if she made a scene.

"C'mere." I grabbed the dog by the scruff of the neck. My cat despises me and is always running away from me, so I'm practiced in nabbing pets. My training had not been in vain.

The dog implored me with sad eyes at first, but then it suddenly raised its head and started sniffing and vigorously licking my fingers.

Startled, I instinctively released it. "Waagh! It slobbered all over me..."

"Oh, you idiot. If you let go...," Yukinoshita said, disconcerted.

But the dog didn't break for the exit and instead gallivanted around my ankles before abruptly rolling onto its back. It showed its tummy and panted, tongue lolling.

What's with this dog? Isn't it being a little too friendly with me?

"This dog is..." Yukinoshita took cover behind my back, quietly peeking around at the dog.

Come on, I don't think the animal is that scary.

"S-Sablé! Sorry he's bothering you." The owner rushed over to us and scooped up the dog in a flash with a rapid-fire bow. The bun on the girl's head flopped a little.

"Oh, Yuigahama," Yukinoshita said.

"Hwa?" came the owner's reply, raising her head with a baffled expression. The hairstyle, the voice, the mannerisms... It was indubitably Yui Yuigahama. "Huh? Y-Yukinon?" Her head mechanically rotated on its axis to me at Yukinoshita's side. "H-huh? What? Hikki? And Yukinon?" Yuigahama looked from Yukinoshita to me and back again, utterly mystified. "Huh? Huh?"

"'Sup," I greeted.

"Oh. H-hi...," she replied. A very odd silence descended upon the two of us. *Whoa, this is uncomfortable...*

While this peculiar atmosphere hovered over us, the dog in Yuigahama's arms yipped. Yukinoshita twitched, and while she didn't hide in my shadow, she did close the distance between us very slightly. She apparently intended to use me as a meat shield should there be any danger.

"...U-uh...um..." Yuigahama gently stroked her dog's head as her gaze wandered around the area between me and Yukinoshita—as if she were measuring just what was between us.

"What a coincidence, running into you here," Yukinoshita said, and Yuigahama jumped a little.

"Y-yeah. Why are you and Hikki...together? Um...it's kinda... unusual to see you two together, like..."

Maybe it was because we hadn't interacted in a few days, but Yuigahama seemed distant, somehow, even with Yukinoshita. Avoiding eye contact with Yukinoshita, she squeezed the dog in her arms tight.

She could ask why all she wanted, but really we'd just happened to bump into each other, so there was nothing going on. Yukinoshita and I just sort of looked at each other, and we both ended up saying the same thing.

"No reason."

Yuigahama cut off any further explanation. "Oh, never mind, actually! Forget it—it's okay. It's nothing… You're out together on a weekend, so it's obvious what's going on, isn't it? I see… I wonder why I never noticed? I thought picking up on social cues was the only thing I was good at…" She forced a smile to her eyes and struggled to make her lips follow suit with a slightly hoarse "Ah-ha-ha…"

Is she making some kind of weird assumption here? Like, does she think Yukinoshita and I are going out or something? Well, if you gave it even a moment's thought, you'd recognize immediately that would never happen. But claiming *We're not going out* would sound kinda, well, dumb, and sorta self-conscious, and just against my sense of aesthetics.

A misunderstanding is a misunderstanding. It is not the truth. And as long as I know the truth, that's enough for me. I don't care what anyone else believes… The more you try to correct a mix-up, the more people misinterpret it and make things worse. I'd given up on that.

The dog in Yuigahama's arms whined a sad *Hween?* up at its owner. Yuigahama muttered, "It's okay…" as she petted its head. "S-see you then. I'll be going…" Yuigahama wilted and, still downcast, began walking away.

Yukinoshita stopped her. "Yuigahama." Her voice resounded loud and clear within the bustle of the hall. That sound was the only thing that reached my ears, as if all other activity around us was behind an invisible barrier.

Yuigahama lifted her head and automatically turned toward Yukinoshita.

"I need to talk to you about us, so could you come to the clubroom on Monday?" the twin-tailed girl asked.

"Oh... Ah-ha-ha... I don't know...if I really want to hear it... Um, like, it'd be kinda meaningless at this point, since, like, I can't do anything, anyway...," Yuigahama said as if she were embarrassed. Beneath her gentle tone and troubled smile was a clear no.

Faltering in the face of Yuigahama's rejection, Yukinoshita's gaze lowered slightly. For a moment, I imagined the volume of the din around us had increased. Yukinoshita spoke hesitantly into the tumultuous racket, as if the words were escaping her. "...I'm not the kind of person who can say things like this without some effort, but...I do want to say this properly."

"...Yeah." Yuigahama's dull response was neither refusal nor acceptance. She momentarily regarded Yukinoshita with some doubt but found something else to look at almost immediately. Then she spun on her heel and strode away. Yukinoshita and I silently watched her leave as her tiny, hunched frame disappeared into the surging throng.

I asked Yukinoshita next to me, "Hey. What do you want to talk to Yuigahama about?"

"Do you know what the eighteenth of June is?" Yukinoshita scrutinized me as if this was a test. Her face approached mine so suddenly, I reflexively retreated a step.

"...Well, I know it's not a holiday."

Upon discovering I had no idea, she puffed out her chest just a little proudly and replied, "It's Yuigahama's birthday... I think."

"Really? ...Huh? You 'think'?"

"I haven't confirmed it from the source." No surprise there, with her communication skills. "So I want to celebrate her birthday. Even if she will no longer come to the Service Club...I want to express my sincere gratitude for everything she's done for us," Yukinoshita announced as she delicately dropped her gaze, clearly self-conscious.

"I see." Thanks to her personality and general perfection, Yukinoshita had been incessantly victimized by the flames of jealousy. Yuigahama was most certainly the first friend she'd ever had. I think she was being honest when she said she was thankful. Though her voice was tinged with resignation, she probably didn't want to lose that friendship.

Agh… This is probably because of something I said to Yuigahama after all, huh? Mildly guilty, I glanced at Yukinoshita. She noticed and squirmed with some discomfort. *Oh, she's probably gonna go,* Don't look, you're creeping me out *or something*, I thought, shifting my attention elsewhere before she could say anything.

She cleared her throat, her cheeks slightly red. "Hey, Hikigaya…"

"Uh-huh?" When I turned around to face her, Yukinoshita was clenching her hands to her chest. I guess that audible gulp meant she was anxious. As if trying to redirect attention from her flushed cheeks, she looked through her lashes at me with moist eyes. This was enough to unnerve even me.

Yukinoshita whispered faintly, thinly, as if the words were struggling to leave her throat. "U-um…would you go out with me?"

"…Huh?"

Komachi Hikigaya is shrewdly scheming.

It was Sunday. The clear skies provided a brief respite from the rainy season. This was the day of my rendezvous with Yukinoshita. The time was just about ten o'clock on the dot.

I supposed I'd showed up rather early. Apparently, this drastic event had thrown me out of whack. I can't believe I actually heard Yukino Yukinoshita say, *I want you to go out with me.*

What do I do…? I guess I should turn her down after all. I was confused when she asked me that… The ludicrousness of Yukinoshita's invitation had robbed me of my capacity for rational judgment. I was resisting the urge to clutch my head and yell out *Gwaaaaagh!* when someone called from behind me.

"Sorry to keep you waiting." Yukino Yukinoshita ambled unhurriedly toward me, bringing a refreshing gust of wind along with her. The soft-looking fabric of her skirt gave her a particularly feminine presence. Her ponytails, dancing lightly on the wind, were tied higher on her head than usual. Perhaps that was her weekend style.

"…I haven't been here that long."

"I see. That's good. Well then, let's go." Adjusting the rattan-weave purse on her shoulder, Yukinoshita scanned the area for someone else.

"Komachi just stopped by a convenience store. Wait just a sec."

"I see… I feel bad for making her accompany us on a weekend, though."

"We don't have much choice. If you and I were to get a birthday present for Yuigahama by ourselves, we'd inevitably come up with something awful. Plus, Komachi was happy to come, so it's no big deal."

"Well, I hope you're right..."

And here's the big reveal. What the heck—is this *World Great TV*?

When Yukinoshita had asked me to go out with her, she'd just wanted me to help her buy Yuigahama a birthday present. And I wasn't even the one she was after. Komachi was who she really wanted.

Well, her logic was sound. Any other time, we would probably rely on Yuigahama for a task like this, but since the present was for Yuigahama, we obviously couldn't solicit her help. And Yukinoshita didn't associate with many people, so Komachi was likely her only other option.

We lingered in silence for about two minutes, and then Komachi returned. Maybe it was because we were joining Yukinoshita today, but Komachi's clothing was rather reserved compared to normal. A summer vest covered a short-sleeved blouse, and underneath that she wore a pleated skirt, knee socks, and loafers on her feet. With that ensemble, she could pass for a classy young rich girl. The newsboy cap sitting lightly atop her head made for a jaunty image. She clasped a plastic bottle of tea in her hands.

"Hey, it's Yukino! Hello!"

"I'm sorry for requesting you to come all this way on a weekend," Yukinoshita apologized.

"No, no! I want to get Yui a birthday present, too, and I'm looking forward to hanging out with you." Komachi grinned brightly. She was quite fond of Yukinoshita in her own way, so I figured she was being honest. *But man, ditzy girls do go for Yukinoshita, don't they? Of the people I know, she's the second most popular with girls after Hayama.*

"The train's coming soon, so let's go." I urged the pair on, and we strolled toward the turnstiles.

Our destination for the day is famous as a popular date spot for high schoolers in Chiba: the beloved Tokyo Bay LaLaport mall. It's the largest hangout spot in the prefecture, with a variety of shops, a movie theater, and an event hall. In sum, the kind of place I would never go.

The interior of the train was fairly packed. We grabbed onto the handholds above us, and the train shook us around for about five minutes. If it had just been me and Yukinoshita, we probably would have remained silent, but since Komachi was accompanying us that day, she tried several different tactics to start a conversation with the other girl. "Have you already decided what to buy, Yukino?"

"...No. I considered a number of things, but I'm just not certain," Yukinoshita said and huffed a small sigh.

I guess Yukinoshita had been browsing that magazine in the clubroom the other day for ideas. I doubted the two girls would have similar tastes.

"Plus, I've never received a birthday present from a friend, so..." Yukinoshita let the comment slip with a melancholic expression.

The remark turned Komachi's expression slightly despondent as well, and silence fell. She struggled to find something else to discuss.

"Hmph, you really are something. Unlike me—I've actually gotten one before."

"Huh? You're kidding," said Yukinoshita.

What a discourteous way to express your surprise. "I'm not. Why would I fake something like that now?"

Yukinoshita nodded her appreciation of my response. "You're right... That was an injudicious way of putting it. I apologize. I can't doubt you all the time. From now on, my faith in your pathetic nature will never falter."

"Hey, if you think that's a compliment, you're sorely mistaken."

"So what was the present? Would you mind telling me, for my information?" she inquired.

"Corn..."

Yukinoshita's big eyes blinked. "Huh?" she replied, as if her ears had deceived her.

"C-corn..."

"What was that?"

"Listen! His family was a bunch of farmers. And FYI, it was really good! My mom steamed it for me!"

"B-Bro, you don't have to get all teary eyed...," said Komachi.

I'm not crying. I am absolutely not crying. This is, you know, my eyes are just watering. "Yeah, back during the summer vacation in fourth grade..."

"Here comes an anecdote...," Komachi commented wearily, but Yukinoshita prompted me to continue with a dip of her head.

"Takatsu came to my house because our mothers were friends or something. It was the first time a classmate had ever visited for my birthday, so I was all worked up. When I opened the front door, he handed me a mysterious object wrapped in newspaper, still straddling his five-speed mountain bike.

"'Today's your birthday, right? My mom told me to give this to you,' he said.

"I replied, 'Th-thanks...'

"......

"'......W-will you come in?'

"'Huh? Uh, I already promised I'd go play at Shin's house.'

"'O-oh...' What the heck. I wasn't invited. I'd thought Shin was my friend, too, so by then I was about to cry.

"Takatsu was like, 'Bye!' and pedaled off on his mountain bike. When I opened the package, I found fresh corn, beaded with the morning dew. Before I could stop it, a salty drop splashed onto the corn, followed by another and another..." I thus concluded my tale.

Yukinoshita sighed softly. "Ultimately, you've never actually received a present from a friend, have you?"

"...You're right! Takatsu and I weren't friends!" I realized I'd been living a lie for the past seven years. Now I was doubting if Shin had been my friend, too.

I guess wringing out the screams of my soul had touched Yukinoshita, if her distant gaze was any indication. "It's true, though," she mumbled. "Sometimes you acquire relationships through your parents' friendships. The adults gather their children together while they're busy talking... I really wished they wouldn't do that."

"Yeah, they totally did. Kids' clubs and after-school day care were rough. I barely got along with kids my own age, and other grades were there, too. I whiled away the time reading alone... I did pick up quite a few good books thanks to that, though, so it all worked out in the end."

"Most of my memories are of reading, too... I've always enjoyed the literary arts, so it was time pleasantly spent."

"Wh-whoa! I can't believe this good weather!" Komachi exclaimed. Unable to take the suffocating gloom anymore, I suppose, she suddenly found the scenery outside the window particularly fascinating. The blue sky was clear as far as the eye could see, heralding the beginning of summer.

Looks like today's gonna be a hot one.

X X X

Immediately after leaving Minami-Funabashi Station, there's an IKEA on the left-hand side. It's a trendy furniture store and one of the more popular spots around here. This region has always had a reputation as a recreation hotspot, and it used to have a giant maze, and after that, an indoor ski hill. This is past tense, of course, because they're no longer there.

Time really does fly. It feels like it's been no time at all, and here I am on the road to adulthood.

Their catchphrase, "Come with no gear at all!" is so nostalgic now. These days it calls to mind unprotected sex. Time really does fly. It feels like it's been no time at all, and here I am on the road to adulthood…

The pedestrian bridge connected directly to an entrance of the shopping mall.

Yukinoshita folded her arms, mulling over the facility map inside the mall. "I'm surprised… It's quite large."

"Yeah," replied Komachi. "It's sorta separated into a bunch of different zones, so it's best to narrow down what you're looking for."

I don't know exactly how big this mall is, but it is the biggest one around here. If you meander around aimlessly, you'll use up the whole day. If we were going to hang out here, we needed to formulate a concrete plan. "That means we need to prioritize efficiency in our search," I said. "I'll take this area." I indicated the right side of the map.

Yukinoshita pointed to the left. "All right, then I'll handle the opposite side."

Great, now we've halved the work. Once we assigned Komachi her target area for maximum efficiency, it'd be perfect. "Then you do this part in the back, Komachi."

"Hold it! ♪" Komachi yanked my finger off the map.

"What? And you're hurting my finger…," I whined.

Komachi sighed at me with a dramatic American shrug, like, *Man, this guy just doesn't get it.*

Hey, that attitude is obnoxious, you know.

Apparently, I wasn't the only baffled member of our group, since Yukinoshita cocked her head and questioned Komachi. "Is there some kind of problem?"

"You and my brother have to stop automatically doing everything solo. We all got together for this, so why don't we shop around as a group? We can give each other advice that way, so it's better."

"But then we won't be able to consider all the options…," said Yukinoshita.

"That's fine! In my opinion, considering Yui's tastes, we'll be good if we just stick to this area," Komachi said as she took one of the pamphlets from the shelf underneath the map and opened it up. She indicated a block farther in on the first floor hosting a number of shops with names like *Love Craft* or *Lisa Lisa* and other things that sounded like cosmic horror or somewhere you'd learn the art of Ripple. I guess the target consumers for that particular cluster of enterprise were teen girls.

"Let's go, then," I said, and Yukinoshita nodded with no objections, either.

And thus, we set off.

The girly district was two or three sections ahead. Along the way, the shops lining the passage sold men's goods, stuff for an indeterminate audience, miscellaneous items, and products from such a multitude of brands as to leave you in awe.

By force of circumstances, I had taken the lead, but usually, I would never visit an enormous shopping mall like this, so I had no idea if we were going the right way. Yukinoshita swiveled her head this way and that, curiously observing our environs with equal uncertainty. But her expression displayed nothing but calm smiles, and at the very least she didn't seem bored. Occasionally, she would stop to inspect some of the wares, but the moment store staff approached, she sensed their impending presence and quietly left.

…Oh, I know that feeling. I really wish they wouldn't try to talk to me when I'm picking out clothes. The employees of clothing stores really ought to learn the art of picking up a loner's *Don't talk to me* aura. It would be great for business.

Eventually, we reached a fork where we could continue to either the right or left block. On each side was an up escalator. Remembering the map from earlier, I turned back to Komachi and gestured to the right. "Komachi, we just keep going straight down that way, right?" But Komachi wasn't there. "H-huh?" I searched for her everywhere but found nothing.

What I did see was Yukinoshita solemnly squishing a weird stuffed panda with fiendish eyes, sharp claws, and glittering fangs. The plump panda bear was Ginnie the Grue, a popular character from Tokyo Destiny Land. "Grue's Bamboo Hunt" is such a popular attraction, you're bound to wait two or three hours to get in.

Tokyo Destiny Land is a popular and well-known place. Funny enough, it's both the pride of Chiba and a source of deep shame for bearing the name *Tokyo* despite its location in Chiba. I'm told that it was built in Maihama because that sounds like "Miami Beach" or something. This concludes the Chiba prefecture lesson for today.

"Yukinoshita," I called.

She returned the plush to the shelf without a word and coolly swept back her hair. *What?* she silently challenged.

Uh, well…nothing, really… Considering her behavior during the recent incident with the cat, not teasing her about this would be the correct choice. "Have you seen Komachi? I think she ran off somewhere."

"Now that you mention it, no, I haven't. Why don't you try calling her?"

"Yeah." I immediately did just that. I was greeted yet again by the unfamiliar jingle. Seriously, why did her cell phone sing? Though the call did go through, Komachi didn't pick up. After I'd waited for a full two loops, I gave up and ended it. "She's not picking up…"

While I had been busy contacting my sister, Yukinoshita's bags had increased by one. Along with her initial rattan-weave purse, she was also grasping a kitschy primary-colored plastic bag. *So she bought it, huh…?* She must have noticed my mild shock, but she pretended not to as she stuffed her purchase into her purse. In an attempt to steer us back on track, she suggested, "Perhaps Komachi found something that caught her attention. It is indeed tempting to pause for a glance when there's such a wealth of goods on display."

"Yeah, just like you." My gaze moved toward her purse.

Yukinoshita suddenly cleared her throat. "Anyway, Komachi knows our destination, so we should just meet her there. There's no point in dawdling around here."

"Yeah, you're right."

I sent a text to Komachi saying, *Call me, you idiot. We're headed to that area you showed us*, and decided to move on.

"...So we go right and then straight ahead, right?" I asked to confirm.

But Yukinoshita just stared blankly back. "Wasn't it left?"

The correct answer was right.

× × ×

The ambiance had clearly changed. Floral and soapy scents wafted around amid a palette of pastel hues and vibrant shades. We had indeed arrived at the sector for girls, with clothing stores and accessory shops, sock specialty stores, kitchen goods stores, and, of course, lingerie shops. From my point of view, what lay before us was an extremely uncomfortable alternate dimension.

"This seems to be it," Yukinoshita said, unruffled.

I, on the other hand, was completely exhausted. "Yeah, I can't believe we took four wrong turns. You're really bad at the geometry part of math, aren't you?"

"You are the last person I want to criticize my mathematical acumen."

"You don't need math to get into a private arts school. I stopped bothering with that subject at the very beginning. So even if I'm in last place, it's no problem."

"Last place? What kind of grade do you need to rank that low, I wonder...?"

"Nine percent puts you in last place. Source: me."

"...Wouldn't you fail the year that way?"

They force you into supplementary lessons and give you a makeup exam. The questions on those are always the same as the review hand-out, though, so after the supplementary lesson, it's all just a question of memorization. Well, it would be a nuisance for the teacher if I were to redo the year. I'm not surprised they resort to strategies like that if there's no issue with attendance.

"So what're you gonna buy?" I asked.

"...Well, perhaps something she uses normally but that's also durable enough to last a long time," Yukinoshita replied.

"Maybe you should get her some stationery or something, then." No matter how you look at it, I think that's the standard gift for a teenage girl.

"I considered that, but—"

"You did?"

"—but it doesn't strike me as something Yuigahama would enjoy... I doubt she would be pleased to receive a fountain pen or a set of tools."

"That's a sound judgment..."

Indeed, I can't imagine Yuigahama would exclaim, *Wow, I always wanted this screwdriver set! Oh, and it even has hex keys! OMG! And a crowbar! Thank you so much, Yukinon!* Though I also get the feeling female mechanics are in right now.

"So you want to find something relevant to her interests?" I asked.

"Yes. If I'm going to give her a present, I want it to make her happy." Yukinoshita wore a calm smile on her face. Yuigahama would have been ecstatic to see that, I think.

"Let's go choose something, then," I said.

"Hold on. What about your sister?"

Oh yeah. Now that she mentioned it, I hadn't heard from her. We wouldn't be privy to that in-depth advice without Komachi. She'd narrowed down the things Yuigahama might like to a specific category, but we couldn't buy anything if we didn't know what to get. I had my doubts about relying too much on Komachi's counsel, but Yukinoshita's ideas were a fountain pen and a tool set, so her judgment was even more questionable.

I checked my phone, but Komachi hadn't returned my text. I figured I'd try calling her again. When I did, I could hear the familiar *doo dee dee doo* as I had every time so far. Seriously, what was this warbling?

"Hello, hello!"

"Hey! Where are you right now? We're here. We've been waiting for you, so hurry up."

"Huh? Oh...there was a bunch of shopping I wanted to do, so I totally forgot."

"I can't believe my own sister's brain has become such a disappointment... Your big brother is a little shocked." *Come on, does she have the memory of a goldfish? No wonder she's always a mess with memorization-heavy subjects*, I thought.

In response, I received an incredibly contemptuous sigh from the other end of the phone. "...Hmph, I guess you won't understand, no matter what I say. Oh well. Looks like I'm gonna be about another five hours, so I'll go home alone. Good luck, you two!"

"Hey, wait, hold on a second!"

"What? Are you nervous being all alone with Yukino? Don't worry! You'll be okay! Probably."

"No, I don't care about that. Are you okay on your own? It's kinda sketchy for a middle schooler to be alone in a place like this..." The mall was packed with people on the weekends. She could get into an accident or some kind of incident. Plus, Komachi was still in a girl middle school. And she was my little sister, so of course she was cute. She could be cheeky and sometimes obnoxious, but I really was worried for her.

"...*Sigh.* I wish you'd care this much about other things. It's me we're talking about here. I'll be okay."

"No, I'm worried *because* it's you." *You'd go off with anyone who just dangled some candy or some cash in front of your face...*

"Bro, who do you think I am? I'm *your* little sister."

Oh-ho, that was rather touching.

"So I'm totally okay on my own! In fact, I've got even more energy when I'm on my own!"

What incredibly sad rationale.

Although, I'm actually peppier when I'm alone, too, so I couldn't argue. You know, when I play video games and stuff, I talk up a storm. *Agh, what's with that?!* or *Oh-ho, here we go!* or *I love you, Rinko,* etc. And then thanks to that, my mother asks me, *Do you have a friend over?* and I have to stammer, *H-huh? I-I'm on the phone...* I can't play *Love Plus* at home anymore.

"I understand... Well, if anything happens, call me right away. Actually, call me even if nothing happens," I said.

"Yeah, yeah. Okay, I'm hanging up now! Try your best, Bro!" And she hung up. All I heard after that was a mechanical *beep, beep, beep.*

You don't need that much effort to buy a present, though…

I put away my cell phone and faced Yukinoshita again. "Apparently, Komachi wants to do some shopping, so she's totally abandoned us."

"I see… Well, she did go to the trouble of coming out with us on a weekend, so I have no right to complain," Yukinoshita said, somewhat disheartened, before continuing as if trying to restore her motivation. "But we did learn what kind of things Yuigahama might like, so now let's just do what we can from here."

Man, I'm super-uneasy about this.

Yukinoshita ignored my anxiety and moved toward a nearby clothing store. She went inside and took some of the items on display in hand, scrupulously inspecting them. I decided to follow Yukinoshita… but I knew I wouldn't last.

First of all, the female customers greeted the man entering their store with caustic glares as if I were some breed of insect. And then the staff marshaled around me like they found me suspicious. They totally got into attack formation just to deal with me.

Wh-why…? There's other guys in the store besides me! Is this discrimination? Hey, this is discrimination, isn't it?! But in truth, the other male customers looked kind of normie-ish. They had scarves around their necks even though it wasn't cold, and they were wearing vests like hunters. To judge the books by their covers, these guys were normies. *What's that weird string on your pants? What do you use it for?*

"Um, sir…may I help you find something?" One of the clerks spoke to me, masking her suspicion with a pasted-on smile.

"Uh, well, um…s-sorry," I apologized reflexively.

My ambiguous apology must have made the staff even more wary, as another clerk showed up. *Oh, crap, she's called reinforcements! It's just one red flag after another! My party is gonna be wiped out!* At this rate, if I stuck around, they were bound to summon more allies. But right when I'd decided to make an immediate escape, someone threw me a rope.

"Hikigaya…what are you doing? Trying on clothes? Can you not keep such activities to your own home?"

"I don't do 'such activities' at home, either! And I haven't even done anything..."

When Yukinoshita and her condescension drew near, the clerks' suspicion waned. Impressive as usual, Yukinoshita. She was a pro when it came to pushing people away.

"Oh, so you came here with your girlfriend. Take your time," the clerk said as if she'd come to her own conclusions, and then she tried to leave.

"Uh, she's not my girlfriend..."

"She's not? Then you really shouldn't be here..." Her eyes went from neutral blue to attack red! I picked the wrong option! At this rate, I could only envision a police report and the ensuing bad ending in my future.

Sigh. "Hikigaya, let's go." Yukinoshita dragged me by the hand out of the crowd of clerks shuffling toward me. That alone halted their approach.

Once we left the shop, my anxiety finally loosened its grip. "...Am I that suspicious?" With that dull expression on my face, my eyes must have looked a million times more rotten than they usually did. One could say this incident had only begot more rot.

Even Yukinoshita spared some sympathy for me and didn't needle me at all for being fishy. "It seems a male customer on his own is viewed with suspicion. From what I could see, all the boys in that store were with their girlfriends."

I see. So it was a girls/couples-only zone, just like *purikura*. In summation, there was nothing I could do here. I lacked the courage to brave that store again. "...I'll be over there, then," I said, motioning to a bench a little ways away. Even though we were outside the store, the area was teeming with females. If I stayed here alone, I could easily imagine all the odd looks I would get. I mean, I get those just by sitting in the classroom at school.

But if I stayed on a bench near the periphery, I most certainly shouldn't be reported to the police. As long as I didn't do anything to invite distrust, I'd be okay. I think I'd probably be okay. Maybe I'd be okay. Anyway, I figured I'd steel myself a little and started for the bench.

"Wait."

"Hmm?"

Behind me, Yukinoshita approached at a brisk pace. "Do you intend to leave this decision up to my tastes?" she asked. "I'm not proud of this, but my personal standards are incongruous with those of the average high school girl."

"So you're aware..." Well, this was the girl whose first idea of a gift was a tool set.

"So, um...it would be helpful if you could give me a hand." Yukinoshita was staring at the ground, as if the request was incredibly difficult for her to make. Her lowered gaze flitted around restlessly.

If she was asking me, she had to be pretty damn stumped. Just so you know, I'd never bought an actual present for a girl before. I *have* presented myself and been totally shut down, though. "Well, I'd love to help you out, but I can't go into any stores," I replied.

Yukinoshita sighed as if resigned. "There's no avoiding it this time. Try not to stray too far from me."

"Huh? What?" I stared at her, puzzled.

Yukinoshita was mildly sullen. "Must I be explicit in order for you understand? If all you're capable of is sucking in and expelling air, that air conditioner over there is far superior to you."

It's true. Those useful machines clean the atmosphere and save electricity and stuff. Before long, they'll even be able to read the air, too. I hope.

"In other words, I'm saying that I will permit you to act as if you're my boyfriend for this day only."

"Now, that doesn't sound arrogant at all." Whoa, she was obnoxious.

Yukinoshita seemed to have perceived my irritation, as she glared at me. "Do you have any objections?"

"Not really."

"I—I see..." Yukinoshita looked sincerely surprised. Disappointed, even.

There was nothing to be shocked about, though. There was no way in hell I'd agree to be her boyfriend, but I didn't really mind pretending. Yukinoshita didn't lie. So if she said this was for today only, then it would be precisely for one day. And if she said "as if you're my boyfriend," she most certainly didn't mean her *actual* boyfriend. That's why I was so comfortable following her suggestion. Just as Yukinoshita had unwavering faith that I was trash, I, too, had absolute confidence that we would never go anywhere. Perhaps this was, in a way, something you could call trust. What the hell. This wasn't peaceful at all, though.

I guess Yukinoshita realized her expression was rather befuddled, as she spun around in an attempt to hide it and replied with something *really* unexpected. "...I thought for sure you would hate the idea."

"Well, there's no real reason to refuse. And, like, don't *you* hate the idea?" I hit the ball back into her court.

Yukinoshita faced me again, now composed. "I don't really care. It's not like anyone I know will see me. I'll be surrounded by strangers, so I won't have to worry about people getting the wrong idea and damaging my reputation." *There she goes, casually treating me like a stranger. Well, not like I care.* "All right, let's go, then," she declared before heading toward the next shop.

I stepped forward, too, keeping pace at her side. I think our lack of expectations might be what made our relationship so comfortable. It's like, you know—they say that packed inside Pandora's box were all the misfortunes of the world, plus hope. It was like that. It was hope and misfortune.

X X X

Things went surprisingly smoothly in the next clothing store. The world was far more straightforward and simple than I had believed. All we had to do was walk together as a young boy and girl, and people assumed we were a couple. Well, it's true, now that I think about it. Even I start mentally chanting curses when I see a high school boy and girl in a pair. Surprisingly enough, maybe that's just how it is.

Yukinoshita's proximity was enough to dispel the misgivings of even the staff who had dogged me so hard I wondered if their training surpassed the Japan national soccer team's. Yukinoshita had forgone all relationships with those around her, so as might be expected, she turned away any approaching staff with only a brief "I'm fine" as she sternly filtered through clothing. Occasionally, she'd take something that struck her fancy and tug it taut from the sides, or top to bottom.

I suspect there may have been something unusual about her evaluative standards.

"Shall we move on?" She swiftly folded the clothing in her hands and returned it all to the shelf. Evidently, she had doubts about their durability.

"Listen, you'll spend the rest of your life trying to make a decision if you're basing it on durability," I pointed out. "I don't think Yuigahama is looking for any bonus to defense in her clothes." *She's fine with the plain clothes. It's not like there are any slimes or skeletons around.*

"…*Sigh.* There's no helping that. I don't know what else to do but base my decisions on the quality of the stitching and material…don't know what Yuigahama likes or what she's interested in." That sigh was deeper than the ones from earlier, and more despondent. She was likely regretting that she'd never even tried to find out.

If so, her chagrin was meaningless. "You don't really need to know, though. In fact, it'd just upset her if you acted like you knew everything when you're operating on meager knowledge. It's like sending peanuts from somewhere else to a Chiba person."

"Your example is so Chiba, I have no idea what you're talking about…," Yukinoshita said, mildly exasperated.

Hmph, so that one wouldn't work for her. Basically, we Chibanese are fastidious when it comes to peanuts. There's a reason we pride ourselves as the number one producer of peanuts in the country. Actually, it's a little weird that a whole 70 percent of the peanuts are from Chiba. By the way, 20 percent come from Ibaraki. They also call it the land of Nanking beans. I wonder why they call peanuts Nanking beans when they're grown in Japan. "To use a more familiar analogy, it's like sending a gift of wine to a sommelier when you don't know much about wine," I said.

"I see… You have a point." She indicated her understanding with a nod of agreement.

Yeah. It's something my dad does a lot with birthday presents. Like how he got a PlayStation and a Saturn mixed up. And how they were out of Super Nintendos and he was like, *Well, Mega Drive, 3DO, they're all the same bleep-bloops, whatever'll be fine.* When you try to make a gift of something you're clueless about, the present usually ends up being crap.

"…So your twisted system of values *can* be of use." She said it like she was half-impressed, but I suspected it was not at all a compliment. "You're right, though. When you're competing in the field in which your opponent specializes, you have slim chances of winning. In order to win, you must go for their weak point instead…"

Even buying presents is a battle for you? Are you from some Amazonian tribe or what? "Well, going for her weak point—that is to say, compensating for it—could work. I think that would fulfill your practicality requirements."

"All right, if that's the case, then…" Yukinoshita must have hit upon an idea, as she headed for the next store.

Stopping in front of the lingerie shop across from the clothing store…actually, I stopped, and Yukinoshita disappeared into the kitchen goods shop beside it. *Am I the only one who finds the isolated underwear stands in a department store far more erotic than this blatant emphasis on sexy and cute?* Also, I think that time in June when they sell school swimsuits is even more erotic.

But back to the point. In the kitchenware store, aside from the basic cooking tools like frying pans and pots, there was a selection of novelty items like oven mitts that reminded me of Puppet Muppet and cutlery sets based on *matryoshka* dolls.

"I see… This is indeed Yuigahama's weak point." Yuigahama is a bad cook. No, an *incredibly* bad cook. I ate her homemade cookies once, but they were terrible, like the charcoal they sell at a hardware store. Joyful Honda, specifically. Anyway, they had tasted about as disgusting as they looked. I wouldn't even call it "taste." "Gustatory stimulation" would be more accurate. I wasn't the only one who had eaten them—Yukinoshita had, too. Though under Yukinoshita's earnest guidance, Yuigahama had attained a minimum level of improvement. If she were to attempt cooking anything more complicated, I doubted the results would be anything decent.

Still, this store was fun. *Whoa, what's with that pot lid? The handle part is open so you can put in spices? That's fascinating. Oh no, I'm acting so stupid.*

The moment I thought all they had were these handy little gizmos, I found they even had a real-deal wok. *Oh man, this makes me want to laugh like* Ka-ka-ka-ka! *and wave it around.* I get like this with DIY stores and hundred-yen shops, too, but just browsing the gadgets and tools made me excited.

"Hikigaya, over here."

I went over when she called me and found Yukino Yukinoshita in an apron. The black was surprisingly light for such a dark color, and on her, it even seemed fresh. The chest was decorated with tiny cat paw prints.

The dainty ribbon ties wrapped around her middle emphasized Yukinoshita's tight waist. She twirled around in a full circle, as if dancing a waltz, to make sure the ties around her neck and arms were secure and test her ease of motion while wearing it. The unraveling ties trailed behind her like a tail. "What do you think?"

"I don't know what I say…except that it really suits you." There was nothing else I *could* say. Maybe it was her black hair, but that kind of modest fashion fit her ridiculously well.

Despite my sincere compliment, Yukinoshita first focused on a full-length mirror to check the shoulders, the ties, and the skirt of the apron. Only the mirror could see the expression on her face. "…I see. Thank you. But I don't mean me. I was asking your opinion about making this my gift to Yuigahama."

"I don't think it would suit her. Wouldn't she be happier with something more fluffy, puffy, and stupid?"

"That's an unkind way to put it, but you're right, so I don't know what to say…," Yukinoshita said and removed the apron before carefully folding it. "So something else from around here, then?" Still holding the cloth, she sought out her next prey. This time she just checked the number of pockets and the fabric and whatnot.

Indeed, checking the fabric quality is necessary. I think asbestos or other fireproof materials would be a good choice. I get the impression Yuigahama would be a fire hazard.

Ultimately, Yukinoshita selected a pale-pink apron without too much ornamentation. "I'll go with this one."

"Yeah, that'll work." There was one small pocket on each side and a big 4D pocket in the middle. You could stuff as much candy or whatever as you wanted in there. It would suit Yuigahama.

Yukinoshita gathered up the pink apron and headed for the register with it and the black apron.

"Between this and that stuffed animal, you've been shrewd about sneaking your own shopping into this trip, huh?"

"…I didn't plan to buy the apron, though."

"So this is an impulse buy? Well, that happens a lot when you go shopping."

"…"

Yukinoshita opened her mouth as if to retort but paused halfway. She averted her eyes and headed off to the register alone.

So it wasn't an impulse buy? I just don't get her. However, one thing I *did* know was that she'd planned to buy that weird panda plush from the very beginning.

X X X

I picked up a few items at the pet store and rang up my purchases at the counter. Yukinoshita was not with me. She hadn't left me behind to go straight home, though. She wasn't *that* callous. I'd said I wanted to do some shopping on my own, and she'd instantly accepted. That was all. Wait, no, that actually was callous.

I thought about calling her, but there was a limited number of places she would go in a shop like this, so I just strolled through the aisles of the pet-goods area toward the cages to find Yukinoshita there, surprise, surprise. She was squatting down with her legs hugged up to her chest, a soft smile on her lips, as she timidly petted a kitten and occasionally fluffed up its fur. Most likely, she wasn't going to meow at it because there were people around. She was so absorbed in petting that cat, it was hard for me to interrupt her.

As I paused, deliberating, the kitty's ears perked up and twitched toward me, and Yukinoshita turned with them. "Oh, that was fast." (Translation: *I wanted to fluff the cat more…*)

"Sorry." I couldn't say for sure if I meant *Sorry for making you wait* or *Sorry for coming back so soon*, but I apologized anyway.

Yukinoshita gave the kitten one last reluctant skritch and mouthed a voiceless *meow* of farewell as she departed. "So what did you get? I think I have an idea, though."

"Well, mainly what you'd expect."

"I see." Her reply was indifferent, but her face betrayed some mild satisfaction. She seemed happy to have been correct. "I'm surprised you'd buy a present for Yuigahama, though," she said.

I didn't know what to say to that. "...It's no big. This is just part of our contest. I've simply decided to ally myself with you for the time being."

"What a rare event... Are you ill?" Yukinoshita's eyes were wide with surprise.

Hey, that's rude. I mean, it wasn't a bad idea to motivate Yuigahama to come back by celebrating her birthday. It was just that in order to do so, I needed my and Yuigahama's relationship to be properly settled. I had a sense that if I didn't do anything, eventually the same thing would happen again. "We've done what we came to do, so let's go," I said.

"Sure."

The time was around two-ish. We'd spent a surprising amount of time at the mall, despite my original intention to go straight in, buy what I needed, and make a beeline for home.

I took the lead until we reached the exit. Somehow I doubted we'd ever escape the place if I let Yukinoshita find our way back, too. I was fine leaving the giant maze that used to be here a relic of the past.

On our way out, we passed an arcade aimed at families and couples. It had medal games, crane games, co-op shooters, racing games that import photos of your face, and *purikura*. Basically, all the machines were for whiling away the time giggling with your friends. In other words, not a place I'd ever visit.

While I tried to forge ahead past it, Yukinoshita stopped in her tracks.

"What? Do you want to play a game or something?"

"I have no interest in games," she said, but she was fixated on the crane machines. Actually, upon closer inspection, that wasn't true. Tracing her line of vision, she was eyeing a single unit—one full of familiar-looking stuffed animals. Gloomy eyes that had witnessed the darkness of the world, claws that could surely slice through both bamboo and beast, and eerily whetted fangs that gleamed in the artificial light. Of course, it was Ginnie the Grue. The stuffed animal emitted such a looming aura of darkness, I understood why they called him "the Grue."

"...Do you want to try?" I asked.

"I'm fine. It's not like I really want to play any games." (Translation: *I just want the stuffed animal.*)

I was mentally interpreting Yukinoshita's statements so skillfully I started wondering if I'd eaten some of Doraemon's weird translation jelly. "Well, if you want it, why don't you just give it a try? I don't think you'll be able to, though."

"That's quite an inflammatory thing to say. Do you think I'm incapable?" My remarks must have irked her. Yukinoshita's typical frigidity had returned.

"No, I'm not trying to diss your skills or anything. This stuff is just hard if you don't have the practice. Komachi has tried it over and over, but she's never succeeded." The sight of Komachi with nearly her entire savings in hand as she inserted coin after coin was depressing.

But of course, comparing Yukinoshita to Komachi wasn't going to quash my classmate's competitive spirit. She inserted a thousand-yen bill into the change machine. "Then I just have to practice," she said, and she piled up the hundred-yen coins beside the coin slot, ready to stick them in one after another. When she slid in the first one, the machine made a stupid, mechanical-sounding *fweeeeh* noise.

Yukinoshita stared intently at the device as if trying to ascertain something—concentrating, unmoving, silent.

"..."

Grave as ever, she seemed to be facing it down with the power of her will.

Wait... Does she...

Does she not know how to work the machine...?

"You move the crane to the side by pressing the button on the left side," I told her. "The button on the right moves it toward the rear. It only moves when you're holding the button down. Once you take your finger off, it stops."

"O-oh...thank you." Blushing, Yukinoshita started the game.

First, she moved the crane toward the right... *Yeah, okay, that's about right.* And then she moved it toward the rear. *Mm-hmm, I think that positioning's pretty good.* Then the crane whined *fweeeeeh* and tried to grab the stuffed animal. *Wh-what's with this crane? Those cries are kinda cute...*

"...I got it," I heard Yukinoshita whisper. When I glanced over at her, she had squeezed her hand into fist and did a tiny fist pump.

But sweet little Crane cried *fweeeh* and dropped the toy before moving back to her original position and falling silent.

Failure.

"See? It's hard at first," I said, trying to console her.

But Yukinoshita just glowered with all her might at poor little Crane. "...Look, I grabbed it perfectly just now, didn't I? How am I supposed to drop it in the chute?" Yukinoshita pressed little Crane for an answer, just like she usually pressed me. She was so intense, I hesitated to speak. She was really scary.

"W-well, it's like, what you did just now moved it to a slightly better position. The trick is to move it little by little." I read word for word the pointers written on the machine.

"I see. So you compensate for the flimsiness of the arm through multiple attempts, huh?" Now that she'd grasped the idea, she put in another hundred yen.

Fweeeh...

"...Ngh! Not again."

Fweeeh, fweeeeh.

"You cut that out..."

Fweeh...

"Agh! ..."

From their voices alone, it sounded like Yukinoshita was bullying poor little Crane. Yukinoshita's face said *calm and collected*, but her hand was swiftly inserting another coin.

She's gonna keep going? At this rate, she'll never win, no matter how many times she tries. "...You suck at this."

"Wha...? Well, if that's how you're going to be, then you must be pretty good yourself, hmm?" Yukinoshita said, glaring daggers at me.

I replied with bursting confidence, "Yeah, because I've been doing this for a long time, like whenever Komachi pesters me to get something for her. It's led to a lot of improvement...on Komachi's part. At pestering me..."

"So *she's* the one who improved...?"

But seriously, when did I first end up being totally at Komachi's mercy,

I wonder…? I have zero dignity as an older brother. "Move aside. *I'll* get it for you," I proclaimed, and Yukinoshita reluctantly surrendered her position to me with intense distrust. "Behold, my secret technique." And then I slowly lifted my right hand up straight overhead.

Yukinoshita watched my hand with brimming curiosity and anticipation.

Not yet…not yet… Timing was key here. And then I caught a softly moving shadow at the edge of my vision.

Now! "U-um, excuse me! I'd like to get this…"

"Yes, sir. This Ginnie the Grue, right? Okay, here we go!"

Fweeh…, little Crane cried, and I heard the soft thump of the toy falling into place. "Here you go, sir." The arcade girl held out Grue-bear to us with a beaming grin. These days a lot of arcades will get the toys for you.

"Ah, thanks," I said. The girl replied with another ear-to-ear smile and left.

Yukinoshita, on the other hand, was side-eying me even more moodily than usual.

"Wh-what…?"

"Nothing… I was just wondering if you're ashamed to be alive."

"Listen, Yukinoshita. Nothing is more precious than life. Shame over ascribing it its proper value is the greatest shame of all. So people who giggle and sneer at me, *Ohh, how embarrassing!* are totally worthless human beings."

"A lovely sentiment, but there was rather too much bile seeping into the conclusion." Yukinoshita flipped her hair in exasperation and breathed a short sigh. "Good grief… I thought you were taking something seriously for once, but then you pull that…"

"I never said I was gonna win it myself. I just said I'd get it for you. Here, it's yours." I pushed Grue-bear toward Yukinoshita.

But she pushed it back. "You're the one who won it. I may disagree with your methods, but I will recognize your achievement." Even with such inconsequential matters, Yukinoshita tried to be proper. *I guess you'd call it being conscientious. Or actually, stubborn. Wait, no, she's just pigheaded.*

But I wasn't about to lose a competition in that arena. "I don't want it, though. And, like, it was *your* money that went into this. You basically paid for it. So you're obligated to accept it," I said, and as I did, Yukinoshita's shoving weakened, and I plunked the stuffed animal into her arms.

"...O-okay." Yukinoshita studied the creature in her embrace, and then she looked at me. "...I'm not giving it back."

"I told you I don't want it." Who would want such an evil-looking stuffed animal, anyway? Besides, she was holding it with such care and reverence, I couldn't ask for it back now. So she did have a cute side. I thought her blood ran colder than that.

Perhaps she noticed my lips quirking upward, since she turned away a bit shyly with ever-so-slightly red cheeks. "...You don't think it suits me? It's easier to imagine Yuigahama or Totsuka with something like this, isn't it?"

"I dunno about the former, but the latter, definitely." Totsuka and stuffed animals go together like cookies and milk. "I guess I'm honestly surprised you like plushies," I blurted.

Yukinoshita didn't react with any indignation, though. She just slowly petted Grue-bear. "...I'm not terribly interested in other stuffed animals. I only like Ginnie the Grue." Yukinoshita took the bear's arm and waved it around. Grue-bear's claws scraped together with a sinister noise. If I could have ignored that sound, it would have been terribly cute. "I've always collected the plushies and licensed goods, but unlike items distributed normally, you can unfortunately only get this one by winning it yourself. I have considered buying from online auction sites, but I always worried it might not be in the best condition, and the sellers could easily post manipulated photos, so I could never bring myself to do it."

H-her rationale isn't cute at all.

I sighed. "Anyway, you like Grue-bear a lot, huh?" In response to this display of her pointless obsession, the perfunctory comment slipped from my mouth.

Surprisingly, Yukinoshita's eyes clouded and focused on something distant. "...I do. I got it when I was little."

"A plushie?"

"No, the original novel in English."

"What? There's a book?" I was so surprised, I asked without thinking.

It was a mistake. Yukinoshita immediately began rambling on and on in a reverie. "The title of the novel is *Hello, Mister Panda*, but the title of the first edition was *The Panda's Garden*. According to popular belief, when the American biologist Rand Macintosh moved to China with his family for his research, he began writing these stories for his son, who couldn't quite adapt to the new environment."

"...Whoa there, Yukipedia," I teased, backing away.

But Yukinoshita was totally oblivious and continued talking. "...The more famous Destiny version emphasizes the characters and features more cartoonish art, but the original novel is excellent, as well. It's a skillfully written metaphor about the cultures of East and West that weaves it all into one coherent narrative. And most of all, you feel the messages of love aimed at his son in every word."

"Huh? That's what it was about? I thought it was just a whimsical tale about a panda who's like, *I'd like to eat lots of bamboo* twenty-four-seven, gets drunk off it, and goes all Drunken Fist."

"The Destiny version does play up that aspect of it; I can't deny that. But that's only one small portion of the original novel. You'll know if you read it yourself. The translation is more than serviceable, but I do recommend reading it in the original language." Yukinoshita must have enjoyed talking about it.

Oh, but I know the feeling. I get like that when I'm talking about topics I like. Back in middle school, I weirded out a potential friend when I rambled on and on about some manga I liked for half an hour. Eventually, he was just like, "You're usually pretty quiet, Hikigaya, but you talk up a storm when it's about manga. It's kinda...uh..."

But I believe it's beneficial to chatter about the things you like to your heart's content, no matter if it's bizarre or unacceptable to the general public. If I have to choose between abandoning something I love or abandoning people who don't even necessarily like me...it's not even a decision.

But still, her recommendation to read the book in English was a little much. I *would* read a certain magical index, though.

"Wait, so you've been able to read English since you were little?"

"Of course not. When I first received the book, I couldn't understand it, but that's what made me want to learn. I read it with my nose half in the dictionary. It was like a puzzle. I enjoyed every minute."

Yukinoshita's eyes were wistful and soft, gazing upon a distant memory, and then she whispered softly, "...It was a birthday present. Perhaps that's why I'm particularly attached to it. So...um..." Yukinoshita bashfully buried her face in the stuffed animal, hiding her expression as her eyes turned toward me. "Um... Thank—"

"Huh? Yukino-chan? Oh, it *is* you!"

A loud greeting cut her off.

When I found the source of that familiar-sounding voice, I was dumbfounded. She was the spitting image of a certain someone I knew, with lustrous black hair, fine, translucent skin, and a fair and well-proportioned face. Her radiant, exceptional good looks accompanied an overall tidy image, and her convivial smile contributed a glamorous appeal.

The woman before my eyes was a stunning beauty. She must have been hanging out with her friends, as she said, "Sorry, you guys go on without me," to the shuffling group of men and women behind her and pressed her hands together in an apologetic gesture.

I was assaulted by déjà vu. Not only that, but something about her was making me tortuously uncomfortable.

"Ugh, my sister..." Yukinoshita's open, artless demeanor vanished in favor of complete horror. Her voice drew my attention, and I saw her crushing the stuffed panda bear in her grip. Her shoulders were rigid.

"Huh? Sister? What?" I visually compared the newcomer to Yukinoshita. She appeared to be a twenty-something. Her outfit was composed of flowing white fabric bordered with fluttering lace, her long arms and legs drawing the eye to her beautiful skin. The ensemble revealed large swaths of her body, but it mysteriously bestowed an air of class on her as a whole. She did indeed resemble Yukinoshita. If Yukinoshita was solidly beautiful, then this woman overflowed with liquid charisma.

"What're you doing out here? Ohhh! You're on a date! A date, I bet! Oh, you rascal!"

"..."

The woman gleefully ribbed her younger sister with her elbow. All she got for her efforts, however, was icy pique.

Oh-ho. Though they were superficially quite similar, it seemed their dispositions were not. Arming myself with an objective viewpoint, I

observed a number of disparities between them. First: their chests. Unlike modest Yukinoshita, the elder sister's bosom was pleasantly full. The juxtaposition of a slender figure with an ample rack was striking. *I get it now! That weird feeling was just the difference in boob size! Wait, no, there's more.*

"*Soooo* is this your *boy*friend, Yukino-chan? Huh?" the woman teased.

"...No. We're classmates," replied Yukinoshita.

"Oh, you. You don't have to be so shy with me!"

"..."

Whoa, Yukinoshita's glaring like hell at her sister.

But her sister was all sunshine, utterly immune to such terrifying antipathy.

"I'm Yukino-chan's sister, Haruno. Be nice to her, 'kay?"

"Uh-huh. I'm Hikigaya." She'd introduced herself to me, so I answered in kind. Apparently, the sister's name was Haruno Yukinoshita. Look, Chii is learning.

"Hikigaya, huh...?" Haruno pensively interposed herself between us for a moment and gave me a swift once-over from my toes to the top of my head.

I shivered in the ensuing chill. I was locked in place.

"So, Hikigaya? Oh, it's so nice to meet you! ♪"

But her beaming smile melted that feeling away. What the hell was that...? Was I nervous because a pretty lady was looking at me?

Haruno was as bright and warm as the sunlight kanji in her name suggested. Though she and Yukinoshita bore similar features, the two of them gave very different impressions. While Yukinoshita was a living glacier, Haruno's expression was ever-changing. I had never realized there were so many different ways you could smile. *So even with the same parts, you can utilize them in different ways to create completely different images*, I thought, impressed.

Though I had figured out what distinguished them, the discomfort tickling my spine still would not go away. Perhaps the source was something else. I inspected Haruno suspiciously.

She met my eyes for a brief second before immediately turning to Yukinoshita. "Oh, that plushie. It's Ginnie the Grue, isn't it?" she gushed, reaching out to the toy. "I really like this guy! Aww, he's so fluffy! I'm so jealous, Yuki!"

"Don't touch it." Yukinoshita's acerbic reply left my ears numb. It wasn't particularly loud, but the finality of the rejection stung my ears.

Perhaps Haruno felt it, too, as her eternal smile froze on her face. "... Wh-whoa there, you startled me! S-sorry! I gotcha—it's a present from your boyfriend, huh? I was a little insensitive."

"I'm not her boyfriend, though," I said.

"Ohh, you're mad, too, huh? You're not gonna get off easy if you make Yukino-chan cry!" Haruno jabbed a chiding finger into my cheek, twisting it around painfully. "Nope!"

Hey, that hurts! And you're too close! Back up, back up, you smell nice! The proximity from which she interacted with people informed me of her social skills. If Haruno was willing to move in this close, she must be terrifyingly adroit.

"Are you done, Haruno? If you don't have any business in particular, we're leaving," said Yukinoshita.

But Haruno showed no intention of listening and continued to prod me. "Come on, come on! Out with it! When did you two start dating?"

"Hey, seriously! Could you please cut that out?!" I said.

But her finger drill persisted, and before I knew it, Haruno was pinned up against me. *Wait, they're touching me! Oh, now they're not. And they've made contact again! A flawless outboxing technique from Haruno's boobs! Is she Muhammad Ali...?*

"...Haruno. That's enough." Yukinoshita's tone was so low the words were creeping along the ground. Not at all attempting to hide her irritation, she briskly brushed her hair behind her and pierced Haruno with a dagger of disdain.

"Oh... Sorry, Yukino-chan. I guess I got a little carried away," Haruno apologized with a weak smile. It was like the set-up with an innocent older sister and a touchy younger sister. And then she quietly whispered into my ear—*Seriously, too close*—"Sorry. She's a sensitive girl...so take good care of her, okay, Hikigaya?"

Right then, that unsettling feeling reached its peak. I reflexively jerked my head away from her.

Haruno tilted her entire upper body to the right in surprise, squinting at me in a silent *Huuuh?* It was so adorable all the men nearby noticed, just for an instant. "Did I do something to make you upset? If I did, I'm sorry," she said, poking out her pink tongue. Her posture ignited a protective urge in me that swelled into a flood of guilt. I had to come up with some excuse for my behavior!

"Oh, uh, not really... It's just, um, my ears are sensitive, so..."

"Hikigaya, don't announce your fetishes to a woman you just met. You'll have no leg to stand on if you get sued." Yukinoshita was gently pressing her forehead as if pained.

As for Haruno, she was back to the old genial smile. "Eh-heh! ♪ Hikigaya, you're so funny!" My excuse must have tickled Haruno's funny bone or something, I don't know, but she burst into laughter and started whacking me on the back. *I'm not kidding. Back off.* "Oh yeah, Hikigaya. If you'd like, do you wanna come have some tea with me? As Yukino-chan's older sister, I need to know if you're good enough for her." Haruno puffed out her chest in a pose and casually winked at me.

"...Drop it already. I told you, we're just in the same class." The severe remark struck with the stinging cold of an Arctic blizzard. It was a brusque rejection of Haruno's teasing. Yukino Yukinoshita's ultimate shutdown.

But Haruno just smirked and brushed it aside. "But like...this is the first time I've ever seen you out with anyone. Of course I'd assume he's your boyfriend. I was just happy for you." She giggled as if she found the whole situation funny. "You're only young once, so you've got to enjoy it, you know! Oh, but don't get carried away, okay?" Haruno placed her left hand on her hip and leaned forward to wag her right pointer finger in a good-humored warning. Then she drew near to Yukinoshita's ear, quietly whispering, "Because Mother is still angry about you living on your own."

The moment she heard the word *Mother*, Yukinoshita tensed up. A curtain of silence descended upon the stage. I even entertained the illusion that the ruckus of the arcade around us had receded like the tide. Pausing for a beat, Yukinoshita embraced the stuffed panda as if confirming it was still there. "That's not really any of your business." As she spoke, she looked not straight ahead but at the ground. Yukino Yukinoshita, who always stood tall and looked you right in the eye. Yukino Yukinoshita, who never yielded to anyone or lowered her gaze, ever.

From where I was standing, this was a shocking phenomenon. Though Yukinoshita could get a little morose sometimes, I had never ever seen her bend her knee to anyone.

Suddenly, Haruno's lips formed into a pleasant expression that didn't reach her eyes. "Oh. I suppose so. That's none of my business, is it?" she said, and she practically jumped away from her sister. "As long as you're aware, that's enough. I guess I should keep my nose out of it. Sorry, sorry." Haruno flashed her teeth with a chuckle as if that would smooth things over and returned the conversation to me. "Hikigaya. If you do end up with Yuki, let's make sure to have tea together. See you later, then!" With one last cheerful grin, she did a little wave good-bye in front of her chest and scurried off. As if her sunny disposition had manifested in an aura around her, I could hardly take my eyes off her until she was entirely out of view.

Then both Yukinoshita and I started walking again, neither of us in particular taking the lead.

"Your sister really is something...," I remarked.

Yukinoshita nodded. "Everyone who meets her says that."

"I'll bet. I get why."

"Yes. Her physique is perfect, she's academically peerless, she's intelligent and athletic, and she's kind and caring to boot. I doubt anyone exists who is as perfect as she is. Everyone sings her praises."

"Huh? You're not much different. Is that your version of bragging?" I said.

Yukinoshita looked up at me, flabbergasted. "...What?"

"When I say she's 'really something,' I mean more like, how can I put this... She's wearing a mask like a fortified armor shell."

A fortified armor shell...or, no, maybe a mobile suit. Anyway, that was the source of the misgivings Haruno Yukinoshita had given me. Perhaps it would be more accurate to say she was ensconced in such an aura.

"Your sister acts like some lonely virgin's ideal woman. She's friendly and unreserved about approaching you, she's always smiling, and she tried to talk to me normally. Also, um...she's a little too physical, and, like...soft to the touch."

"Are you even aware of how disgusting you sound...?"

"D-don't be stupid! I meant her hands, her *hands*! Her hands were soft!" My excuses did nothing to lift the weight of Yukinoshita's scorn. In an attempt to bring the conversation back, I raised my voice a little. "But an ideal is just an ideal. It's not reality. So it comes off as sorta fake."

I doubt anyone is more of a realist than a foreveralone. The Three Non-Connection Principles of the Foreveralone are carved into my soul: The foreveralone shall neither possess hope nor manufacture weaknesses in the heart, nor shall he permit the introduction of anything that sounds too good into foreveralone territory. This model soldier who grapples day and night with the ultimate enemy that is reality will not be deceived by such cheap tricks.

In this world, though there may exist the "good woman," there is no such thing as a "yes woman."

—Hachiman Hikigaya

I came up with a line that could pass for a pithy quote, and I engraved it on my soul as such.

Yukinoshita regarded me somberly. "...So despite the putrefaction of your eyes...or no, *because* of it, you can see through these things, can't you...?"

"Was that supposed to be a compliment?"

"It was. It's high praise."

That's news to me...

Yukinoshita crossed her arms in displeasure, and her eyes took on a faraway look. "It's just as you say. That's my sister's social face. You know about my family, right? My sister is the eldest girl, so she was always taken to political events and parties to introduce herself. That's how she formed that mask... I'm impressed you could tell."

"Yeah, my dad taught me all about that stuff. He told me to watch out for women selling paintings at sketchy galleries and stuff like that. I'm wary of people who get into my personal space when we've only just met. A long time ago, someone like that strung my dad along and manipulated him into taking out a loan." I heard my mom was hopping mad after that happened. Anyhow, my extracurricular education has borne fruit, since I've never fallen for any of that stuff so far. I don't think I ever will.

Yukinoshita breathed a short sigh and put her hand to her temple. "Haah… What a stupid reason. My sister would never believe something like that bested her facade." Her aggravation was evident.

That wasn't the only reason I could tell, though. "Also, though superficially you two are similar, the way you smile is totally different." I know Yukinoshita's real smile. Not one of flattery or deception, nor a smile to cover something up, but the real deal.

Yukinoshita's strides lengthened, and she took a few steps ahead of me. "…What a stupid reason." She spun around wearing her usual, slightly stony expression. "Let's go," she said quietly, and I nodded. We reached the exit without exchanging a single word.

I didn't ask any questions of Yukinoshita, and she made no move to do so of me, either. There were probably things I should have asked and things we should have discussed. But we chose to maintain our usual distance, neither of us intruding on the other. The time we passed together was cold. We were merely two strangers sitting beside each other on the train. When we arrived at our station, Yukinoshita stood from her seat first, and I followed suit.

After we passed through the ticket gates, Yukinoshita paused for a moment. "I'm going this way," she said, pointing to the south exit.

"Okay. Bye," I replied and started to the north.

Then I heard a soft murmur at my back. "I had fun today. See you."

I instinctively doubted my ears. When I jerked around to look, Yukinoshita was already marching away, showing no sign she would acknowledge me. In the end, I watched her go until she was completely out of sight.

I dunno... Ho stuff.
Talk about? I mean, she generally talks with Yukinoshita. A lot of the time I'm just listening.
Yeah, yeah. But, well, I think she's a good person.
She's really nice to everyone. Actually, that's the part of her I can't trust, though.
That remark just erased what little desire I had to trust them.
Regarding Yui Yuigahama

I've gotta find out what's up with him this time for sure!

That's no good. No girl is nice to everyone, you know? You need to have more faith in girls! 'Cause we're only nice to people who make it worth our while!

5

Despite it all, **Yoshiteru Zaimokuza** wails alone in the wasteland.

Monday. Given that it means "day of the moon," you'd think there'd be more butts involved, but of course, it was nothing so sexy. The thought of another week of school was enough to draw a sigh from me. *Another week of school…* I had a serious itch to cut class, but of course, with no one to take notes for me or collect extra handouts, I was forced to attend more often. It costs money to go to school, and yet I still want to skip, so I bet I'll end up skipping constantly when I get employed. You don't even have to pay for that. No, I wouldn't want to cause trouble for my coworkers by shirking my duties, so I'd prefer never working in the first place.

But normies are always spouting stuff like *Oh man, school is such a drag. Ah-ha-ha! And I lost my textbook over summer vacation!* so why do they adore school so much? They show up every day, right? Perhaps espousing views one doesn't actually hold is a core tenet of normiedom. In sum, the way of the normie is founded upon deception.

Barely in time for morning homeroom, under cover of chatter and noise, I entered the classroom. Inside, a number of colonies had formed. There was the coed Normie Squad One, the boys of Normie Squad Two itching to make a pass at the girls, the sports club jocks who hadn't actually made the teams, the nerds, the main unit of girls, and the quiet girls. And a few loners here and there. These loners could be further classified into a few different types…but whatever.

When I walked into the classroom, everyone was engaged in conversation, and no one noticed me. No, that's not right. It'd be more accurate to say that no one cared. Weaving through the various social islands in the classroom, I advanced toward my own seat. Nearby was a gaggle of normies and the nerd group.

People in cliques stress out over every little thing. When they arrive too early, they're like, *I guess the others aren't here yet...* There's an endearing quality to the way they fidget with their cell phones and pretend to brush back their hair and glance at the classroom door. They're highly group conscious, so they don't stray beyond their own cliques much. When they're alone, they don't try to mingle with other factions. When you think about it, they're actually exclusionary. Discriminatory, even.

In other words, paradoxically, loners are the true philanthropists. Loving nothing is equivalent to loving everything. Damn, it's only a matter of time before they dub me Mother Hikigaya.

I took my seat and figured I'd zone out. I stared at my hand vaguely, and an array of inconsequential ruminations sprouted up one after another, like *Oh yeah, my nails are a little long*, or *Huh? Is my lifeline getting shorter?* so I wasn't bored. I'm an old hand at wasting time.

What a worthless skill...

X X X

I employed several of these useless skills, and before I knew it, class was over, and school was done for the day. I worried I might have honed that skill a little too well and unlocked my Stand power. I briskly packed my things and rose to my feet.

The girl in the seat beside me hadn't spoken a word to me today, either. Maybe the reason English education in Japan doesn't work is because they force you into pairs for compulsory conversation.

When I arrived at the Service Club, Yuigahama, who had left the classroom before me, was already there, though not inside the room. She was taking deep breaths in front of the door.

"...What're you doing?"

FWIP
FWIP

"Hyagh! …Oh, H-Hikki. U-uh, well, I dunno? There's just kind of a weird vibe in there…" She averted her eyes awkwardly.

"…"

"…"

Both of us were silent.

We both silently looked down, avoiding each other's eyes. Then I noticed the door of the clubroom was slightly ajar. When I peeked in through the crack, I saw Yukinoshita in her same old spot, reading like she always was.

I guess Yuigahama was hesitant to go inside. That was no surprise. She hadn't attended in a week. Be it school or a part-time job, if you suddenly ditch, it's hard to face everyone when you return. I've experienced that three times because I skipped work on a whim. Each time, I felt so awkward that I never went again. Actually, if you include the jobs where I never attended once, I guess it was five times. Thus, I was sympathetic to Yuigahama's reservations.

"Come on, we're going in." That was also why I half-dragged her in with me. I made sure to open the door as loudly as possible to draw attention to us.

The noise likely irritated Yukinoshita, as her head jerked up. "Yuigahama…"

"H-hey, Yukinon…" Yuigahama raised a hand weakly and replied with strained cheer.

Yukinoshita returned to her book as if nothing had happened. "Don't just stand there. Come in. Club's begun already." Her downward gaze appeared to be an attempt to hide her face, but her cheeks were red enough that even I could tell. Also, what was with the way she said that? Are you a mom ushering in your runaway kid who's come slinking home?

"Y-yeah…," Yuigahama replied and took her customary seat beside Yukinoshita. But she pulled the chair out farther than usual, leaving a person's-width space between her and the other girl.

I settled into my normal position diagonally across from Yukinoshita.

Yuigahama would usually be fiddling with her cell phone, but today she was seated on the edge of her chair, her hands resting stiffly on her knees. Most likely, she was trying so hard to tune out Yukinoshita's presence that she ended up extraconscious of her, as she was frozen stock-still.

This was not a comfortable, languid quiet. This silence was tense. I was hyperaware of the sound of my own squirming. Even the smallest *ahem* reverberated in the room, and I couldn't ignore the sluggish ticking of the clock counting off the seconds. Nobody said a word. But all three of us had perked up our ears so as not to miss any ostensible attempt to break the ice. When someone sighed, we immediately zeroed in on that person.

What a long silence…, I thought. I checked my wristwatch, but not even three minutes had passed. *What the hell? Is this the Hyperbolic Time Chamber?* It was so bad I could feel the increased gravity and atmospheric pressure weighing down on me. I watched the second hand of the clock go *tick tock*, and once it had completed its circle, I heard a soft voice.

"Yuigahama." Yukinoshita snapped the book in her hands shut, sucked in a breath so deep her shoulders rose, and then slowly exhaled again. She quietly faced the other girl and opened her mouth as if about to say something, but nothing came out.

Yuigahama's body was turned toward Yukinoshita, but her eyes remained glued to the floor instead of making contact. "U-uhm…you wanted to talk about…you…and Hikki, right?"

"Yes, I wanted to talk to you about our future…," Yukinoshita began.

Yuigahama interrupted her. "L-look, you don't have to worry about me at all. It's true I was surprised, or, like…a little startled, I guess…but you don't have to go out of your way for me, you know? In fact, this is a good thing, so I think we should celebrate and enjoy it…"

"S-so you caught on… I just wanted to celebrate it properly. Besides…I'm grateful to you…"

"O-oh, no… I haven't done anything worth any thanks. I…haven't done anything."

"It's very like you to lack self-awareness about such matters. Still, I am thankful. Besides, one doesn't celebrate these things because of some act on the part of the recipient. I just want to do it."

"…Y-yeah."

I suspected they weren't having the same conversation. It was like they were putting keywords first and filling in the blanks in their own heads. Yuigahama was equivocating to avoid confrontation, and Yukinoshita was communicating in implications to disguise her shyness, creating a mismatched conversation that was all mood and no substance.

Yukinoshita was bashful and crimson cheeked as she expressed the gratitude she usually never voiced. And every time Yuigahama saw the other girl's face, her own expression darkened a shade, occasionally covered with a forced smile. Her narrowed eyes were moist.

"S-so, um…" Yukinoshita started to say something and then fell silent.

A tiny window of time passed. *Searching for words*, *timid*, *fearful*, *hesitant*, or *tentative* would all have been apt descriptors for Yukinoshita right then. Objectively timed, the silence probably wouldn't have amounted to ten seconds, but the heavy stillness lasted too long for her to continue. The three of us gazed pointedly away from one another in the hopes this weird moment would pass.

"U-um…" Yuighama spoke as if she'd made up her mind about something, and that was when it happened.

A panicked banging on the door rang through the quiet clubroom.

Yukinoshita softly closed her book, faced the door, and called out, "Come in."

But there was no response from the other side of the door. All that reached our ears was a sound like a horse snorting. *Fushururu*.

Yukinoshita and I looked at each other, and she nodded. Apparently, that meant for me to go investigate.

Go look yourself…, I thought for an instant, but it would be awkward telling a girl to check out the source of that ghastly panting sound. I advanced toward the door, each step closing the distance between me and the mysterious respiration. There were only two sounds remaining in the quiet room: my footsteps and the panting. When I arrived at the portal, I gulped audibly. The thought of nothing but a single wooden panel separating us from that nameless presence stirred my apprehension. I put a hand to the door and timidly slid it open.

A large, black shadow popped through the gap and reached out to wrench the door wide. "Wahhhh! Hachiemoooon!"

"Oh, Zaimokuza… And hey, don't call me that."

Our enigmatic visitor was in fact Yoshiteru Zaimokuza. Even though we were halfway into June, he was clad in a black trench coat. Gasping in the heat, shoulders heaving, he entered and grasped my shoulder. "Listen, Hachiemon! These guys are so mean!" Zaimokuza continued, heedless to my request not to call me that. He clearly didn't care.

What a dick… He was grating on my nerves, so I elected to shove him back out. "Sorry, Zaimokuza. The Service Club maxes out at three. Right, Gian?"

"Why are you looking at me?" Yukinoshita's expression was half bemusement and half pique. *But never mind that right now.*

"Hey, wait, Hachiman," said Zaimokuza. "This is no time for jokes. If 'Hachiemon' is not to your liking, I can settle for 'Ninja Hachitori.' Lend me your ear."

"The biggest joke in the school is telling *me* not to mess around…" This was a bombshell.

"Hngh! This is my chance!" Exploiting my momentary distraction, Zaimokuza skated into the room, but the slide was the only acceptable part of his entrance. He swooshed well enough, but his trench coat was filthy. "Feh-hm, no sign of the enemy, huh…? It seems my infiltration was a success," he said, making a show of scanning the area. The whole role-play must have left his mind immediately thereafter, though, as he yanked out a nearby chair totally normally.

If you're gonna do it, stick with it until the end.

"Now then, men," he announced. "Today, I am calling on you for counsel on a certain matter."

"I don't really want to hear about it, though…," I told him.

All of us eyed him skeptically. Yukinoshita seemed particularly uninterested in any further engagement, as she had returned to reading. *Man, you sure switch gears quickly.*

But Zaimokuza grinned broadly and lifted one hand, stopping me. Every last one of his little idiosyncrasies was so irritating. "Come, hear my tale to its bitter end. The other day, I informed you of my aspirations to be a games writer, right?"

Yeah, now that he mentioned it, that did sound familiar.

"Didn't you wanna write novels or something...?" Yuigahama tilted her head.

"Ngh... Indeed I did. 'Tis too long a yarn to spin here, but basically, a light novel author lacks a stable income, so I relinquished the dream. I figured it'd be better to be a full-time formal employee after all."

"That was a short story... It took you two sentences," I remarked. "And it's not like I care, but stop directing everything you say toward me."

Zaimokuza was as terrible as ever at talking to girls. He'd never taken his eyes off me this entire time.

The vibe in the room was relaxed. No, actually, maybe a more accurate descriptor would be "completely apathetic." Zaimokuza was the lone island of enthusiasm in a rising sea of ennui. "Phmph. So about my career ambitions..."

"If this is just another plot or setting outline, I'm not looking at it," I said.

"Pa-hem, pa-hem. Such was not the purpose of my journey here. There have arisen in my life those who would interfere with my ambitions. I think they're probably jealous of my talent."

"What did you just say?" I was indignant. No, one could even call the sentiment genuine ire. *He says he has talent?!* I was inches from flying into a rage and punching him in the face.

"Hachiman, do you know of the UG Club?"

"Huh? The *yuugee* what? *Oh*?" The word wasn't familiar, so I answered his question with another question.

Yukinoshita, who was still reading, replied as she turned a page. "It's a new club that was established this year. The acronym stands for 'United Gamers.' It seems their focus is to study games entertainment in general."

"Ohh, so it's basically a games society."

"Yes. This school doesn't allow the more casual clubs like this, and so their hobby is treated as an official club. But when you consider the actual scope and nature of what they do, it's probably clearer to call it a society, I suppose."

I didn't know we had something like that at our school…

"So what about this *yuugee* club?" Yuigahama asked, pronouncing the acronym a little oddly.

Zaimokuza paused again briefly before responding. "Uh…oh yeah. I was at the arcade yesterday, and unlike at school, I can converse with people at the arcade. So I was speaking of my dream to write for games to my fighting-game buddies."

Such a graceful way of putting it, "speaking of his dreams." But those are really just his delusions. The guys he'd strong-armed into listening must have suffered, too.

"All and sundry prostrated themselves before my grand ambitions in a storm of commendation: 'You can do it,' they said. 'We're cheering you on.' 'Of course the Master Swordsman can pull off these impossible feats with ease.' 'That's so exciting!' 'I look up to you, man,' et cetera."

Listen…nobody's saying that stuff sincerely. They're making fun of you. But I couldn't tell Zaimokuza that, obviously. Seeing him reveling in the memory of that moment, I couldn't bring myself to burst his bubble.

"However! Among the crowd there was one man who turned to me and said, of all things, 'It'll n-n-never happen, you're just d-d-dreaming!' But I'm an adult, so at the time I just said, 'Y-yeah, that's true.'"

Lame. Sir, you are lame.

It seemed the mere recollection was enough to enrage Zaimokuza, as he started gasping and panting. He retrieved a two-liter plastic bottle from his bag and took several gulps to quench his thirst before he opened his mouth again. "But I am not adult enough to back down after a challenge like that!"

"Are you an adult or aren't you…?" Yukinoshita muttered, rolling her eyes.

Zaimokuza paused for an instant, flinching in horror before he continued. "And so after those fiends left, I made an inflammatory blog post about the Chiba community of Arcanabros. Hmph, no doubt it left their faces bright red with rage."

"Whoa… You're so terrible, it gives me the shivers. I actually find that kinda cool," I said.

"Hrrm. And now I hear he goes to our school… When I looked at the response this morning, I saw it had been decided that we would settle this with a match. The community is afire with fervor… Hey, do you think they hate me?"

"I dunno… But there's nothing wrong with settling it through a game. Just go kick his ass."

"Ha-ha-ha-ha! 'Tis not possible. In the realm of fighting games, he is far more skillful."

"Huh? Aren't you supposed to be really good?"

"Well…I suppose I could beat the average player, but there are many greater than I. Did you know, Hachiman? Among the top-tier competitive gamers, some even have professional contracts."

"Professional…? You can be a pro in this stuff?"

"Indeed you can. The world of fighting games has dark and unholy depths. The man I speak of is not so proficient I'd call him a pro, but he's definitely better than me," Zaimokuza said, sounding frustrated.

Yukinoshita snapped her book shut. "I understand, more or less. In other words, you're soliciting us to help you win this fighting game or whatever."

"Nay! Feh! Hachiman, you fool! Thou speakest lightly of action games! 'Taint so superficial they kin be mastered in a wee fortnight! And more to th' point, wot do ye folk ken of fightin' games?"

He had combined so many dialects I couldn't understand a word of it, but his anger, at least, made itself clear. I wish my far more formidable irritation would get across to *him*. *Don't say that stuff to me. Say it to Yukinoshita. Come on.*

Yukinoshita gave Zaimokuza a look usually reserved for scraps of garbage. Openly revolted, Yuigahama was muttering, "Ugh…"

"Thus I would like to either cancel the competition somehow or make it into a game that I can definitely win. So bring out those secret gadgets, Hachiemon."

"Sometimes, I seriously start thinking you're even more despicable than I am..."

It doesn't trouble me when I'm the one saying reprehensible garbage, but hearing someone else do it makes my skin crawl... Somehow restraining the urge to hit Zaimokuza with a chair as he chuckled "tee-hee" to himself like a little brat, I glanced over at Yukinoshita.

Of course, she shook her head. *Well, color me surprised.*

"Sorry, but no," I said. "You clearly brought this on yourself. If you're not ready for the consequences, then don't stir up shit in the first place." The Service Club was not about bailing out everyone who came to us. It was not an all-powerful magic lamp to grant any wish, nor was it a robotic helper to solve any problem. The club just helped you help yourself. And that was why we weren't going to lend a hand to someone who had dug his own grave. It was harsh, but it had to be said.

Zaimokuza went silent for a while. Maybe he was reflecting on his behavior. "Hachiman," he rasped my name with considerable anguish.

I replied, *What?* with my eyes alone.

Zaimokuza released a deep sigh. *Pfwooo.*

Huh? Was that just a sigh? What a weird noise.

Hfwoo. "You've changed, Hachiman. You used to seethe with fighting spirit... In your visage, I could see a quiver like a bow string's pulse."

"Don't break into falsetto. My face has never looked like that. What're you trying to say?" I fired back.

Zaimokuza shrugged his shoulders and snorted a laugh. "Ahh, hmm, it's nothing. You just go giggle and titter away with the girls. 'Twould not be the sort of thing you'd understand, anyway. 'Tis better for you to doze in your dream of normalcy. I have no need for a warrior who has forgotten the battlefield."

"Hey. Wait. I don't remember ever 'giggling and tittering' away. I don't have a girlfriend, either. Oh, though I have giggled with Totsuka—"

"Silence, boy!" He cut me off with a command like the snap of an enormous white wolf. His words resounded within the quiet clubroom, and a momentary silence fell upon us.

But just before everything went totally still, I thought I heard a quiet "...Huh? You...don't have a girlfriend? Uh, uh...huh?"

"Listen, Hachiman. Imagine if I lost the match. Things would get so awkward, I wouldn't be able to visit the arcade anymore. Then when you and Totsuka go, you won't have me to show you around. Is that not so?"

Ahh! H-he's right! What a conundrum! I have to help him win somehow!

Not. Obviously.

"Uh, but we don't really need you to show us around… I hate to say it, but you were just in the way."

"Duh-heh," Zaimokuza chortled disconcertingly, and the two girls quietly inched even farther away from him. Before I knew it, Yuigahama and Yukinoshita had shifted closer to each other.

Huh. I'd always believed Zaimokuza was the type who always ruined the mood, or maybe just disturbed it. And he really was. He destroyed good vibes, but he also deftly torpedoed the bad ones, too. He probably didn't do it deliberately, but I figured the Service Club should show some appreciation for this. I felt a little guilty for saying no to him now.

Perhaps Zaimokuza was perceptive enough to detect my vacillation, as he grinned and followed up on his attack. "Ha-mmph. This Service Club or whatever you call it is laughable. You offer no assistance to one before you, and you call this service? You can't actually save anyone, can you? Don't just talk big! Show me with your action!"

"Oh, Zaimokuza. You idiot…"

It was the height of summer, yet my spine was perfectly cold.

"……I see. Then we will prove it to you." Yukinoshita pierced Zaimokuza with an icy glare, and I heard a little *eep*.

See? What part of this looks like idle frivolity to you? This is legitimately terrifying.

X X X

Just like the Service Club's room, the UG Clubroom was in the special building, but on a different floor. Our space was on the fourth floor, and theirs was situated on the second. Their room was smaller than the others on the second floor, enough to be mistaken for a prep room. The décor was precisely what you'd expect of a brand new club: a piece of paper on the door reading UG Club in marker.

"Let's go in, then..." By some twist of fate, we'd all come down here. I looked back at Zaimokuza, Yukinoshita, and Yuigahama.

Zaimokuza answered with a pretentious "Hmm." Yukinoshita offered neither a response nor any kind of expression. And Yuigahama stood a little ways away with visible unease.

"...Are you coming in?" I asked her, just in case. My impression was that Yuigahama had merely tagged along by force of circumstance. Though she was essentially a member of the club, she hadn't attended for the past few days, and we didn't know if she was going to continue, either. If her plan was to gradually disappear, it would probably be better to let her go if she wanted.

"Y-yeah...," she replied, hugging herself. "I-I'm coming, but... Hikki, you don't have a girlfriend?" Her question was incredibly random. *Look, "but" is a contradictory conjunction. The transition between your clauses doesn't make sense.*

"No, I don't."

"What a foolish question, Yuigahama," Yukinoshita admonished, lightly patting Yuigahama on the shoulder. "This boy could never manage proper interaction with the opposite sex."

"Leave me alone," I said. "I don't need a girlfriend. There's no greater agony than the theft of one's time. If a girl woke me up in the middle of the night with some tearful phone call, I know I'd instantly dump her." I wonder why normies like to expose their painful relationship stories. It's like how old people boast about their illnesses or how office workers crow about how busy they are. There's nothing more infuriating than people vaunting their own masochism. What, are you Misawa?

"Whoa. You're a dick...," Yuigahama said in disgust. But for some impenetrable reason, her eyes were smiling. "Oh. B-but, like, you went out with Yukinon, didn't you? What was with that?"

"If you're referring to the Cat and Dog Show the other day," Yukinoshita interjected, "we just happened to encounter each other. I was accompanying him and his sister only because Komachi invited me. Didn't I tell you?"

"Yeah, that's right," I said. "Anyway, not like I care, but can we just go in? Zaimokuza has nothing to do, and he's staring out the window."

"H-hold on, just hold on for a second," urged Yuigahama. "So you two aren't actually going out?"

"Of course not......," I replied. So she really did assume all that bull. *If you paid any attention to our interactions on a day-to-day basis, obviously that would never happen. Get a clue.*

"Yuigahama, some things are enough to anger even me, you know." Yukinoshita emanated an aura of chilly wrath with a countenance of naked displeasure.

"Oh, sorry, sorry! Never mind. S-so...let's go on in." Flustered, Yuigahama rushed up to the clubroom. In contrast to Yukinoshita's grumpy demeanor, Yuigahama rapped on the door with perfect cheer.

A quiet, languid "Hellooo" sounded in response. That probably meant it was okay to enter.

Upon opening the door, what greeted us was a mountain of boxes, books, and packages. They rose up and up like walls or partitioning screens, creating a maze. To envision a similar scene, imagine a bookworm's study piled high with books crossed with an old-fashioned toy shop.

"Huh? Isn't this the UG Club?" Yuigahama gaped dumbly as she inspected a nearby box. The somewhat subdued package bore a pattern of skulls and roses. The writing on it was all in English, and it was definitely foreign. "This doesn't really look game-ish..." Yuigahama's surprise was reasonable. Usually the term *game* refers to video games.

"Is that so? This sort of thing is just what I would expect," said Yukinoshita. "I suppose you were imagining it would be bleep bloopers, weren't you?"

"Bleep bloopers?" I said. "How old are you? Even my mom calls them Nintendos."

"But they go *bleep bloop*, don't they...?" Yukinoshita remarked, disgruntled.

To my knowledge, games these days do not go *bleep bloop.*

"Well, you don't seem like the type to play games, Yukinon."

"And you do, Yuigahama?" Yukinoshita replied.

"Hmm, my dad likes them, so I do enjoy watching him play. I play them myself sometimes, like *Mario Kart* or puzzle games like *Puyo Puyo.* And *Animal Crossing* or *Harvest Moon* on the little thingies."

I presumed by "little thingies" she meant handhelds. "You play more games than I thought," I said.

Yuigahama turned around to face me and nodded. "Oh y-yeah… You know, like when everyone else is doing it, you just kinda…"

Well, recently some games have begun incorporating elements to make them tools for communication. Some people do enjoy them the way Yuigahama does.

"And then the new FFs and stuff. The graphics are super-pretty and really cool! And they'll make you cry buckets like a movie! Plus the chocobos are super cute."

Ptoo. The moment Zaimokuza heard Yuigahama's explanation, he pretended to spit. Of course, we were indoors, so he didn't actually spit… *He* didn't, *right?*

Zaimokuza usually never addressed her at all, so when he suddenly snapped, Yuigahama seemed taken aback, or rather, she reacted as one does when confronted with a creeper. "Wh-what? You're freaking me out…" Frightened, she slipped behind me to conceal herself in my shadow.

Zaimokuza moved in for another strike. "…Filthy casual."

"Wh-what?!" said Yuigahama. "I dunno what that means, but it's making me mad…"

"Give it up, Zaimokuza," I said. "I understand how you feel. But in moments like these, it's actually best to bask in your own superiority and think to yourself, *I'm the only one who* really *knows, not like this trash.*"

"Oh-ho, Hachiman. That's such a positive perspective."

"And one that reflects the nadir of human nature…," Yukinoshita added in exasperation. "Video games… I doubt I'll ever understand them."

"Oh, I don't know," I replied. "I seem to remember there's a Ginnie the Grue game out."

"Huh? Ginnie the Grue? Why are we talking about that all of a sudden?" Yuigahama questioned, her expression confused.

Ah, so Yuigahama doesn't know that Yukinoshita is fond of Grue-bear. Although perhaps words like *obsessed* or *maniacal* would be more apt.

"Well, like—"

"Hikigaya, what are you talking about?" Yukinoshita aggressively cut me off.

"Huh? What are you—?"

"I have no idea what you're talking about. We'll discuss this later." Yukinoshita's eyes were stern.

"O-okay…" It appeared she really didn't want her affection for Grue-bear to be public. Why not? Was she embarrassed? *If she likes something that much, she should just be proud of it. And, like, what does "We'll discuss it later" mean? Does she want to know about that game without revealing that she's a fan of Grue? I don't get it. I don't get her standards for shame at all.*

Well, there was no need to call attention to it. I don't exactly enjoy the dissemination of information about things I like, either. Why do elementary schoolers always immediately tell everyone about your crushes?

Yuigahama muttered, "Grue-bear?" curiously. She didn't seem satisfied.

"So anyway, I wonder where the club members are?" said Yukinoshita.

"Yeah, good point. Someone answered when we knocked…" Yuigahama's thoughts shifted toward finding these people. *Wow, Yukinoshita. You're seriously a manipulator.*

The clubroom was no bigger than a prep room, which was to say not large at all. Only the stacks of boxes and haphazardly arranged bookshelves made it hard to see.

"Fhnph. Backlogs of unplayed games and unread books always pile up the highest in the areas where you spend the most time. Therefore, we'll easily find them if we head for the highest stack."

"Oh-ho, Zaimokuza. Wow. But you need to bestow your brilliant insights upon people other than me." *You never talk to anyone but me, and it's sad, Zaimokuza.*

Anyway, we set our sights on the highest tower, as per Zaimokuza's advice. Though the screen of boxes blocked our view, once we got closer, we could hear voices. We circumnavigated the boxes to discover two boys.

"Sorry for walking in on you guys. There's something we wanted to talk to you about," I said.

The two boys, presumably of the UG Club, looked at each other and nodded, then turned back to examine me. Well, this *was* the first time they'd ever seen me. If an unknown visitor darkens your door out of the blue, I suppose you would look at him like that.

I decided to perform my own inspection, and that was when I observed that their indoor shoes were yellow. Yellow is the first-years' color. In other words, these two were in the grade below us.

"Hmph! You are first-year lads, I see!" The moment Zaimokuza realized these two were younger than him, his manner swiftly turned pompous.

I had no trouble with his readiness to change his attitude. I despise the oppression of social hierarchies and seniority-based systems, unless I'm the beneficiary. So I hopped up on my high horse along with Zaimokuza. It was just, you know, a negotiation strategy to assume the psychologically superior position. It wasn't at all because I'm a jerk or anything. "So I heard you kids have been giving Zaimokuza here some cheek, huh?" I said. "Go ahead. Trash-talk him some more."

"H-huh? H-Hachiemon?!" Zaimokuza implored me silently, but it wasn't the least bit cute. *I mean, even if you are older, you're waaay below them on the social ladder.*

"Stop fooling around and get to the point." Yukinoshita gave me a cold glare.

When the first-years saw, they whispered to each other surreptitiously. "I-isn't that Yukinoshita from second year…?"

"I—I think so…"

Whoa, for real? Was Yukinoshita famous? Well, she was good-looking, after all. She also had her distinctive aura of mystery. It was nothing extraordinary for her to have admirers in other grades. When I was in middle school, I knew the names of cute older girls, too. That was the extent of my knowledge, though.

"All right. You two have business with this guy, don't you?"

But before I could beckon him over, the guy in question shoved his way to the front. "Fwa-ha-ha-ha-ha-ha! 'Tis been a long time! You talked big yesterday, but now the time for regrets is past! I shall now teach you a lesson, as both your *elder* in life and your *elder* in school!" Firmly highlighting the "elder" part, Zaimokuza aggressively presented himself.

The UG Club pair, however, received him with all the warmth of a refrigerator. "Hey, is this the guy you were talking with before? Whoa, this is painful."

"I know, right? He's so bad it's hard to believe." They snickered in a condescending and exceedingly stereotypical manner.

In the end, Zaimokuza was the one shaken up. "Uh, H-Hachiman? D-did I just do something weird?"

"Relax. This isn't the only time you've been weird."

Zaimokuza had almost entirely broken character.

I pushed him back with a firm pat on the shoulder. "We're the Service Club. We're basically like counselors. Zaimokuza said he had a dispute with you, so we came here to resolve it. So, um...who's the one he fought with?" I asked indifferently.

One of the boys timidly raised his hand. "Oh, that's me. I'm Hatano, a first-year. And this is..."

"Sagami, also a first-year..."

The one who had introduced himself as Hatano was skinny—and a little on the hunched side. He sported glasses with no frames and sharp corners, perhaps a reflection of his sharp mind and sharp ideas. His friend, also slender, looked like a pasty middle schooler. His glasses were a little more rounded, inspiring the next generation. To be honest, I didn't have any particular desire to remember their names, so I decided to distinguish them by their glasses.

"I heard you're going to have a competition with Zaimokuza, but you're good at fighting games, right? If you guys settle your score that way, it'll be obvious before the match what the outcome will be. So why not try another kind of competition?" This proposal was absurd, if I do say so myself. It was like approaching a soccer player and suggesting, "Let's play baseball instead!" This kid was not going to voluntarily relinquish his advantage.

Of course, he indicated that he was not on board with the idea. His lack of head nodding indicated a polite refusal.

"At least make it another game or something. You have so many," I said, gesturing toward the ramparts around us.

"Well, I guess..."

"Okay, then..." Though their responses were subdued, they oozed confidence. Clearly, they held some assurance in their ability to win. It seemed the name of United Gamers was not for show. "But if we're switching games, we need to get something in return...," Hatano said with mild reserve.

Well, they had made one concession for us. It was only natural to put forth their own conditions to even the scales. I nodded and waited for them to continue.

"...Okay, how about Zaimokuza groveling to you? If we lose, I'll personally take responsibility and force him to say 'I'm eternally sorry for getting carried away,' or something," I suggested. I was sick of waiting, so that was good enough.

"Huh? Me?" Zaimokuza dropped out of character again. *You've got no right to refuse, though.*

"Well, I guess that's fine..." Mild-mannered as ever, the UG Club accepted those terms.

"Then I'll let you pick the game. Don't choose anything too complicated. A newbie can't do well in a game with a steep learning curve, and that'd make it no different from a fighting game." In fact, I think the reason fighting games have been going downhill for so long is because it's hard for new people to get into them. Even if you find one you'd like to try out at an arcade, the regulars like the Guiltybros or fans of even older titles are usually occupying it, and you can't join in. And even if you do edge your way in, they'll immediately wreck you, making you swear off playing it anymore. In the future, they should designate a special area for casual gamers.

"Then...we'll take a game everyone already knows and tweak it a little."

"*Hrrm*...do as you will. What is the name of this game?" Zaimokuza asked.

The pair pushed their glasses up their noses. "I'm thinking we'll play a game called Double Millionaire." The proposal sounded innocent enough, but their glasses flashed deviously.

X X X

The cards slid against each other softly as he shuffled them.

Millionaire is played with a standard deck of playing cards. It's also known as Beggar or President.

"Um, you know the rules, right?" Hatano asked hesitantly.

I nodded. Yukinoshita was the only one to tilt her head with an invisible question mark floating above it. "I've never played it...though I have played poker."

"Okay. I'll explain the rules, then." Sagami provided a brief summary. "One, you deal all the cards to the players equally."

In reality, such egalitarian distribution isn't feasible, not even for cards.

"Two, the game starts with the dealer. The dealer for the first round plays the first card from his hand, and after that, everyone takes turns playing their cards on top of it."

In reality, people forget about my turn and have no qualms about butting in ahead of me.

"Three, the cards are ranked. From lowest to highest, it's three, four, five, six, seven, eight, nine, ten, jack, queen, king, ace, two. Jokers are wild."

In reality, power is determined not by raw ability but rather by affluence and connections.

"Four, the players can only put down a card higher than the one already on the pile. If someone plays a pair, you have to put down a pair."

In reality, even incompetent weaklings who cannot succeed are sent to the front lines as sacrificial pawns, scapegoats, or a warning to the rest.

"Five, when you have no cards you can play, you're allowed to pass."

In reality, there is no passing.

"Six, if all the other players pass, and it goes back around to the player who put down the first card, then that player starts the next pile. All the cards on the first pile are then discarded."

In reality, you can't discard the past.

"Seven, repeat the above until someone runs out of cards. That player is the millionaire. Second fastest is the rich man, then the poor man, then the beggar."

That's the only part that's just like real life. What the hell. This is depressing.

"Also, the millionaire can take two good cards from the beggar and exchange them with any two cards from their own hand."

In other words, this is a microcosm of modern Japan, where the winner has the upper hand and permission to eternally exploit the loser. Ugh, what an awful game.

"I see. I get the idea." That explanation seemed enough for Yukinoshita since she nodded. As always, she was quick on the uptake.

"Wait, what about local rules?" Zaimokuza asked.

Hatano waved him off. "Yeah, yeah, of course." He had absolutely no respect for Zaimokuza.

"We've got a beginner here, too, so why don't we just go with the most mainstream ones?" I suggested. "Are you okay with the Chiba rules?"

"Um…what are the Chiba rules like?" Sagami asked with some concern.

Huh? He doesn't know Chiba rules offhand? Whatever. I'll just explain it.

In Millionaire, it's fair to say that the local rules are the crux of victory and defeat. There exists a diverse array of local rules you can add to the basic rules, and combining them together can complicate strategy exponentially. "Well, there's revolution, eight enders, the ten discard rule, three of spades strong, jacks reverse, fleeing the capital, locked cards, staircase style, and joker doesn't end it. That's about it."

"Oh, I think it was like that at my school," said Yuigahama.

"Hmm. No five skip or seven handover, huh…?" added Zaimokuza.

These rules differ not only by region, but even between elementary schools. Once you're grown, differences in local rules with Millionaire can even start fights, so it's best to agree on them from the start. People even argue over what to call the winner and loser of each round. It's like 'cops and robbers' versus 'jailbreak.'

"Hikigaya, do you mind explaining?"

Oh, whoops. We'd been conversing under the assumption that everyone understood us, but Yukinoshita had never played Millionaire before. So I briefly elaborated on each rule. Under the *revolution* rule, if you play four cards of the same number, it reverses the ranking of all cards in play. In *eight enders*, after playing an eight, you discard the whole pile and start a new one. For the *ten discard rule*, when you play tens, you can remove an additional number of cards from your hand equal to the number of tens you put down. *Three of spades strong* means the three of spades can beat a joker, and *jacks reverse* means that when you play a jack, the ranking of the cards is reversed for everyone's next turn only.

Yukinoshita nodded occasionally as I explained. Well, you can't truly grasp it if you don't do it yourself. Practice was probably the fastest way to pick it up.

"We agree to your suggested local rules."

"So you will accept our Double Millionaire rules." The pair's glasses flashed again.

The air hung oddly heavy, and I quietly gulped.

The next moment, both boys had broad smirks on their faces. "The rules are the same as regular Millionaire."

"The difference is that you play it in pairs."

"Pairs?" I asked. "So in other words, you and a partner have to decide together?"

The UG Club pair shook their heads in perfect accord. "No. You trade places and take turns putting down cards."

"You're not allowed to talk with your partner."

...That meant the game would require evaluating not only your opponents but also your partner. It was surprisingly strategic... In that case, though, the problem was selecting a partner. I glanced to my side.

"Heh-heh-heh... Don't presume you can beat my deck."

I don't want to team up with Zaimokuza...

"The strongest card is the joker, hmm? I see... Can you play a joker after an eight?" Yukinoshita recited the rules to herself to ensure she understood them. She had a lot of talent, but she'd never played Millionaire before. Plus, divining her thoughts was a formidable task. If her team failed, she'd probably chew out her partner, too.

So, the only remaining option is Yuigahama... She'd played Millionaire before, and she knew the same local rules as me. Most important, she was a relatively straightforward person, so she was easy to read. I looked to Yuigahama, figuring if I needed a partner it might as well be her. Our eyes met at exactly the same moment.

"Y-Yukinon, let's be a team!" She immediately broke contact and clung to Yukinoshita's shoulder.

"Huh? Oh, sure," Yukinoshita replied.

Figures. I had erroneously assumed the choice of my partner was mine to make. It is laughable for one who is never chosen to attempt to choose another.

Now Yukinoshita and Yuigahama were confirmed as a pair, my partner was automatically decided for me. Once again, the leftovers formed an alliance. Zaimokuza also had a wealth of experience with this, as he glided over in front of me and tossed a remark over his shoulder. "Hachiman. Can you keep up?"

...He was more than welcome to leave me behind.

X X X

Hatano swept everything off the desk, and Sagami carried in three chairs. Now the stage was set for the battle. For the first round, Sagami, Yuigahama, and I occupied the seats. The rule was that each time we played a hand, we'd trade places with our partner. For the quickest transitions, each partner stood behind each chair. I didn't know the UG Club's strategy, but Yuigahama was likely going first because Yukinoshita was unfamiliar with the game.

Sagami finished shuffling the cards and dealt them out one by one. The fifty-four cards were divided into piles of eighteen.

"All right," Hatano declared. "Let's begin the Double Beggar competition between the UG Club and the Service Club. This is a five-match competition. The ranking of the players after the final game will determine the victor."

Each of us picked up our respective hand and fanned it out.

"This is effectively a two-on-one team competition, so we're going to make the first move..." Though Sagami's announcement was polite, he played a card from his hand as if his initiative was a given fact. Well, ultimately they were playing against two pairs: me and Zaimokuza, and Yukinoshita and Yuigahama. We would be in the clear if either of our teams won. In fact, the best strategy would be to cooperate throughout the game. Allowing our opponents the initial move was only fair.

The first round ended without incident.

Perhaps all of us were testing the waters because we expended our cards in a reasonable manner.

"Ha-ha-ha-ha! It's time to d-d-d-duel! Monster card!" Zaimokuza was the only one being obnoxious. "I summon the Ten of Clubs! Once the Ten of Clubs has been successfully summoned, the Card Effect means that I can choose one card from my hand to send to the Graveyard. I set down my fifteen cards, and my turn ends."

Each familiar-sounding turn of phrase stirred up old memories within me. "Man, I'm getting nostalgic... I used to play against duel bots, too."

"Duel bots? That's the first time I've heard of this," Yukinoshita said, looking curious.

"It's like poker bots. They're for people without friends."

"I don't think that's what poker bots are for," she replied.

Oh, is that right? I thought for sure they were just for playing poker by yourself.

"I usually used two decks. I had tons of Miracle of the Zone and Magic cards and stuff, but I didn't have anyone to play with..." Zaimokuza's enthusiasm abruptly dampened, and he handed me the cards. Matches are the bread and butter of collectible card games, so they're no fun without friends to challenge. Although thanks to the Game Boy version, I have a wealth of experience with computer opponents.

Once Zaimokuza had finished being insufferable and shut his mouth, silence enfolded the room. The only sounds came from cards sliding out of hands and slapping onto the pile. We went around the circle a few times in this manner, and the competition continued without incident. Perhaps it was thanks to the ten discard rule and playing triples, but everyone's cards decreased steadily.

Eventually, Zaimokuza and I had two cards remaining, and Yukinoshita and Yuigahama had three. Remarkably, the UG Club still had five cards left. Despite Double Beggar being their idea, they didn't appear particularly adept. Their strategy revolved around getting rid of their weakest cards first with no additional stratagems. If this was how they were going to play, this would be an easy win.

Yuigahama played a six of spades, and then I played the eight of hearts I'd been saving. Only one left now.

"Zaimokuza."

"Aye."

I laid our last card facedown on the desk and surrendered the seat to him. Zaimokuza plopped down with the declaration, "'Tis my turn!" Yes, we noticed. "Now it ends! Trump Card: Open! ...Checkmate!" He triumphantly put down our last card.

Yukinoshita must have been saving a card, too, as she played the two of clubs. The UG Club passed, and she immediately handed her remaining two cards to Yuigahama, who laid down a pair to end the round. Both teams were out, and the Service Club finished in first and second place.

"Fwa-ha-ha! That was pitiful! Did you enjoy tasting my power?!" Zaimokuza roared as if this triumph were entirely his accomplishment. *It must be pretty mortifying to have a guy like him lording victory over you*, I thought.

But checking the UG Club's reactions, I saw their expressions were nonchalant. "Oh dear, Hatano, we lost. Oh no."

"Yeah, Sagami. We were careless." Despite their words, they didn't seem cowed in the slightest. In fact, I could have sworn they were enjoying themselves.

Huh? What're they up to? I peered at the UG Club pair. Something was fishy.

They smirked. "We're in trouble, huh?"

"Yeah, so much trouble."

"I mean, if we lose, we have to strip."

"I mean, if we lose, we have to strip."

The pair spoke in unison and immediately shucked off their vests as if shedding their disguises. *Sure, it looks cool, but that's pervert behavior, you know.*

"What?! What the hell is that rule?!" Yuigahama smacked the desk in protest.

But their smirks only broadened. "Huh? Isn't it normal to take off your clothes if you lose?"

"Yep, yep. You have to strip if you lose with both mah-jongg and rock-paper-scissors," his buddy added.

Uh, there's no strip rule for rock-paper-scissors. The loser only has to go buy the winner juice or something. They were right about mah-jongg, though.

"All right, time for round two…"

"H-hey, hold on! Listen to me!" Yuigahama demanded a halt to the game.

Ignoring her, Hatano swept up the cards and started shuffling. He swiftly dealt.

"Yukinon, let's go. Going along with this would just be stupid…"

"Would it?" Yukinoshita replied. "I don't mind the rule, though. We only have to win. Besides, this is a competition. Of course it entails risks."

"Huh?! B-but I don't wanna do this!"

"I see no problem. While the variety of local rules in the game can be confusing, as long as the cards are ranked in a fixed order, there's no change in the fundamental strategy. If we can remember which cards have been played and predict which ones remain in our opponents' hands, I doubt we'll lose so easily. I've also discovered several methods of achieving victory in the final stages, so it's not difficult to predict what our opponents will do based on the number of remaining cards in play."

"M-maybe you're right, but…unnngh," Yuigahama groaned, teary eyed. At this point, all she could do was rely on Yukinoshita. As long as the other girl was on board, Yuigahama's hands were tied.

…Maybe I should try to put a stop to this. I doubt Yukinoshita would listen to me, though.

"Come! Quickly! Let us begin battle now!" While I hesitated over what to do, Zaimokuza sat down and accepted the cards from Hatano.

"All right, let's get started." Yukinoshita also picked up the cards spread before her on the desk, fanning them out in her hands in one sweep. Behind her, Yuigahama looked glum.

"First, the card exchange, then." Hatano took two cards from his hand and passed them over to Zaimokuza.

In Millionaire, from the second round on, the millionaire and the beggar must swap cards. The beggar takes the two strongest cards from his hand, the millionaire takes any two cards from his hand, and they exchange them. The cards we received were a joker and a two of hearts. Good cards.

"Hrrm…" Zaimokuza removed two cards and handed them over with great delight. They were a king of spades and a queen of clubs.

"What?! Hold on, what are you doing?! Why aren't you handing them bad cards?!" I demanded.

He quietly closed his eyes and replied with dignity, "…'Tis the mercy of a samurai."

Why you little… Do you just want to see the girls naked?

The UG Club guys accepted the cards from Zaimokuza and smirked.

I—I see… They're…they're playing against both guys and girls, so they established the strip rule to invite discord between us. What an advanced psychological tactic!

...These guys are idiots.

× × ×

I had thought the UG Club were just a couple of fools, but in the second round, their strategy turned so brilliant it was unrecognizable. Fearless of the risks, Hatano played aggressive hands like triples, and Sagami reliably reduced the cards in their hand with skillful use of the card effects. They employed such wildly different tactics each turn, it was impossible to predict what they would do next. In a steady march toward victory, they slowly rid themselves of cards. Before I knew it, they had only two left.

The Yukinoshita/Yuigahama pair and I doggedly held our own, eventually coming to a point where the girls had two cards and us boys had four.

Yuigahama's right hand wavered. We were near the stage that would decide the victors and the losers, so she was probably contemplating how to win. "I-I'll go with this." After some deliberation, she played the card she'd probably been saving as her trump card, the two of clubs.

Fortunately, both of the jokers were in our hand. So the best strategy would be for us to complete the stack so Yukinoshita could play on a new pile and finish. *Okay, at this rate, we'll have no problem*, I thought. But then, an ambush came from an unforeseen direction.

"Whoops, my foot slipped!" No sooner had Zaimokuza vigorously toppled against me than a card fluttered onto the table. It was a joker.

"Huh?! Watch it, Snowflake, or I'll kill you!" Yuigahama threatened as she leaped from her seat with a clatter, but Zaimokuza merely whistled to himself. *You think that's gonna cover up anything?*

Zaimokuza triumphantly played the three of spades. Hatano casually put down an eight and discarded the pile. Sagami took over, putting down his last card, the ace of spades, and went out first.

At this point, either me and Zaimokuza or Yukinoshita and Yuigahama would have to strip. There was an ace on the table. With some regret, Yukinoshita passed. My turn came around.

"Hachiman… I have entrusted my…no, *our* dreams to you." My shoulder felt warm where he was gripping it. When I looked at his face, he was wearing a calm smile like that of a warrior advancing to his death.

Hey, he hasn't forgotten that if we lose, he'll have to grovel to them, has he…?

With Zaimokuza's passionate hopes weighing on my shoulders, I fanned out my cards. A four of spades and a joker.

Hatano pumped a clenched fist as if he were silently yelling, *We're comrades, aren't we?!*

Sagami quietly lowered his eyes, pressing his hands together silently in prayer. I heard a tiny whisper of "God…" from him.

Had I ever before been entrusted with so many peoples' hopes? No, I had not. In that moment, I felt those unshakable bonds. My finger brushed the joker. Zaimokuza, awaiting my next action, let out a whoop of joy. That cry made Hatano and Sagami leap from their chairs, eager to burn this crucial moment into their retinas.

I heard a quiet voice. *"Ha-chi-man… Ha-chi-man."* It was a tiny, hardly audible little whisper, but before I knew it, it had swelled into a loud cheer. Just like the first-place runner's return to the stadium during an Olympic marathon, it was a passionate, stirring scene.

But amid that fervor, Yukinoshita was blasting me with enough glacial ire to freeze me solid, and Yuigahama was groaning, her lips pursed into a stock-straight line as she glared at me through her tears.

The UG Club guys and Zaimokuza disregarded them, continuing their cheers of glee.

The room was awash with crazed enthusiasm, confusion, chaos, and passion.

Yet an irresistible impulse bubbled up inside my body, manifest in uncontrollable laughter. "Heh… Bwahhh-ha-ha-ha-ha!" Everyone stopped breathing as I bellowed.

I wonder how many of them heard me whisper "Pass" right after that.

There was a momentary hush.

"Listen up! There's nothing I despise more than stuff like coed strip games and stupid punishments for losing like you're at a drinking party with a bunch of idiotic college kids! In fact, I *loathe* them!"

My voice shook the atmosphere like thunder from the heavens.

Just as the silence returned, I heard a deep, deep exhalation from Yukinoshita. "You're an idiot. What an idiot...," she muttered in exasperation.

Next, a rough holler roared through the room. "Hachiman! What are you doing, you fiend?! This is no game!" Zaimokuza seized me by the lapels.

"Calm down, Zaimokuza. You're right, this isn't a game."

"Hmm? That sounds rather cool, but what's it supposed to mean?" he asked.

I ignored Zaimokuza's question and shifted my gaze to the side.

"Hey, hey, what're we gonna do? That guy isn't joining in..."

"Yeah, he's seriously not picking up on the vibe here..."

Hatano and Sagami exchanged whispers.

"Too bad for you," I said, "but I'm bad at joining in and I'm atrocious at picking up on vibes, so your tricks won't work on me."

"H-Hachiman...what do you mean, 'tricks'?!" Zaimokuza stuttered.

"The strip rule isn't because they want to see us get naked," I explained. "It's a psychological tactic. They're using the fact that we're on gender-segregated teams to split us apart." Yes, by shackling us with the manacles of a strip rule, they had nurtured a smidgen of doubt between the Hikigaya/Zaimokuza pair and the Yukinoshita/Yuigahama pair. There were two levels to their plan. If us guys betrayed the girls, it would create an advantage for them. Even if we didn't, they would only need to break the trust between teammates, and once the pressure caused us to make a mistake, they'd reap the benefits.

"I—I see...ah...ha! Now that you mention it, I've heard of this kind of tactic before! The secret technique of the siren... They use 3D women as bait while they employ their witchcraft upon you in order to invite insurrection! It is known as...the honeypot! Heh, that was a close one. 3D really is pig disgusting, after all!"

"Oh. Yeah. Well, that's close enough, so whatever." Plenty of adults have gotten caught in honeypots after all.

In any case, if things went on like this, the UG Club's scheme would have Yukinoshita and Yuigahama drowning in their suspicions while Zaimokuza and I would likely struggle to even communicate. And if Yuigahama and Yukinoshita were to pull out of the game, the Service Club would lose, no ifs, ands, or buts about it. To think the UG Club had plotted to sow discord not only within the Service Club, but also each pair… They were fearsome indeed.

But their scheme was over now. I fixed Hatano with a narrow glare. "You also tried to use mob mentality by getting us all riled up, weren't you?"

"Ngh. So you noticed."

"You looked so blandly typical at first glance, I thought we could easily get you on board…" *Ouch, Sagami. That was kinda mean.*

I swung an index finger toward the UG Club and forcefully declared, "Mob psychology doesn't work on me…because the mob always excludes me!"

"…"

"…"

Hatano and Sagami quietly averted their eyes, smiling uncomfortably. I guess you'd call that half pity and half sympathy. Ultimately, they clearly regarded me as an abject human being.

Ahem. "Anyway. That won't work anymore," I said, clearing my throat to sidestep the awkwardness.

The two UG Club boys looked at each other… "I see. It seems we must get serious."

"Prepare yourselves… Playtime is over," he announced with a low chuckle.

I shuddered. *They're called the United* Gamers, *though…and now they say they're going to stop playing?*

X X X

The UG Club guys weren't kidding when they announced they'd play seriously. They fired off a steady barrage of plays even sharper and dirtier than round two, cornering us in a relentless fight. They leveraged their initial advantage of being the Millionaires and clobbered us with high-ranking cards like jokers and twos at crucial junctures. We lost the third and fourth rounds. Having already shed my socks and dress shirt, I reluctantly put my hand to my pants. I was at my final line of defense: my favorite pair of undies.

"Fsheh. So I must finally remove this coat…" Beside me, Zaimokuza began sloughing off his coat, seeming very grumpy about it. So far, he had removed his socks, fingerless gloves, and wrist weights. His pants and dress shirt were totally untouched.

…Why does this feel so unfair? Why am I the only one in my underwear?
"Damn it…" A little teary, I slid off my pants as modestly as I could.

I suddenly sensed eyes on me, and when I searched for the source, I found Yuigahama's. She looked despondent and apologetic.

"…Hey. Don't watch. Or are you interested?"

"Wh-what?! I-I'm not watching at all! Like hell I'd be interested! Don't be stupid!" she yelled with all her might as she slapped the table. *Hey, you don't have to get all purple and angry. It's a joke. Really.* Yuigahama threatened me with a snort, but her aggression gradually diminished, and she eventually lowered her gaze to the floor. "…Um, Sorry. Thanks."

"Not like I did anything… No reason for you to be thanking me. I'm just doing what I want."

"Hrrm. Not that it matters to me, but when you say such things whilst so unclothed, you look like a defiant pervert," Zaimokuza said with a half smile.

You're the last one to talk, you jackass…

Oh, I almost forgot to mention— Once I started stripping, dear Yukinoshita began to pretend I wasn't there. She didn't spare me a glance and just completely ignored me. I expected no less.

X X X

The cards were dealt for the fifth round. I had only one life left: my boxers. In other words, this was a battle I absolutely could not afford to lose. This was not to be confused with the battles that characters on TV absolutely cannot afford to lose and, for some reason, do so surprisingly often.

"All right… We're gonna win this…" My instincts were focusing, my body overflowing with determination.

"Pfssh! Says the guy in his underwear trying to play it cool!" Zaimokuza burst into laughter.

When I surveyed the rest of the group, both the UG Club guys and Yuigahama were desperately trying to restrain their laughter. Upon closer inspection, even Yukinoshita's shoulders were trembling.

You guys are awful. "Hey, Zaimokuza…" Unsurprisingly, rage welled up within me. The corners of my mouth twitched.

Apparently, Zaimokuza realized how angry I was, as he affectedly cleared his throat with a *hom-hom*. "Calm down now, Hachiman. Games are something to be enjoyed. Relax."

"Why, you…" *He's talking like* he's *the reasonable one here?!* But just before I could give him a piece of my mind—no, five pieces—a sigh stopped me.

"I see. So that's how you view games. Hmm." It took me a moment to realize it was Hatano who had spoken. His manner now was clearly different from his timid impression from early. Now he had a transparently aggressive edge.

"That's like…how should I put it? It's a…certain uninitiated perspective? Well, it's not a bad thing in and of itself, but to stay at that level is a little…lacking." Sagami took over. The way he spoke was both circumlocutory and arrogant.

"Ngh…" Zaimokuza started to say something, but in the face of the pair's attitudes, he stopped. They both wore blatant contempt.

Hatano snorted. "Well, whatever. It's over now, anyway."

"Let's begin the final match," his partner added.

"Y-yeah," I agreed.

In accordance with Sagami's direction, each of us took our places on the battlefield. Zaimokuza had the initial move. First, he had to exchange cards with the UG Club.

As Hatano selected his cards, it looked as if he were also searching for a remark to toss in our direction. He plucked two cards from his hand and flung them at us. As Zaimokuza reached out to add the cards to his hand, Hatano followed up with his question. "...Why do you want to make games, Master Swordsman?" Maybe this "Master Swordsman" was the alias Zaimokuza used at the arcade. All I heard was *Master (LOL) Swordsman*, though.

Zaimokuza forgot to pick up the cards in front of him as he took two cards from his own hand and slid them across the table. "Hrrm. Because I like them. I think it's obvious to turn what you like into a career. As a regular employee at a game company, I'd have a stable lifestyle, too." He said this in a placid manner, but the last bit illuminated his true intentions.

"Ha! Because you like them, huh? There're a lot of people like that lately, who think that's enough to pull it off. So you're one of them, eh, Master Swordsman?"

"What are you trying to say?" I guess that got his goat, as Zaimokuza slammed down his first move, a pair. He scraped his chair back roughly and stood, handing me the cards.

Yukinoshita added another pair to the pile.

"You're just using your dreams as an excuse to escape from reality," our opponent continued.

"Wh-what basis do you have...?" Zaimokuza stopped there, at a loss for words.

Sagami took the silence as a cue to toss another couple of cards onto the stack.

I fanned out my hand. In the opening stages of this game, if you have to follow up on a pair, it's a good chance to get rid of some cards. As I deliberated, I studied the fourteen cards.

...Fourteen?

Noticing that I was short, I peeked under the desk, thinking I must have dropped some. And indeed, two cards had fallen. The cards that Zaimokuza had forgotten to add to our hand had apparently dropped down there when he had shaken the table a moment ago. I picked up the cards and added them to my stock. They were a four of diamonds... and the fourth six. I could go for a revolution.

But I had to save it for a while. If I went for it, I'd have to do it after midgame and when we were the first player on a pile. After some approximate mental calculations, I placed a pair on the stack of gradually rising numbers. Yuigahama and Hatano continued the trend. *Two aces, huh…?* It didn't look like anyone could play on that. After two passes, the players switched with their partners, and Sagami put down a card.

"Master Swordsman, you're shallow. And I'm not talking about what I said before, your uninitiated perspective, but rather the fact that you never go past that point. You just graze the surface, giggling to yourself all the while."

Oh-ho, nice one. Let him have it, Sagami. I almost wanted to cheer the guy on. Yukinoshita also nodded wordlessly in agreement.

"Nghhhh!" Zaimokuza handed the cards to me to restrain himself from responding. I accepted them and played the next number in the sequence with no fanfare. I guess Sagami's remark had hit Zaimokuza hard, as he stopped yelling and pretending to duel like he had been.

Yukinoshita played next, and Hatano glanced at the card she'd put down with a cold smile. "Attempting to create a game when you don't even know what games are is just laughable. A lot of young game designers are like that lately… They try to make a product even though all they've ever played are video games. Their ideas are uninspired, and they lack innovation. They haven't cultivated the proper soil in which to grow original ideas. You can't make video games just because you like them." He emphatically slapped his next play onto the table.

"Nghh." Zaimokuza's moan rang through the room.

A few turns went by, and the game progressed to the UG Club's advantage. When it was Zaimokuza's turn again and he faltered, unable to choose a card, Sagami spoke. "Master Swordsman, you have no skills or anything you can take pride in, no? Games are just your security blanket," he taunted.

There was nothing Zaimokuza could say to that. He just handed me the cards with frustration and silently passed.

I accepted the cards from him and took my seat. Sagami's accusation really stuck with me. As for why, his reveling in tearing down a deluded M-2 type was disheartening and uncomfortable. It hurt to watch, like he was a weary adult on a tirade about drumming the harsh realities of the world into a kid with dreams.

I passed, and the UG Club got to play the first card in the new pile. Hatano very slowly drew one, two, three cards. Of course, we had just passed, so there was no way we could play on them. Yukinoshita also passed.

"By the way, Master Swordsman, what's your favorite movie?"

"Hmm, let me see. *Magic*—"

"Whoops, not counting anime."

"Ngwah?!" Once anime was no longer an option, Zaimokuza had nothing. *Oh-ho, nicely done, painting him into a corner.* ...But if anime didn't count, I couldn't really think of anything, either. If I had to pick one, I'd say *The Professional.* I'd like to take in a young girl, too.

As if mocking the tongue-tied Zaimokuza, Sagami swept the kings off to the side and played a new card. "See? You can't come up with one, can you? What about your favorite book, then?"

"...Hmm, among recent ones, *My Girlfrie*—"

"Aside from light novels."

"Oof!" The interruption came so abruptly Zaimokuza bit his tongue—hard. He theatrically flung his head back to face the ceiling and did not move from there, as if he'd just taken a heavy uppercut. He was still standing, but only barely. Utterly debilitated, he swayed on the spot. *Are you one of those hypersensitive kids these days who can't take criticism or what?*

The UG Club pair sneered at Zaimokuza's state. "In the end, you're a fraud. You don't understand the essence of entertainment. We're actually studying the origins of gaming and entertainment from the ground up. It's embarrassing to watch a half-assed guy like you declaring he's going to write games." As Hatano said, the clubroom was indeed overflowing with an assortment of entertainment. Given the stacks of boxes packed with board games and the scattered dice, probably for tabletop RPGs, the two UG Club guys obviously took their hobby seriously.

On the other hand, Zaimokuza would never do anything like that. All he did was oink away at moeblobs... He had no chance of winning here. His loss was warranted. Of course he needed to be put in his place.

But still, it rubbed me the wrong way. I didn't really care if Zaimokuza was the butt of ridicule. I couldn't argue with their dismissal of him. But there was something undeniably off about their arguments. I just couldn't pin down why exactly they annoyed me.

We were approaching the finish line. The UG Club had five cards remaining, Yukinoshita's team had six, and we had eight. Though their lead was numerically small, the quality of their cards was unquestionably superior. The UG Club had the joker we had given them. The further we progressed into late game, the more the inequalities set in the early game would influence our strategies.

Yuigahama judged that it was time to make her move and silently confirmed with Yukinoshita before laying down a triple. Of course, at this point in the game, nobody could play on that.

Yukinoshita took over and sat in their chair. "I've heard both sides speak, and the UG Club's argument holds water. Hikigaya, if you want what's best for Zai...Zai...*him*, you should guide him down the right path." Yukinoshita started a new pile, smiling as if she were testing me, and the UG Club continued after her.

Well, she was right. If Zaimokuza was serious about his aspirations to be a game writer or a light-novel author, he should make a proper effort instead of dribbling his delusions onto paper and declaring the ensuing scribbles "the best plot ever that I just came up with." He could be spending his time studying the scriptwriting in Hollywood movies or copying down eminent works. I think Hatano's and Sagami's efforts were honestly praiseworthy, and Zaimokuza's laziness undoubtedly did deserve criticism.

But that's not... That alone *isn't necessarily right.* I believe extolling the "right" way to do things is what's truly lazy. Following the textbooks, completing the curriculum, fulfilling the quota... Isn't that just playing it by the book and sticking to tradition? Isn't that merely leaning on the achievements of the ones who came before you, relying on their authority, and painting over your own identity before you've even made something of yourself? What's so praiseworthy about entrusting your sense of what's right to someone else?

"I don't think the UG Club's method is necessarily correct," I said. "...Oh, but it doesn't take much thought to know Zaimokuza is in the wrong, though."

"I see," replied Yukinoshita. "Well, you're his friend, so if that's your opinion, perhaps you're right."

"We're not friends." If we were, I'd probably be taking his side right now.

But this won't click for an idiot like Zaimokuza until he's compelled to dig his grave with his own two hands. Nothing I could say would matter. A loser of Zaimokuza's caliber will even blame other people for the very things that forced him to give up. If he was going to be like that anyway, he might as well taste vicious defeat before he wholly, utterly desists.

"You know...," Yuigahama said quietly, slightly embarrassed, "I don't really get games, and I don't know a lot about them, but..."

No one else said a word. Slowly but surely, her earnestness attracted the attention of every person in the room. I waited for her to continue.

Yuigahama had been fixated on the cards in her hands, but she quietly raised her head and looked me square in the eye. "Even if you didn't start out right, and even if you didn't do everything you could... If you're sincere and not fake about it... I don't think it's wrong to have that kind of...affection."

I wonder who she's talking about.

As that thought crossed my mind, I heard the scrape of Zaimokuza's shoes against the floor as he shifted. "...Yeah. You're right," he admitted. "...And it's true. I don't have anything to be proud of." His words carried none of his typical contrived bombast. His voice was trembling so violently it was pathetic, but while he stuttered, he absolutely did not stop. "That's why I'm staking everything on this. What's so weird about that? Aren't you guys the same?!" Zaimokuza wailed, sniffling, shoulders trembling. His breaths were ragged, and his watery glare was unmistakably that of a defeated man.

Hatano and Sagami regarded Zaimokuza and his pitiful state with revulsion. Perhaps they detested not only Zaimokuza but their former selves, too.

I was sure they also loved games. They had dreams. But dreams are too heavy to bear on your own. As you mature, you discover the realities of your future and your inability to chase down the impossible. You learn about your maximum monthly salary of two hundred thousand yen pretax, the tragically low employment rate of alumni from prestigious universities, the annual suicide rate, rising taxes, and unreliable pensions that offer no return even after you've paid into them.

You constantly absorb facts like these. Any reasonably mature teen would figure them out. Everyone jokes around like, "Get a job and you lose," but that statement isn't necessarily untrue. In this world, the pursuit of dreams leads to a life so painful and frustrating the mere thought of it is enough to merit a sigh.

Passion alone wasn't enough. That was why these guys compensated. They educated themselves, compared themselves to the dreamers, and comforted themselves by saying, *No, we're different.*

They didn't want to give up, no matter what. How dare Zaimokuza defy their choices?

"...You don't know a thing about real life. It's nothing like your ideals."

"I've known about real life for a long time!" cried Zaimokuza. "My friend from the arcade who always posted about how he was going to be a writer got a regular office job! I know another guy who bragged that he got to second-stage applications, and now he's a NEET! I know about real life..." Zaimokuza's fist was clenched in the air, tightly, like his nails might break the skin. "When I talk about becoming a light-novel writer, I know ninty-nine percent of people who hear it are thinking, *Don't waste your time dreaming about that crap* or *Open your eyes to reality, kid*, and snickering on the inside. But still, I..."

...Of course. We know reality.

We know terrorists won't suddenly invade our classrooms and zombies won't infest the city while we barricade ourselves in a hardware store. When a normal person hears your plans to write games or light novels, to them, it's just as absurd as those stupid fantasies. Nobody's going to sincerely attempt to support you or stop you. Even if you're serious when you explain, nobody will take you seriously. Thus, you eventually cave and sneer at the people with their heads still in the clouds and at yourself for ever having dreamed. You laugh to hide the truth.

So why could Zaimokuza—crying, sniffling, voice trembling—keep talking about his dreams?

"I'm certain now... Even if I can't be an author or a game writer... even so, I'm going to keep writing. I don't love writing because I want to be a writer! I want to become a writer...because I love writing!"

I honestly envied him. I envied the artless, foolish honesty in his ability to justify his path with the words *because I love it* with no doubts, no pessimism. How irrational can you get? He was so ridiculously straightforward it was noble, even.

The strength it took to announce honestly that he loved something was nearly too much for me. I'd taken the pure-hearted innocence necessary to make such a declaration with conviction, devoid of any pretense or irony, and I'd locked it away.

So *if*—if Zaimokuza—if *we* could win this match, I'd be willing to take a chance on believing in him.

I wouldn't if we lost, though.

"...Zaimokuza. It's your turn." I pushed the fistful of cards at Zaimokuza.

He pressed his hand to his chest as if to find his heartbeat before he accepted the cards and stepped forward to sit in the chair. "...No matter what you say to me now, I'm not giving up," he murmured at a lower pitch than usual as he passed me by.

Stop that. You're gonna leave that cool remark ringing in my ears.

He inhaled deeply, calming his shaking, tearful voice. "...Phew. Apologies for the wait. Let us settle this duel." We had eight cards left. A jack of spades, an eight of clubs, a three of hearts, and a four of diamonds...and all four sixes. "Eat this! Infinity Doom!" The card zipped from his hand and slammed down as Zaimokuza supplied his own sound effect. "Bam!"

Oh, I get it. The number eight on its side is an infinity sign, and the "doom" is because it's an eight ender.

"Hachiman," he began.

But before he could give me advice along with our hand, I stopped him. *You don't need to finish. I know.*

I took the seat and fanned out the cards. If we were going to use them, now was the time. We could use this move precisely because we'd been on a losing streak, because of our ongoing weakness, and because we had not succumbed. Was it willpower? Perseverance? Spiritual fortitude? Keeping your nose to the grindstone?

It was none of those. I'd been trying for this from the very beginning. No loss up until now had been a defeat. Those paltry defeats here and there were merely the foundation for our success. Defeat isn't defeat until you acknowledge it as such.

The man at my back would surely deny his losses until the bitter end. Ergo, he was closer to victory than anyone. Even if every avenue is cut off, and his hopes come to nothing, so long as he can raise a noble cry, so long as he can remain on his feet with nothing to lean on but his own pure will…

…then he will do so, and he will call it his dream.

Such an illusion, the kind no one else can hinder, is precious. Thus, only a handful of people can attain that rare reality.

The whole situation sent an involuntary shiver through me. This really felt like the climax. I was only half aware as the line I'd so longed to say fell from my lips. "I won't. Will you?"

"No. I won't," he replied.

As if on cue, the two of us stood back-to-back and spoke as one. "We're not gonna lose today!" I grabbed the four cards and slammed them on the table.

"The End of Genesis, T.M.R.evolution Type-D!"

Shut up, Zaimokuza. Just "revolution" is fine. Why did that sound so cool? You'll convince me you actually have talent.

Yuigahama gave a strained smile, and Yukinoshita let out a sigh that resembled a scoff. Shrugging her shoulders, she said, "Pass."

Hatano and Sagami eyed Zaimokuza bitterly, as if something had lodged in their throats. No surprise there. I mean, way back when, they must have played around like that, too. But eventually, they had come to a

number of realizations, and mere affection for games ceased to be enough. So they had sought out excuses. Perhaps that instant of hesitation was over choosing a card, or *perhaps* it was over the path they'd walked. "Pass..."

"Well done, Hachiman. Leave the rest to me." Unable to hide his excitement, Zaimokuza snatched the cards from me with a smile.

"Sword of the Knave! Reverse Mode!" The name was supercool, but as you can guess, it was just a jack of spades.

"Hey, wait! You moron! The jacks reverse rule nullifies revolution!" If you use jacks reverse when revolution is in effect, then of course, it reverses again. In other words, since the opposite of opposition is approval, in this situation, the jack makes the number order normal. What we should have done was play a low number to get rid of it.

"Huh? ...Ah!" Zaimokuza's eyes widened, and he blinked, finally realizing his own error. What a dick. He had just been concentrating on how good it felt to yell out his moves...

He was a total reject after all. We'd declared we were going to win, but that wasn't going to happen now. Zaimokuza doesn't have a Zetsuei, and I'm no Shell Bullet.

Yuigahama waffled for a bit, then chose to pass, and Sagami instantly followed with a two of spades. Since the UG Club had the joker, there was nothing the rest of us could play to beat that.

Hatano and Sagami looked at each other and let out a pair of deep sighs. The UG Club pair started a new pile, and revolution resumed. They had three remaining cards. Our side had two cards each, but now that they controlled how the pile began, I had no doubt they would come up with a winning strategy. "Well, I respect your enthusiasm, Master Swordsman," Hatano said, grasping two cards between his fingers. "But this is reality." He raised his pair of cards as if to swing Death's scythe.

So we're not gonna make it, huh...? If Zaimokuza hadn't made that stupid mistake, we could have won. But there's no point in saying that now. There's nothing else to be done... We're going to have to strip.

But right as I imagined my fate, Yukinoshita, who had been silent the whole time, spoke. "You got me... No matter how I do the math, there's no way I can win," she moaned as she pressed a hand to her forehead.

Hatano must have been surprised to hear her, as he stopped short.

"Huh? How can you tell, Yukinon?" asked Yuigahama.

"You can tell if you count all the cards in play, can't you?" replied Yukinoshita. "And then if you subtract our cards, you can deduce what's in your opponents' hand, right? Plus, there's the card exchange between the millionaire and the beggar. The UG Club took the highest cards this round, so it wasn't difficult to pick them out."

"Are you the computer grandma or what…?" *Yeah, I'll just memorize every card that's been played!* was a method I'd thought up way back in elementary school, but no one can actually do that. Memorizing the cards is hard enough without having to concoct your strategy at the same time. Plus, when you get swept up in the thrill of the game, you stop caring. At most, you can pin down the twos and jokers.

…Actually, maybe she's just an idiot.

"The UG Club will use their joker as an eight for an eight ender and finish off with the seven of diamonds. Hikigaya and his partner hold the three of hearts and a four of diamonds. Our loss is definitive," Yukinoshita said, sounding irritated as she set her cards on the table and stood.

Wait, you seriously know what cards we're holding? Are you an Alter user?

Yukinoshita bit her lip in frustration, her cheeks flushed with embarrassment as she put her hands to the hem of her summer vest. Her fingers trembled with humiliation, and she couldn't quite grasp it. The sight made me anxious. Huffing a short sigh through clenched teeth, Yukinoshita steadied her slim, long fingers and squeezed the hem tight. Slowly lifting it up, she began exposing the blouse hidden underneath it. Her smooth, white porcelain skin softly peeked through the gaps between the buttons.

Whether I liked it or not, my eyes couldn't resist her. Well, I did like it, though. I gulped. That was when I heard rustling.

What? Stop being so loud. Shut up, I'll miss this, I thought, glaring at the source in time to see Hatano let a single joker fall onto the table. But apparently, he didn't have time to worry about that right now, either. He apologized, saying, "Sorry," but he immediately went back to ogling Yukinoshita and didn't even pick up the card… Geez.

Seriously, be more careful. Now then..., I thought, returning to the scene at hand, but my vision was totally obscured.

"Stop right there. Okay, that's enough." A girl's distinctively soft hands were covering my eyelids. When I gently removed them, I saw Yuigahama scowling at me like I was utter trash.

"What?" I asked.

But Yuigahama sullenly chose not to reply. She jerked her head away, her bun wagging at me in displeasure. "Yukinon. You don't have to strip, you know?" Yuigahama squeezed Yukinoshita's hands in her own, stopping her from undressing.

Yukinoshita slowly relaxed the tension that had made her stiff. She gave Yuigahama's hands a weak squeeze in return. "...Rules are rules. I feel bad for dragging you into this, though."

"Oh, that's not what I mean. We can win this," Yuigahama said, snatching their cards off the desk. "Here. The three of spades."

Hatano had just dropped a card onto the pile, face-up.

"Geh!" Sagami's ejaculation of surprise resembled something out of Mitsuteru Yokoyama's *Romance of the Three Kingdoms*.

"Geh!" His partner Hatano's shocked expression could have come straight out of *Ultimate Muscle*.

The three of spades. Normally, it was one of the lowest-ranking cards, a three. But under our special rules, it was the only card that could top the wild card, the joker. What's more, now that revolution was in effect, the three was the highest-ranking card. In this game of Beggar that so mirrored modern society, it offered a glimmer of hope, albeit fleeting.

"Here, Yukinon." Yuigahama cheerfully handed a dumbfounded Yukinoshita their final card. Yukinoshita shyly accepted it along with Yuigahama's little smile, and thus the goddess of victory smiled upon their queen. The light of the setting sun shone into the clubroom, casting a tiny victory pose in silhouette.

These moments of victory were all too brief. While the taste, such as it was, still lingered on our tongues, I spoke to the UG Club. "It's not about hating or loving the game, or having the knowledge or not. Life is just...a game of chance."

Whether or not your dreams come true is up to luck, as is victory and defeat. Source: *Tottemo! Luckyman.* What the hell, man, the difficulty on this game is ridiculous. Anyway, whether or not Zaimokuza's dreams would come true would also boil down to luck, I suppose.

I sighed and admonished Zaimokuza and the Service Club with my smile. "Don't you think it's too early to be giving up on or rejecting dreams?"

"Hikigaya," said Yukinoshita. "Put on some clothes already."

× × ×

A lukewarm breeze was blowing through the open hallway when we left the UG Clubroom. Maybe it was due to stewing in anxiety for so long, but my shoulders were particularly stiff. Putting a hand to my shoulder, I twisted my neck until it made a nice cracking sound. Beside me, Yuigahama stretched high with a groan, and Yukinoshita stifled a small yawn.

"Um, I'm sorry."

"For laughing and stuff." Hatano and Sagami quietly bowed their heads with contrite expressions. The fact that they were apologizing was perhaps proof that their hearts had been in the right place. It had to be why they couldn't hold back their remarks when they'd first heard Zaimokuza pontificating about his delusions. In a way, they were the only ones who had taken Zaimokuza seriously when he'd talked about his dreams. If they had not done so, they would never have considered criticizing him.

Oh, I'm not like them, though. I believe from the bottom of my heart that Zaimokuza is scum and reject him entirely.

"Mm-huh? ...Fwa-ha-ha-ha! So long as you understand! Come now, just you wait a few years. I shall send my stunning Yoshiteru Zaimokuza Presents video game out into the world!" Obnoxiously enough, Zaimokuza's head had swelled even larger.

But the UG Club boys were willing to excuse it with a smile. "Yeah. We'll be looking forward to your game, Master Swordsman."

"Well, the company will own the copyright, so it won't really be yours."

Zaimokuza's laughter instantly faded. "Wh-wha—? Wh-what do you mean?" he stammered.

Hatano and Sagami looked at each other before launching into a detailed explanation. "Products from a company generally become the intellectual property of that company."

"With stuff like games, the joint copyright goes to the company."

"It depends on your contract, but I believe writers are often work-for-hire."

"Under work-for-hire, no matter how successful the property is, you won't receive any compensation beyond your initial payment."

"S-seriously?!" Zaimokuza dropped his bag with a thud. "Th-then… maybe I won't… Yeah, screw that."

What a tool… He snapped right back to talking like the real Zaimokuza… I…I wanna deck him…

Fearing my fist might connect with Zaimokuza's temple at any moment, I desperately restrained myself. The UG Club boys only smiled awkwardly, as pity had eclipsed their frustration.

"Nghh. If my share is minuscule even if I write a big hit, then there's no point. Being a light-novel author was the better idea after all! My, my, now that I've decided, there's no time to waste! I must be getting started on my plot outline…," Zaimokuza said, picking up his bag. Arms still crossed, he began briskly striding away. "We must part, Hachiman! Fare thee well!"

I replied with only a flip of my hand, shooing him away. He waved back, beaming with joy.

That was…the biggest waste of time the Service Club has engaged in since its inception.

"He's kinda weird," Hatano said with a sigh.

"I know, right? Nothing good comes of getting involved with *that*," I replied.

"Uh, you guys are pretty weird, too, though." This time it was Sagami who spoke, and his expression was rather frosty.

"Huh? Hey, how can you say that? I'm as commonsense as they come!"

"In what culture is your attitude considered commonsense? Associating with a freak like you is utterly exhausting," quipped Yukinoshita.

"Uh, but you're sorta odd too, Yukinon...," Yuigahama coolly fired back, then looked at Yukinoshita and followed up with an uncomfortable *ta-ha-ha*.

But Yukinoshita didn't seem particularly offended, and a gentle smile appeared on her face. "Indeed. It seems both Hikigaya and I are somewhat abnormal...so it's good to have a normal person like you around." Illuminated in the fading light, Yukinoshita's cheeks flushed a faint crimson.

Yuigahama gaped at her in a daze, her mouth slowly curving into an expression of joy. Her eyes grew slightly moist as she latched onto Yukinoshita's arm and squeezed. "...Y-yeah!"

"You're smothering me...," Yukinoshita muttered quietly, but she made no attempt to untangle herself.

"Let's just go back to the clubroom," I suggested, starting to walk there. Yukinoshita and Yuigahama trailed a few steps behind.

Well, for now I'll assume they've made up...

The one I talk to most is Miss Hiratsuka…but she's too old to be called a girl.

Totsuka, I guess. Yeah, Totsuka. It's Totsuka. Definitely Totsuka.Today we were discussing the best way to eat a chocolate cornet. Totsuka's the type who tears off little pieces. Apparently, that's because he can't open his mouth very wide, and if you look at it, his mouth really is small and supercute. Anyway, he tried biting into it for me, and he licked the chocolate off his lips… W-well, that part was, like, *man*! When he saw me watching him, he looked away like he was so embarrassed. That expression!

Hey, wait. I'm not done talking. After that—

H-hey, wait, I said! Listen, come on, please! And then Totsuka had some melon bread, and…!

Hmm…he may be my brother, but he's hopeless.

Which girl do you talk with the most?

She's gonna smack you if you say that to her… Who other than the teacher?

Regarding

Saika Totsuka

Agh…

Oh, Bro. Are you okay with beef shabu-shabu for dinner?

Welp, I'm going shopping! ♪

6

Finally, **his** and **her** beginning ends.

I arrived in the clubroom and glanced at the evening sun slowly setting into Tokyo Bay outside the window. On the eastern side, the curtains of night were falling in a wash of pale indigo over the sky.

"What do we do now…? I even went to the trouble of baking a cake," Yukinoshita commented with a sigh. She'd noticed the color of the sky, just like me. It was indeed nearly time to go home. The bell would probably ring right as we cut the cake.

Yuigahama tilted her head, confused. "A cake? Why a cake?"

"What do you mean, 'why'? Oh, I haven't told you yet, have I? I asked you to come here because I wanted to wish you a happy birthday, Yuigahama," replied Yukinoshita.

"Huh?"

"You haven't been coming to the club lately…and, um…I wanted to encourage you to put in the appropriate effort to show up. Also, uh…I suppose you could call this a symbol of my gratitude." Yukinoshita cleared her throat quietly with a little *he-hem*, as if to draw attention away from her shyness.

Before she had even finished speaking, Yuigahama glomped her. "…You remembered my birthday, Yukinon!"

Uh, she didn't remember it. She just guessed it from your e-mail address, you know.

Still, uninterested in how it had come about, Yuigahama tearfully basked in her lingering joy.

"Regardless, it doesn't look like we can do this today," said Yukinoshita. I guess she felt smothered after all, as she attempted to peel Yuigahama off her as she spoke. Yuigahama resisted a little, then clapped her hands as if she had an idea. Yukinoshita took advantage of the distraction and smoothly slipped free.

"Okay, then let's go somewhere. Like…out," suggested Yuigahama.

"Huh? But we can't just…" Yukinoshita floundered in the face of such a sudden proposal.

But Yuigahama rolled right over her objections and insisted, "Come on, come on!" with a wink that said, *Leave it to me!* "I'll make the reservation and everything, so don't worry about it! It's fine! I'm already superhappy you got a cake for me."

"There's more than just a cake, though…"

"N-no way, you got me a present, too?!" Yuigahama's eyes sparkled at Yukinoshita. Heedless of the fact that she had peeled her off just moments earlier, Yuigahama again closed the gap between them.

Wary of another glomping, Yukinoshita replied, "Yes, well…I'm not the only one, though," she said, implicating me with a glance.

"Huh? You mean…" Yuigahama deciphered the other girl's meaning and gave a vague, awkward smile. "Ah…ah-ha-ha. I totally didn't expect you to get me a present, Hikki. Since, um, like…recently… things have been a bit…weird." Yuigahama's eyes met mine, and we both immediately broke the contact.

When Yukinoshita was with us, I could overcome the weird unpleasantness by pretending not to notice it. But Yukinoshita had deliberately dragged me into the conversation this time, and I figured that was a message to acknowledge that something happened and get my ass in gear to resolve it. Considering how insensitive she typically was, she'd sure chosen an odd time to butt in.

I pulled a small package out of my bag and casually passed it straight to Yuigahama. "…It's not necessarily for your birthday, though."

"Huh?"

I was drowning in an atmosphere that made it extraordinarily hard to speak, but I forced my mouth to move as properly as I was able, even as I felt in danger of stuttering. "I've been thinking a little. I guess… let's call it even with this, you know? Me saving your dog and you trying so hard to be nice to me. Let's wipe the slate," I said, forging ahead without waiting for her response. "I mean, there's no reason to force yourself to go out of your way for me. The person who hit me paid for my hospital bills with insurance and came with the lawyer to apologize, or so I heard. So there's no reason for you to pity me or worry about my feelings." With every phrase that left my mouth, I felt an unpleasant pressure around my heart as if something were squeezing it. Nevertheless, I'd never be able to end it if I didn't say this. "Plus, I didn't save the dog because it was yours."

For a brief moment, Yuigahama looked at me with incredible sadness, but she lowered her eyes right away.

"I wasn't thinking of you as a particular individual who would owe me, so there's no need for you to repay your debt to me individually, either. But…like…I dunno…I do want to pay you back for how friendly you've been to me. Once you subtract this, we're at zero. We're even. You don't have to worry about me anymore. So we're done with all this," I finished, and when I released a breath, I felt the load on my chest leaving me along with the exhalation. Now the situation could be resolved, and we could put this behind us—both the awkward misunderstandings and the misguided attempts at self-preservation. Though both of those would probably happen in the future, anyway.

I avoided Yuigahama's eyes, watching only the tight, hard line of her lips. "…Why do you think of it like that? Like I feel sorry for you, or I'm forcing myself to be considerate? …I've never once thought of it that way. I just…" Her voice was trembling, quiet as a whisper. Yukinoshita and I only listened silently. It was all we could do. There was nothing either of us could say. A faint darkness lurked in the corners of the clubroom. Only the tiniest rays of sunlight still slanted in. "Like… it's so complicated, and I don't really know anymore… I thought it was a lot simpler than this…" Her tone was a little brighter than it had been, but she was likely forcing that cheery veneer, lending her words no more substance than so much air.

An icy comment cut through the ambiguity. "It's not that complicated." Yukinoshita stood with the setting sun at her back. A sea breeze from the open window swished through her hair. "Hikigaya doesn't remember saving you, Yuigahama, and you don't remember ever feeling sorry for him. You were both wrong from the start."

"Yeah, that's true," I agreed.

Yukinoshita nodded. "So I think Hikigaya's proposal to end it would be the correct choice."

We began in error, so obviously the ensuing events left us in error, too. No matter the emotions involved, that answer didn't change, I was sure. Even if...*if*...those feelings were something special. If that sentiment was born due to an arbitrary accident, if it was directed at me because of my sacrifice, or if it would have developed for any altruist who had saved her dog, then I couldn't accept it as the real thing.

If I had done that favor for her without recognizing her as herself, then she had received it without recognizing me as myself. Thus, her feelings and her benevolence weren't for me. They were for the person who had helped her. That was why I didn't want her to get the wrong idea.

I've stopped bothering getting my hopes up and watching them die when all of it's just in my head. I expect nothing from the start, I expect nothing in the middle, and I expect nothing up until the end.

Yuigahama was silent for a while before muttering a few words. "But ending it...? I kinda... I don't want that."

"...Don't be silly," said Yukinoshita. "If it's over, then you should just make a new start. Neither of you is at fault."

"What?" I asked, startled.

Cool and composed, Yukinoshita swept back the hair resting on her shoulders. "Though there is a difference between you two in that one helped and one was helped, you were both equally victimized by the traffic accident, were you not? In which case, the cause of it all was the perpetrator of the accident. That means..." Yukinoshita paused for a moment. During that brief interval, she fixed me, then Yuigahama, with a firm look. "...you two...can make a proper start," she said, wearing a smile that was both gentle and vaguely sorrowful. I couldn't distinguish what was in her narrowed eyes in the sunset glow. "I have to go report to Miss Hiratsuka that we've recruited the additional member she requested," Yukinoshita added as if she'd just remembered, then curtly spun on her heel and marched away faster than usual, out the clubroom door without turning back.

Now it was just Yuigahama and me. Yukinoshita had said her piece, so I supposed she had no reason to stay, but this awkward vibe could go straight to hell.

Furtively eyeing me, Yuigahama searched for the right moment before gently, tentatively concluding the conversation. "Um…uh… I-it's good to be back." The words needed no follow-up, but for some reason she bobbed her head in a bow.

"Y-yeah…" I had no idea what was so good about it.

Something still didn't sit right for me. I had a sense that Yukinoshita had wheedled me into this. *Sophistry is supposed to be my specialty. I can't believe she beat me at my own game.* I smiled wryly.

Yuigahama poked me in the back. "…Hey, can I open it?"

"Go right ahead." Now that I'd handed the present over to her, it was in her possession. No need to bother requesting permission to open it.

Yuigahama carefully undid the wrapping paper, and her face lit up. "Wow…" She gasped.

A round silver tag lay in the center of a braid of black leather. It would pair nicely with brown hair. The item was well chosen, if I do say so myself. I got *something* out of buying so many presents for Komachi over the years. I happen to be an expert on running errands for her.

Yuigahama appeared satisfied with my selection as she gently studied the present. "H-hold on a second," she said and instantly spun away from me. In less than thirty seconds, she was facing me again and fidgeting with her bangs. "H-how does it look?" She averted her eyes a little bashfully. The black leather adorning her white neck struck a lovely contrast with her brown hair in the radiance of the setting sun. It suited her perfectly.

I really didn't want to tell her…but at times like these, it was undoubtedly wisest to get it over with. "Uh…that's a dog collar, though." *Why does it look so good on her?*

HFF!
HFF!

"Huh?" Yuigahama's face changed color before my eyes. "Wh-why didn't you say that earlier?! You jerk!" she yelled, hurling the wrapping paper at me.

Uh, can't you tell? Well, I guess it is adjustable, so…

"Honestly, geez! I'm gonna go reserve us a place now!" Fuming, Yuigahama removed the collar and stalked toward the exit. But when she opened the door, she halted.

"Thanks. Jerk." Without a glance behind her, she left me with those two words and slammed the sliding door shut before I could reply.

"Agh…" Alone in the classroom, I let out a deep, deep sigh and looked at the empty space by the window Yukinoshita had occupied earlier. Yuigahama and I had been sitting not two meters from that spot, but for some reason, the distance seemed impassable, as if an invisible line divided the space between us.

Before long, we would learn the facts—the truth that unmistakably separated us from her.

Bonus track!
"Like, This Sort of Birthday Song."

This bonus track is a prose adaptation of the drama CD that came packaged with the *My Youth Romantic Comedy Is Wrong, As I Expected*, Vol. 3 special edition copy. This script details an episode that occurs soon after the events of Volume 3. We recommend you listen to it after you have finished reading this book. Also, please understand in advance that, as the text has been revised, some parts do differ slightly from the vocal track.

Birthdays.

On one of these auspicious days, I was delivered into the world, and on many others, traumas were delivered into my life. Birthday parties where I was the only one not invited, for example. Times when my classmates singing the birthday song touched my heart because I believed it was for me, and then it turned out to be for someone else with the same birth date. Birthday cakes that misspelled my name… Oh, and about that last one—what the hell was my mom doing? Don't get your own son's name wrong.

Perhaps the reason babies cry upon being born is not from the emotions of their nascent existence, but because they are experiencing loneliness for the first time after being separated from their mothers. Thus, loneliness begins with one's birthday.

As a wise man once said, never forget what it was to be new. Therefore, spending your birthday alone is the correct course of action, and frittering the day away chumming it up with friends is wrong...though the desire to celebrate someone isn't, I think.

X X X

One day, I was going down the hallway of the special building. A few meters ahead of me, I caught sight of a student of mine humming contentedly as she walked along. Her name was Yui Yuigahama. She's a generally cheerful girl, but that day she seemed to be in an especially good mood.

"Hmm, hmm, hummm! ♪"

"Hey there, Yuigahama," I called out to her. "You sure look chipper today. Something nice must have happened for you to hum like that in the hallway."

She came to a stop and replied with a warm smile, "Oh, Miss Hiratsuka. Well, it's my birthday today. And I think Yukinon is gonna throw me a...birthday party? Or something."

A birthday...? Yes, at that age, they're still enjoyable, but at mine... whoops, strike that. Anyway, it would be fun for her, so she should have a proper celebration. Once she reaches my age, she might not be able to accept those "happy birthday" wishes quite as graciously.

"Oh-ho, so today's your birthday, huh? Happy birthday. I'm glad you're getting along so well. I'm pleased to see how much Yukinoshita's grown as a person, but on the other hand...agh." Without warning, the face of another student rose to mind.

I suppose Yuigahama was thinking along the same lines I was, as the corner of her mouth quirked upward as if she didn't know how to respond. "...Yeah. W-well, Hikki's like...um, he's generally pretty crappy, but he can be nice on occasion and, like...give people presents... and stuff."

When I saw her reaction, my face relaxed into a smile. "Oh? I never brought up Hikigaya's name at all, though."

"What?! No way! Was that a trick question?!" Yuigahama floundered in surprise. *But it wasn't.*

"If you must classify it, I'd call it a leading question. But never mind that. You're someone I can count on when it comes to those two. They're a hassle, but be a good friend to them." *Hmm. Did I just say something rather teacher-like?* I thought to myself, and Yuigahama herself seemed stunned for a moment.

She blurted out her simple and naive impression. "S-sure… Miss Hiratsuka, you kind of remind me of my mom."

"Gwagh! I-I'm not old enough to be your mother…though…" Instantly, a blow like a blunt weapon struck my heart. Struggling to keep my legs steady, I grinned back at her.

Flustered, Yuigahama continued. "O-oh, n-no! I didn't mean it that way! It's more like…you're…mom-ish? Like *a* mom, not *my* mom, specifically. You'll be a good mother, Miss Hiratsuka! If you just get married!"

Wheeze. "Ngh! It hurts all the more because I know you're not trying to…" When confronted with *iaijutsu*, drawing and attacking in a single motion, the moment right after the strike is when you're most vulnerable. That means that if I hadn't read in *Rurouni Kenshin* that one must always prepare for the follow-up, I would have failed to react in time and collapsed from the shock just now. But it was okay. She was essentially complimenting me. I could still go on. *It's not time to give up just yet! Go, Shizuka!*

While I was busy cheerleading myself, Yuigahama spoke up, as if she'd just thought of something. "Oh, I know! Why don't you come to the party, too, Miss Hiratsuka?"

"Hmm. While I appreciate the offer, I'll have to sit this one out. I have another get-together today."

"Are you going to a birthday party, too?"

"N-no, not exactly… I'll die before I tell her I'm going to a matchmaking event." *…Let's change the subject before she asks me what kind of get-together it is.* "Anyway, should the birthday girl be hanging around here? Aren't they all waiting for you?"

"Oh, right! See you later, then!" she chirped.

"See you. Have fun." I watched her dash off and then looked out the window to the sky slowly darkening overhead. "...Agh, I want to get married."

X X X

Yukinoshita and I were reading together in the silent clubroom. This was nothing out of the ordinary. What made this different from usual was that for once, we had plans after this.

"Hey, Yukinoshita," I said. "Can we just end club now? Even if we continue, all we'll be doing is reading..."

Firmly fixed on her paperback, Yukinoshita turned a page and replied, "You're right. We'll be celebrating Yuigahama's birthday after this, so we won't be able to engage in any Service Club activities. Do you have any objections?"

"No, no objections. In fact, I feel lucky to get the day off. I'm thrilled Yuigahama was born. Thanks to her, there's no more club today."

"I can't tell if your perspective is too narrow or too broad... You're as shallow as ever." Vexed, Yukinoshita closed her book.

But I was exasperated, too. *You just don't* get *it, Yukinoshita. You don't* understand. "Don't be stupid. Being deep isn't necessarily a good thing."

"I was under the impression it was preferable, or am I wrong?" Yukinoshita expressed the very objection I had predicted.

"A deep river has a fast current, your vision can't reach the bottom, and your feet can't, either. So paradoxically, if I am shallow, I am calm, easy to see through, and grounded," I replied with a smug chuckle.

Yukinoshita looked bewildered. "Inexplicably...I've come to understand that you are a great man..."

"Inexplicably...I've come to understand that you're being insincere..." *That's odd. I think I'm a pretty solid guy.*

But a baffled Yukinoshita was tilting her head. "Huh? But you lack even a single laudable trait."

"Why are you giving me that cute puzzled look? The discrepancy between your expression and your remarks is causing me unnecessary pain," I said.

Yukinoshita spared me no concern. "I apologize. My nature is fundamentally honest."

"That's not what you should be apologizing for. Look. If you ignore how I don't have friends or a girlfriend, I'm basically high caliber," I expounded.

Yukinoshita softly pressed a hand to her brow as if her head hurt. "Generally speaking, those are fatal deficiencies, though… Well, not that it matters. I myself have a few objections with that particular prevailing notion."

"You got that right. To declare 'the more friends and girlfriends the better' is to deny the individual. Among those lauded by the world as the greatest, the most prominent individuals, the geniuses, there are some who have no friends at all. Well, more to the point, *you're* a genius, ranked top in our grade, capable of anything, and *you* don't have any friends, either."

"I—I have one…," Yukinoshita protested shyly. She was most likely referring to a mutual acquaintance of ours.

"Yeah, Yuigahama. But you know, I said *friends*, plural, and that typically implies you have more than one. You don't have friend-*zuh*!"

"You're splitting hairs again…," Yukinoshita said bluntly and with condescension.

That was when the door to the clubroom opened. "Yahallo! Hmm? What're you guys talking about?" That particular idiotic greeting arrived along with Yui Yuigahama.

"Oh, Yuigahama. Oh, Hikigaya was just insisting that he's a great man and refuses to back down."

Yuigahama clapped her hands as she burst into laughter. "Ah-ha-ha! That's rich."

"Don't shoot me down right out of the gate. C'mon, calm down. I'll explain my greatness point by point. First, I've got a decent face, so that's plus one point."

"But you've got a rotten look in your eyes. Minus one," said Yukinoshita.

"Plus, you're tooting your own horn there…" Yuigahama chimed in. The girls were so generous with their subtractions.

"Ngh! W-well… I'm here at a school that'll put me on track for university. Plus one," I retorted.

"There's a possibility you'll repeat the year. Minus one," replied Yukinoshita with indifference.

"Ah…ah-ha…ha. I—I don't think I can talk. I'll leave that one for now." Yuigahama tittered uncomfortably.

W-well, so far my points had been kinda…on the abstract side. Or like, one could contend a lot of it was subjective. But this time, I would come up with points that were both concrete and rock solid. "Then how about this? In the arts category, I'm ranked third in our year in Japanese. Plus one."

"But your grade in math is nine percent, the lowest mark in the year. Minus one," Yukinoshita retorted.

"U-ughhh. Mine is twelve percent… I-I'll leave that one." Yuigahama was nearly crying.

What else, what else… "Nghhhh… A-also…I have a deep and abiding love for my sister?"

"That's just a sister complex," said Yuigahama. Both girls wordlessly told me, *Die, pervert.*

"Minus two points," announced Yukinoshita.

"Why was that two?! Damn it! Is there anything else…? I—I can't. I can't think of anything…" I tried to scrounge up something else, but there was nothing.

Yukinoshita smiled mercilessly upon me and my troubles. "Are you done already? We have more."

"What…did you say?" *She has more dirt on me? Come on, do you have heaven's memo pad or something?*

Yukinoshita quietly averted her eyes and muttered softly. "Like… how you actually got Yuigahama a birthday present. Plus one point… or not."

"Huh? Did you say something?" I asked.

"Nothing important. Come on, let's get going. The cake has fruit in it, so it would be best to eat it while it's still fresh." Yukinoshita coolly deflected my question, pushing her chair back.

"Y-yeah...," I replied. Yuigahama and I followed suit and stood.

"Yay! Cake! What kind of fruit is in it, Yukinon? Watermelon?!" she said.

"The first thing that comes to your mind is watermelon? Your cooking skills are terrible as ever," muttered Yukinoshita.

× × ×

We left the clubroom and trudged down the hallway. When we arrived at the first floor, I remembered the e-mail from my sister. "So where are we going now? Komachi said she wanted to come, too, so I'd like to invite her."

Yukinoshita nodded.

"Why not?" Yuigahama replied. "We're headed to the karaoke place by the station. They're charging a flat rate after five. You know, the 'free time' deal."

"Okay, gotcha. I'll e-mail her, then... 'Free time,' huh? I'm not a fan of that." Unpleasant memories rose unbidden to my mind.

Looking grumpy, Yuigahama asked, "Huh? Why? 'Free' means you can do whatever you want. It's a great thing."

"Freedom is not necessarily an unequivocal good. Freedom means no protection, no shelter," Yukinoshita said.

That seemed rational, so I nodded, too. "That's exactly right. Be it field trips, school-wide outings, swimming classes... I never knew what to do when they said we had free time, and I was constantly stressing over it. I didn't have anything to do when we went to the pool, so I swam about two kilometers."

"That's essentially endurance swimming," Yukinoshita remarked.

Yeah, that was clearly beyond the scope of the class, huh? It was rough...

"Ha-ha-ha!" Yuigahama laughed. "It's easy to deal with field trips and stuff, though. All you have to do is be quiet and reserved and keep three steps behind."

"That sounds like a rather unpleasant *yamato nadeshiko*...," Yukinoshita replied.

As this pointless conversation continued, we arrived at the school entrance, and abruptly, I detected boisterous laughter from somewhere nearby.

"Fwa-ha-ha-ha-ha-ha! Hachiman!"

...Oh, must have been my imagination.

"But why karaoke?" I asked.

"Ngh? Heh-heh-heh-heh-heh... Hachiman..."

Yuigahama pondered for a moment. "Why? 'Cause people won't get mad at you even if you're supernoisy, and you get all-you-can-drink beverages."

"Ho-mmph... H-Hachiman? Hello?"

"Plus, I hear for birthdays they'll let you bring in the cake," she added.

"You should still ask the staff first, though," Yukinoshita said.

Yes, that cackling was just my imagination after all. Yukinoshita, Yuigahama, and I continued our conversation. "Huh, but, like...it's Yuigahama's birthday. So why was she the one reserving the karaoke?" I asked.

"...! I-it's not like I had a choice!" Yukinoshita replied. "I don't know how to plan these sorts of events."

"Oh, don't worry about it!" Yuigahama said. "Also, like, you know...I'm just happy people are coming to a party for me, and I'm even happier when I think, like, *Oh, Yukinon's relying on me!*"

"Yuigahama..." Yukinoshita trailed off.

"Eh-heh-heh." The two of them blushed rather shyly and shared a smile.

All of a sudden, a black shadow stomped its way into our group!

"JUST A MOMENT! DON'T LEEEEAVE MEEEE!"

The fierce bellow made both Yukinoshita and Yuigahama cower. By the way, so did I.

"Eek!"

"Waugh!"

"Yaaagh!" I cried. "That scared me! ...Oh, it's Zaimokuza. Huh, where'd you come from?" He was there? Really?

"Ga-hum, ga-hum! If you ask from whence I came, first I must needs prove that I exist at all, though?" He cleared his throat in a contrived manner before spouting a bunch of self-important nonsense. What a pain in the butt.

"Oh, that sounds like it'll be exhausting, so forget it... What is it? Do you want something?" I asked.

Zaimokuza folded his arms arrogantly and replied, "Hmph. After our last meeting, I went straight to drafting a premise for my new light novel... I'll permit you to see it if you want."

"Why are you acting like I'm beneath you? And don't give us a plot or an outline or whatever. Bring us a complete draft."

"Hwa-ha-ha-ha! Come now, this time the outline alone is so stunning, you'll be back for more! Come, behold my work!" He shoved a stack of papers at me.

"Right now? Sorry, but we've got things to do. How about later?" I casually rebuffed him.

Suddenly, he gazed off into the distance and began to ramble. "Fleh. Have you heard this tale before? The god of luck, Caerus, has only one lock of hair near his forehead. So you cannot let him slip by you...muh? Hey, Hachiman, if you miss his bangs, why can't you grab his hands or feet or something?"

"I don't know. Don't quote myths you don't really understand... If you're in such a hurry about your story, anyway, go have some message board evaluate it."

"That would be impossible. If one of the other *wannabes* were to post something like *Lulz this guy's writing sux so bad lolol whoever wrote this is a talent vacuum rofl*, I would choose death." Zaimokuza meaningfully emphasized the English word *wannabe*.

"Let's try cultivating some thicker skin before we polish our creative strengths, shall we?" Zaimokuza was so pathetic, I found myself kindly chiding him.

Yukinoshita peered up at me. "Hey, Hikigaya, what's a wannabe?"

"Oh, I'm not completely sure, but I've heard that's what they call people who aspire to be light-novel writers." I'm sure there are various theories on this, but my guess is that it comes from the English *I wanna be such and such*. But I don't really know.

Yuigahama, who knew no more than I did, made an appreciative noise. "Ohh...I thought it was those animals at the Chiba Zoo."

"...There're no wallabies in the Chiba Zoo, though," I said.

"Yuigahama, it's eastern gray kangaroos that they have there," Yukinoshita replied in all seriousness.

Yuigahama's face reddened as she protested. "I—I know what kangaroos are! But, like, you know, there's those tinier ones, aren't there? I got it mixed up with those!"

"...Do you mean meerkats?" Yukinoshita suggested.

"Yeah, that's it! Tsk! I was so close! ...Next question, please."

"No, you weren't close, and we're not doing the Trans-Chiba Ultra Quiz, either," I said. *Also, you know way too much about the Chiba Zoo. You're weirding me out, seriously.*

"Hyagh! Who cares about marsupials or whatever, anyway?!" Zaimokuza thumped his draft as he became more insistent. "I have confidence in this one! Thus far, I have been called a stinking garbage wannabe, but 'tis only a matter of time before they drop a word or two from that title..."

Yukinoshita put a hand to her jaw and gave an appreciative nod. "I see. So from now on they'll simply call you stinking garbage, hmm?"

"Why take out that part...?" I commented. I imagine the correct assumption was that they would drop the "stinking garbage" part and call him a plain wannabe. *Wait, you're gonna make them take the nasty parts out and then stick with being a wannabe?*

But Zaimokuza's fearless smile was brimming with assurance. "Heh. You'll understand how different this one is soon enough, once you've read it... Hmm? By the way, Hachiman, what is this business you're on today?"

"Huh? Oh, it's Yuigahama's birthday, so we're having a little party."

"What?! The celebration of her nativity?! Is this perhaps what they call a...*baasudei* in English?!"

"Well, yeah. There was absolutely no need to bust out the English, though."

Trembling like a leaf, Zaimokuza said, "Oh-ho...so the old legend was true… When a certain personage's seventeenth birthday arrives, the Master Swordsman General shall also hasten to give her his blessings."

"You're kinda freaking me out…" Yuigahama swiftly cringed away and retreated behind me, her human shield.

"Old ladies always go wild whenever they hear the word *birthday*, though, don't they?" I said. "I dunno, Chibanese are just sensitive to the subject of birthdays."

"Is that so? I've never paid them much mind, though." Yukinoshita quizzically cocked her head.

"Well, in elementary schools in Chiba, seating charts are based on your birthday, right?" I replied.

"Ahh! You're right, they were!" Yuigahama spoke up in agreement. "I was surprised when I started high school and we were suddenly in alphabetical order."

"You're right. It seems that determining the order based on date of birth is unusual compared to the rest of the country," said Yukinoshita.

"Indeed so. And 'tis an anomaly that can bring about tragedy…"

"Where's this coming from, Zaimokuza?" I asked.

Zaimokuza's know-it-all expression darkened. "…Two days before, everyone said happy birthday to the guy in the seat in front of me. Three days later, they said it to the guy behind me."

"Ahh, got it," I said.

"They completely snubbed you, huh?" remarked Yukinoshita.

I guess that kind of thing can happen when your birthday is during the school year. My birthday is in the middle of summer vacation, though, meaning I've never experienced anything similar myself. So I could easily accept his claim. "When you think about it, then, Chiba is a rough prefecture for a loner."

"Ma-hom. Why are you looking at me like this has nothing to do with you, Hachiman?"

"Nobody wants anything to do with him, so everything has nothing to do with him." Yukinoshita grinned broadly.

"Why do you have to smile when you say that? I don't wanna hear it from you. Everything has nothing to do with you, too," I replied.

Yukinoshita swept her hair back with a hand and a generous helping of self-assurance. "Indeed. I don't want anything to do with anyone, either..."

"Huh?" A disappointed Yuigahama gave Yukinoshita a few sharp prods in the back.

"Yuigahama, could you not poke me like that?"

"Hmm..." Yukinoshita's request did not stop Yuigahama, and she continued jabbing at the other girl as if she was grumpy about something.

Unable to bear it, Yukinoshita lightly cleared her throat. "Ahem... I amend my statement. While there are exceptions, I don't want anything to do with most people."

"Yukinon!" Yuigahama leaped upon Yukinoshita.

"You're smothering me...," Yukinoshita muttered in a complex mixture of gladness and annoyance.

Ignoring the pair, I said my farewells to Zaimokuza. "So yeah, Zaimokuza, we've got some stuff going on, so I can't today. Later." We parted with him and set off once more.

But there were footsteps close behind us. "Ahem. What a coincidence. I just so happen to have no plans today..."

"I see. It sure is nice to have nothing going on. Anyway...why are you following us?" I asked, gently implying that he should stop.

Zaimokuza, however, did not get the message. "I am so bored, ah, so very bored! I have naught to do, so mayhap I might go on a quick jaunt before I head home. Whoops, now that I think of it, Hachiman, wh-where are you guys going?"

"The station."

"You don't say! ...What a coincidence. I was just about to pass through thereabouts today on my way home. This might perchance be fate... So this is the choice the world has made..."

"..."

His performance was annoying, so I ignored it.

Zaimokuza sank deep into thought, glancing at me from time to time.

Yuigahama, repulsed by our exchange, quietly whispered in my ear. "Hey, Hikki. About the Special Snowflake..."

"'Snowflake'? Is that your nickname for Zaimokuza?" *Isn't that kinda mean?*

Yuigahama seemed unconcerned, though, and continued. "Yes. Don't you think Snowflake wants to be invited?"

"Yeah, I get that, but..." I trailed off.

Yukinoshita shrugged her shoulders. "So you do understand...*sigh*. But so long as Yuigahama is okay with it, I see no problem with inviting him. I'd rather give up now than have him follow us indefinitely."

"Hmm... I dunno," said Yuigahama.

"If you do invite him, though, you have to take due care of him until the end," commented Yukinoshita.

"Are you my mom or what?" I said. "Hey, Yuigahama. Can we let him come?"

Yuigahama considered it for a bit. "Hmm...well...it's not like I don't know him, and he *is* your friend, so...okay."

"Thanks. He's not my friend, though."

"H-he's not...?" Yuigahama had this odd expression that was not quite shock and not quite disgust.

Turning my back to her, I spoke to Zaimokuza. "Zaimokuza, why don't you come, too? To Yuigahama's party, I mean."

"Hrrm? Oh, but I am a man driven. My internal deadlines hound my heels, and it is crunch time even now, but...even so, 'twould be rude to refuse such an invitation. Very well, I shall accompany you."

"Damn... I wanna smack this guy..." *I have no idea why he puts on that self-important persona. As usual, he talks big, but it's all hollow.*

Even Yukinoshita seethed with a hint of murderousness in her eyes. "He's far and away more insufferable than I had imagined..."

"W-well, hey, the more the merrier, right?" said Yuigahama.

"No need to force yourself," I told her.

Yuigahama made the best cover-up smile she could. "Ah... ah-ha-ha-ha-ha-ha! Oh, there's Sai-chan!"

"Wh-what?! Did you say Totsuka?! H-hey, Yuigahama...the more the merrier, right? *Right?!*"

"Huh? Y-yeah, but... Wait, where are you going?!"

I barely heard Yuigahama's question as I dashed away as fast as a certain combat butler, quick enough to set a personal record.

"He sure ran off in a hurry...," commented Yukinoshita.

"Totsukaaa!" I cried out. "T-today is Yuigahama's birthday, a-and we're having a little party, s-so...d-do you...want to c-c-c-come too?!" As my cry echoed in my ears, I somehow sensed that Zaimokuza was wailing behind me.

"Uh. Hannngh? He wasn't doing that with me at all, was he?! Hey, hey, he's acting different now!"

X X X

The train station at twilight was hustling and bustling with people and cars. The five of us made our way through the throng.

"Sorry, Totsuka," I apologized. "I feel like I dragged you into this."

"Oh, no, it's okay. I was just thinking about going over to give Yuigahama a present. And I'm really glad you invited me, you know?"

Totsuka was so cute, I cried delicious tears. *Sob, sob, sob.* "I'm so happy that Totsuka is coming t—ah! No, no, Totsuka is adorable, but he's a guy. Stay calm; don't be led astray, Hachiman Hikigaya! Stay calm, like a Buddhist monk. Don't give in to temptation. Breathe in, out...in...out... Focus and still your spirit... The way of the Buddha has no need of women... The way of the Buddha has no need of women... Wait, Totsuka's a guy, so that won't work! Asceticism is useless!"

"What kind of nonsense are you muttering to yourself? Here, we're at the karaoke parlor." By the time Yukinoshita's icy admonition had pulled me back to reality, we had arrived at our destination.

Karaoke is one of the foremost pastimes of the high schooler. I mean, there has always been an unbreakable connection between students and music. Choir recitals, for instance. Actually, why do normies get into fights during practice for those? One girl goes like, *The boys aren't even trying to sing properly!* and bursts into tears, and everyone in the class rushes after her. It's a familiar youthful cliché. But in reality, behind the scenes, they're saying stuff like:

"Anyway, why is A-ko crying all of a sudden? It's hilarious.*"*

"I dunno, it's less funny and more, like, annoying."

"I know, right?! She totally wants to be in charge!"

"But, like...isn't she taking a long time to come back? Should we go get her?"

"Oh man, is this like that thing where everyone goes? Oh my god, we're totally living out our youth, aren't we?"

...That sort of exchange. Gosh, those celebrations of youth sure are magnificent, aren't they? Wonderful!

When the automatic doors parted and we entered the karaoke parlor, a cacophonous deluge washed over us.

"Oh! Bro!" Komachi, who had arrived ahead of us, leaped up from the sofa when she spotted our group and rushed over.

"Oh, Komachi. You got here first, huh?" I said.

"Heya, Komachi," Yuigahama greeted.

"Hello, hello! Thanks so much for inviting me today," Komachi replied.

"I'm glad you're here. Thanks for coming!" said Yuigahama.

"Oh, don't thank me! When I heard it was your birthday, Yui, I just had to come."

While the pair exchanged pleasantries, Yuigahama let out an affectionate sigh. "Aww... You're so sweet, Komachi... It'd sure be fun to have a little sister like you. I wish you could be my sister... Wait. I—I didn't mean..."

"Y-you jerk! H-how can you say that?!" I demanded. "Komachi is *my* little sister, and mine alone! I won't give her to anyone!" I'd never, *ever* give her to anyone.

Yuigahama sighed again, differently from before. "There it is. Hikki's sister complex... Agh..."

"I apologize for my brother..."

"Don't worry about it. It's not your fault, Komachi..."

Ngh, now I'm starting to suspect I did something wrong. I have to retreat for now. "Anyway, we haven't checked in yet, right? I'm gonna go do that." When I started for the counter, I heard voices pipe up behind me, but the background music drowned it out.

"I-I'll come, too," said Yuigahama.

"Hrrm, then I shall join you. Because there is nowhere I belong!" announced Zaimokuza.

"...What a sad reason for a third wheel to butt in..."

X X X

Good, good, good. They've got a weirdo tagging along, too, but it looks like Yui is doing her best, and in Komachi terms, that's a relief.

When my brother headed toward the front counter with the others in tow, Yukino came to talk to me. "Thank you for your help the other day, Komachi."

"It was no big deal," I replied. "You asked me to, after all... My brother's always causing you trouble, so I don't mind helping you whenever to make up for it." Well, in Komachi terms, the "help" I was talking about was a different kind of help. *Tee-hee.*

"What are you talking about?"

As always, Totsuka was too cute for words... *He just looks so fascinated, and...ah! Bad Komachi. No.* "Oh, nothing much. Yukino, my brother, and I recently went to buy Yui presents together."

"Oh, really? That sounds like fun. I'd like to go out with you guys, too."

"Yeah! ...I get the feeling my brother would rather go out with just you, though...ahh! My brother is starting down a strange path... I'm worried..." This was a fairly serious concern of mine. At home, when my brother talked about school, it was mostly about Totsuka. It was so bad he'd practically scheduled a *Totsuka Today* segment into the regular broadcast schedule.

"I don't quite know what you're talking about, but it seems you are in a difficult situation as well," said Yukinoshita. "I sympathize..."

"Now that it's come to this, everything hinges on you and Yui..." Yukino is the queen of aloofness, but in Komachi terms, I have high hopes for her, you know?

"Me and Yuigahama? ...What could be hinging on us? I'm not terribly confident in my ability to deliver corporal punishment."

"I'm sorry. I mean without violence."

"I see. Inflicting mental and emotional distress *is* my forte."

"Th-the way you said that with a grin is making me uncomfortable..."

X X X

The clerk at the front counter rang us up. "The reservation is for Miss Yuigahama, is that right? You're in booth 208. The microphone and touchpad are in the room. When you're out of time, we'll call you on the booth phone."

"Okay! Thank you very much." Yuigahama took the tray with the receipt.

While she occupied herself with that, Zaimokuza spoke to me. "Hey, Hachiman."

"Hmm? What?" I asked.

"Was that her ladyship, your most honored younger sister?"

"Yeah..." I had a bad feeling about this...

"...I see. By the way, Elder Brother, what might your most honored younger sister's name be? And her age and hobbies, in detail?"

"No way am I telling you. And if you call me 'Elder Brother' again, I'm gonna punch you."

"Hrrm. How cold, Dear Sib."

"You're not allowed to call me that, either!"

X X X

We had finally assembled in the karaoke booth after getting beverages from the drink bar. Each of us held our glasses in hand.

In a thoughtful gesture for the rest of us who couldn't manage to start this thing, Totsuka raised his glass high. "Um...a-all right, then. Happy birthday, Yuigahama."

We all toasted along with him, clinking our glasses. "Happy birthday," said Yukinoshita.

"Happy birthday!" added Komachi.

"May you enjoy a felicitous new year."

"Uh, Zaimokuza, while that is a form of congratulations, you don't say it on someone's birthday," I said.

After everyone had offered their congratulatory greeting, the birthday girl raised her hands and replied, "Thank you so much, guys! O-okay, I'm blowing out the candles, now!" *Fwooo!*

"Yaaay!"

"Wooo!"

After Yuigahama blew out the candles, we had another toast, and for some reason or another clapped. Very birthday-ish.

Then, a brief silence...

"..."

"Huh?! Wh-why's everyone gone quiet?!" Yuigahama said, startled.

"This is kinda awkward somehow, like...we got too excited at a wake or something..." Komachi seemed uneasy.

Yukinoshita and I, however, dealt with the silence calmly. "It's not that," she said. "I'm just unaccustomed to this sort of thing."

"I don't know what people do at birthday parties and after parties and stuff, so I'm lost," I added.

"I agree most profoundly," said Zaimokuza. "Although I am never invited to after parties."

"Me neither, ever since I went that one time," I announced with an utter lack of concern, as if this were incredibly ordinary.

For some reason, this made Zaimokuza burst into noisy, victorious laughter. "Mwa-ha-ha-ha-ha-ha! That is nothing! Is being invited once not enough? What a trifling reason to tout yourself as a loner...*laughable!*"

"What did you say?! It sounds like I have to explain this to you, because you don't understand. I was only invited because the entire class was obligated to participate, all right? You haven't even been to one party, so there's still a possibility you could enjoy yourself at one. I'm one step ahead of you."

"Wh-what?! Ngh, I should have expected nothing less of a pro loner."

"What a tasteless dispute... I'm invited every time, but I've never once accepted. May I propose that I'm the winner here?"

"Erk!" I flinched. "You're so miserably competitive." I don't know what the condition for victory was in that conversation, but Yukinoshita counted herself the winner, apparently.

Sensing we were spoiling the mood, Totsuka interjected, "Come on, this is a birthday party. Let's talk about fun stuff, okay? Right, Yuigahama?"

"Huh? Oh, I'm having a lot of fun, though," Yuigahama asserted. "Nobody's ever thrown me a birthday party before, so I'm pretty happy…" I think she genuinely was. The peaceful smile on her face was exuding joy more and more.

"That's surprising. I thought you were *jooshy polly yey* 365 days a year," I said.

"What's with the random English? I don't get it. …Wait, *is* that English?" asked Yuigahama.

"I'm not sure… Didn't Miura and her crowd throw you a party out of pity, at least?" I asked.

Yuigahama adopted a thoughtful pose for a bit. "Hmm. It's not like I never had the opportunity to do something like that. It was just, like, I was always the celebrater rather than the celebratee, and I was usually the one organizing everything, like serving everyone and stuff, and before I knew it, it was over…"

"Oh… Well…sorry, I guess," I apologized reflexively. *What a sad story.*

Yuigahama awkwardly looked down. "Oh…yeah. It…doesn't really bother me."

"…"

Both of us fell silent.

Komachi broke in with a strained smile. "…And now it feels like we're at a wake again… I can't take this! Let's just drink some cola, Yui!"

"Oh, o-okay!"

"Woo!" Komachi and Yuigahama clinked their glasses to cheer things up.

While they busied themselves with that, I sighed.

"…Haaah."

I really am no good with these kinds of social functions. Part of it is because I don't get invited to after parties or class parties and stuff, so

I'm unaccustomed to them. But I also simply have doubts about parties in general. Everything strikes me as an act where everyone raises their voices in unison and pours so much effort into being festive. I bet if all those normies were to stop screaming, they wouldn't be able to take the ensuing anxiety. If they shut up for a minute, they might realize they're dull human beings. And thus, they force themselves to chitchat, move the conversations along, and stage a theatrical show of merriment. It's a display to ward off threats, puffing themselves up to look bigger.

"Haah..."

"Hachiman? What's wrong? You're sighing." Totsuka peered at my face.

"Oh, yeah. It's just, this...like...birthday party? At the end of the day, I don't know what to do."

"U-um...eat food, say cheers, do party tricks, and stuff? And...cut the special cake together?"

"That sounds like a wedding..."

"Ah-ha-ha, you're right. But it's a celebration, all the same, so... Shall we...cut the cake?"

"We'll be just like newlyweds, Saika." Without meaning to, I gave him a pointed stare.

"H-Hachiman...y-you're playing dirty... You can't just suddenly... call me by my first name..."

"Stop! Okay, that's enough! *I'll* cut it." Yuigahama interposed herself between us, bringing me to my senses.

"...Ah! That was close!" I said. "The mental image of Totsuka in a wedding dress flitted through my mind for a moment there. How strange. I mean, Totsuka is a guy."

"...Uh, that really is strange. And, uh...gross." Yuigahama was super weirded out.

I gave her a soft smile. "Yeah, it's strange. But it's not gross. Totsuka's a guy, so he should wear a tux!"

"You've already decided to marry him?!"

Right then, something banged violently against the wall.

"Whoa, that scared me!" I said. "See, you're being so loud, you made the neighbors angry."

"Oh, sorry. That's weird. It's supposed to be soundproof. Well, whatever," Yuigahama muttered, reaching for the knife we'd borrowed from the karaoke parlor's kitchen. "O-okay, I'm cutting the cake. H-Hikki, will you hold the plate down? U-um, I don't mean anything by, like, how we're doing it together..." The latter half of her sentence disappeared into mumbles, and I couldn't make it out at all. *Are you me when the hairstylist asks what I want, or what? Enunciate. Come on.*

"Hey, today's your birthday, so why don't you sit back and relax? Totsuka and I will cut it. It's okay."

"H-huh? I-I'd feel bad for Sai-chan, though..."

"You're not gonna feel bad for me? Then...Komachi."

"Huh?" said Komachi. "If I cut it at this point, it'd be like...low Komachi points. At home when we're alone together would be fine, though, *blush, blush*. Oh, and that just now scored major Komachi points."

"...You're so obnoxious. Zaimokuza, then." I attempted to ask him.

"...Uhhhhh." Yuigahama's expression said, *No way.*

"Hey, that look kinda makes me feel sorry for him," I gently protested, out of pity.

Beside me, Zaimokuza clenched his chest and began groaning. "Hrrngh! The sealed door within me opens! Yes, it was back when I was but a lad completing my military training at a regular elementary school. Mayhap it was a strange twist of fate...but when I volunteered to hand out rations, a single Valkyrie, in tears, refused the curry I served her..."

"See? You stirred up old trauma, and now his character's messed up...," I said.

"Oh, i-it's not like I don't want him to do it. It's just, like...you know...I want him to go wash his hands or something," muttered Yuigahama.

"Heblagh!" It looked like that was the finishing strike for Zaimokuza.

Yukinoshita watched them both with irritation, huffed a short sigh, and took the knife in her hand. "Hmph... I'll take care of the cake. I'm excellent at cutting."

"Yeah, I bet you are. Like cutting people off or making cutting remarks."

"And you're good at being cut off," she retorted.

"Why'd you put that in the passive voice? And that's because, you know...I'm Buddhist. My goal is to become a Buddha through severing ties with the physical realm. I'm way up there, from a Buddhist perspective."

"There you go again with your feeble knowledge of Buddhism... Buddhism is, in essence, a religion that attaches little importance to the indirect ties of *pratyaya* that you describe. Gautama Buddha, in fact, advocated the existence of *pratyaya* in the form of *hetu-pratyaya*."

"...Here she comes, the great Yukipedia."

"What is that questionable nickname? Well, whatever. More important, I'm cutting the cake, so hold the plate," she said.

"Okay." As ordered, I gently pressed the plate down.

Yuigahama, in a panic, tried to stop us. "H-hey! Hold it! I'm gonna do it after all! I-I can't let you guys cut the cake together..." I couldn't hear most of the latter half of that. *Are you like, you know, me when a police officer stops me on my bicycle and checks for a criminal record? Articulate. Come on.*

I guess Yukinoshita heard her, though, as she regarded Yuigahama with some curiosity. She didn't comment on whatever it was, though. "Oh? Okay, go ahead."

"Huh? Yay! Yeah, yeah! I'll do it! I'll do it!"

"Hold the plate good and still, Yuigahama," Yukinoshita said.

"You and me?! U-ugh... My feelings are so complicated now."

X X X

Yukinoshita swiftly inserted the knife into the cake.

"Those are some damn even sixths," I remarked.

"Not really. It's not so difficult." Yukinoshita stood with poise before a cake divided into perfect, precise slices.

But Yuigahama, who was watching, reacted with some surprise. "Whoa, it's true! Are you blood type A, Yukinon?" she asked.

"What are you basing that on?"

"Well, I mean, you're so methodical."

"She's not methodical," I said. "She's more like a neat freak or a perfectionist or something."

"What nonsense... How is there any relation between blood type and personality?" Yukinoshita, who apparently was not fond of blood-type personality theory, was producing her characteristic chill.

Totsuka neutralized it with his warm, balmy voice. "Oh, I'm type A, though. I *am* often picky about details."

"Oh? You'd make a good bride, Totsuka," I said.

"D-don't tease me, Hachiman..." Totsuka blushed a hot red.

Beside him, Yukinoshita turned her frigid energy toward me. "Not that I care, but my impression is that you're treating him very differently from me."

What extreme temperature fluctuations. Does this booth have a desert climate?

The one who ruined the atmosphere was, of course, a professional at such tasks: Zaimokuza. "Hrrm. But blood-type personality theory may not necessarily be untrue. 'Tis a popular belief that AB types have dual personalities, and I find that to be peculiarly fitting. I feel that I, too, could suddenly awaken to my other identity at any time...ngh! Not now! Calm thyself, my right hand!"

"If you're going to play those games of yours, could you do it outside? Anyway, what type are you, Yuigahama?" asked Yukinoshita.

"Me? I'm type O," Yuigahama replied.

Komachi clapped her hands in agreement. "Offhand O, huh?"

"What the heck. So is type A *aff*hand?" I asked.

"Oh dear...," said Yukinoshita. "If Yuigahama is type O, blood-type personality theory is starting to sound more believable."

"Huh? Hey! Am I really that careless?" Yuigahama asked.

"Yui, it's okay! I'm type O, too," said Komachi.

"What's so okay about that...?" I inquired.

"Huh? I can...give her blood if something happens?" Komachi replied.

Inundated in a wave of offhand, careless remarks, Yukinoshita shuddered. "How accurate... This is becoming more and more plausible..."

"So what type are you, Yukino?" Komachi asked. "You've got to be type A, right?"

Yukinoshita replied readily. "Type B."

"Oh. Well, I believe in blood-type personality theory now," I said.

"Are you trying to suggest something?" she asked.

"Oh, I mean, you're totally my-way-or-the-highway, or, like, selfish, or maybe I'd call it arrogant. Basically, I think it's on the mark."

"If that's your reasoning, then you must be type B, too."

"My brother is type A, though." The moment Komachi said it, everyone froze.

"What?" Yukinoshita gawked in disbelief.

"Huh?!" exclaimed Yui.

"Hey, your combined shock is striking me as kinda mean, guys," I said.

"Pffshhht!" Zaimokuza sputtered. "H-Hachiman, you're t-t-type A?! No, no, 'tis preposterous! An irresponsible, unpunctual, uncooperative loner like you, type A?! No matter how you look at it, you are nothing like a farmer. Thank you very much."

"Damn it… I wanna punch you…" I restrained my right fist from connecting with Zaimokuza's jaw as it so desperately wanted to.

A little dismayed, Totsuka commented, "S-sorry, Hachiman… I think…I'm sorta surprised, too."

"T-Totsuka…" Tears unwittingly sprang to my eyes.

"Oh, b-but I'll give you blood if anything bad happens to you!"

"T-Totsuka!" A cry of joy unwittingly sprang from my mouth.

Apparently, I wasn't the only jubilant occupant of the room, as happiness played across Yukinoshita's face, too. "What a relief. It's thanks to you that I can again discount all blood-type personality theory."

"Hey," I protested. "You can't say something like that with such a sweet smile on your face. That hurts!"

"Oh, I'm sorry. There is the possibility a complicated family situation led to them lying about your blood type. Perhaps my comment was indeed thoughtless. I apologize."

Yukinoshita had a belligerent way of asking forgiveness.

"You can't say something like that in front of my real sister. I don't know what I'd do if I found out we're not actually blood related." I keep myself in check because we're close kin, but if we weren't, I'd be showering her with loads of love, seriously.

Yuigahama must have sensed that, as she had clearly lost patience and snapped at me. "That's sister-complex level! Or maybe you're just a pervert!"

"Well, in Komachi terms," Komachi butted in, "if we weren't related, it would be okay, though. Oh, I bet that scores high Komachi points."

"In societal term, it's scoring low points!" cried Yuigahama. "You're kinda weird, too! You guys really are brother and sister!"

"Well, my brother and I have different blood types, but we have fairly similar personalities. I guess it's nurture after all."

"Yeah, yeah," I said. "Like how we both like celery, and we're both demanding." Plus, we hate summer and are willing to compromise.

"How do you raise a person to become *that*...?" asked Yukinoshita. "I'd like to meet your parents sometime..."

"Please do, please do!" Komachi said, cheerful as could be. "Our parents would be moved to tears if they were introduced to you."

Yukinoshita responded with utter bafflement. "Hmm? And why would that be?"

"Huh? Why? Because that'd mean my brother..."

"Hikigaya?"

"...Uhh, nothing... That's so weird. I thought I triggered that flag." Komachi mumbled something unintelligible.

Yuigahama cleared her throat, drowning out Komachi. "Ahem. I-I'd kinda like to meet them. Ah-ha. Or not."

Komachi's eyes promptly sparkled. "Please, please *do* come over to our place, Yui. It's a done deal, it's a done deal! ♪"

"S-sure!"

Those two sure get along well. But they had neglected one crucial fact. "Give it up. We have a cat. You don't like cats, do you?"

"O-oh dear! Th-that's right!" Yuigahama melodramatically yielded.

Totsuka's reaction to the word *cat*, however, was a far cry from hers. "Oh, your family's cat is so cute, Hachiman!"

"You think?" I replied. "He's cheeky, he smacks the floor with his tail when you call his name, and when you see him at his water dish in the middle of the night, he could seriously pass for some kind of demon.

Also, when I come home he goes crazy huffing my stinky feet." *No, actually, that's the way cats act toward people they don't care about. Well, I have to admit it's still cute, though.*

Totsuka was apparently a cat person, and he disputed my assessment of kitty flaws. "Huh? That's adorable! Yeah… I'd like to pet him again sometime. Could I…come to…your house?"

"S-sure…sometime soon. When my parents aren't home."

"Ngh? Why only then?"

I shouldn't have to explain that, Zaimokuza.

My heart all a-flutter over Totsuka's charm, from the corner of my eye, I saw Yukinoshita fidgeting.

"H-Hikigaya… U-um…I would…also…"

"Huh?" I replied. I hadn't quite heard her.

But Yukinoshita shook me off.

"N-never mind. More importantly, the cake's divided, so let's eat."

"Ah. Oh yeah. Komachi, get me a fork."

"Okeydoke!"

Accepting the fork from Komachi, I thought I heard a soft little murmur, accompanied by a sigh.

"…Haah…cats."

X X X

Yuigahama forked some cake into her mouth and, after a few seconds, released a sigh of appreciation. "Mmm! Your homemade cake is so good, Yukinon!"

"Oh? I'm glad you enjoy it."

"It really is yummy!" agreed Komachi. "You'll have no trouble getting married! Right, Bro—"

Abruptly, another vehement thump sounded from the neighboring room.

"Eep!"

"Not again… Our neighbors are a little rowdy." Fed up, I glanced at the wall.

But Totsuka smiled a crooked smile and shrugged his shoulders. "Yeah. But karaoke always gets loud… Oh, is there peach in this?"

"There is," replied Yukinoshita. "Since they're coming into season."

Yukinoshita's cake really did taste quite fancy, with all those fresh peaches in it. I savored the delicious dessert with relish.

Suddenly, Zaimokuza commented, "Did you know, Hachiman, that in ancient China, peaches were prized as the secret to eternal youth? A truly auspicious fruit, indeed."

"Wow. That's some great trivia, but why am I the only one you're sharing this with? Not that I have no sympathy."

"You're so good at baking, Yukinon," Komachi gushed, impressed.

Yukinoshita, however, reacted with neither pride nor modesty. She was simply composed. "It's nothing impressive. You cook at home, don't you, Komachi?"

"Yeah. Both our parents work, so I do the cooking. Oh, but my brother used to do it."

Yuigahama leaped to her feet in an exaggerated gesture of surprise. "Whaaat?! He did?!"

"Yeah, 'cause knives and the stove and stuff were too dangerous for her until she was ten or so," I said. "Which means I can take pride in my ability to cook better than almost any sixth grader."

"What a dubious claim to fame…," Yukinoshita said, unsure how to react.

It wasn't, though. It was a perfectly respectable reason to be proud. "And I can do pretty much all house chores at a sixth-grade level. I'm ready to be married off as a househusband whenever! No way am I ever entering the workforce! Get a job and you lose!" I declared loudly.

Yukinoshita softly pressed her temple as if her head ached. "There he goes again, spouting nonsense with a rotten look in his eyes…"

"Huh… So you can cook, too, Hikki," said Yuigahama. "I've gotta get good, too… I still haven't been able to give him proper cookies…"

"Oh, all this talk about cooking reminds me." Yukinoshita rummaged around in her bag, withdrew something, and handed it to Yuigahama.

"Huh? Wh-what is this?" wondered Yuigahama.

"It's your birthday present. I don't know if it will suit your taste, though."

"Oh," I said. "The thing you found after going through all those idiotic magazines that make no sense and you would usually never read."

Yukinoshita shot me with a glare. *Yikes.* "You may keep your mouth shut."

"Yukinon… For me? Thank you. Can I open it?"

"Y-yes, go right ahead." Yukinoshita was a little shy.

Yuigahama flashed her an especially bright smile and unwrapped the gift. "An apron… U-um, thank you! I'll take good care of it!"

When Yukinoshita saw Yuigahama's sincere delight, she looked somehow relieved. "Personally, I'd be happier if you used it rather than delicately hanging it up as a decoration."

"Yeah! I'll use it with love!"

"I'll give you mine then, too." Totsuka, after watching their exchange, also rummaged through his bag. "Here. You always have your hair up, right, Yuigahama? So I bought you a hair clip."

"Thank you, Sai-chan! Actually, this is so cute. Your tastes are even girlier than mine…"

"And I'll give you this." Komachi had also gotten her something and pulled a carefully wrapped present out of her bag. "Here. It's a picture frame."

"Thank you, too, Komachi-chan!"

"I actually really wanted to give you a photo along with it, but all the photos at home just have those rotten eyes… He must have some appeal that doesn't show up in photos."

"Oh, so he's got that rotten look even in pictures, huh…? Hey, but it's not like I wanted one, anyway!" Yuigahama said, but she looked happy.

Zaimokuza, who had been thus far only watching the presentation of gifts, abruptly ruffled his hair. "Hrrm. Alas, alack. As I was invited so uncharacteristically suddenly, I came unprepared."

Indeed, it had been out of the blue. In fact, it would have been cause for concern if he *had* gotten her a present.

Apparently of similar sentiment, Yuigahama gave him a casual smile and a warm reply. "Hey, don't worry about it at all, okay?"

"And thus! I present you with an autographed copy of my brand-new manuscript!"

"Don't worry about it at all, okay..." Though her statement was almost exactly the same, its temperature had dropped to absolute zero.

"Duh-heh. What a rejection, hrrnk. Now that it has come to this, I shall bestow upon you a mix CD of my top one hundred anime songs."

The moment I heard that, I automatically grabbed Zaimokuza by the shoulders and stopped him.

"Don't do it, Zaimokuza. Anything but that."

"Ngh, wh-why? 'Tis unlike you to so tearfully stop me from doing something." He looked at me with bewilderment.

"I suppose I have no choice," I said. "I'll tell you. This is about a friend of a friend of mine, though..."

"Th-this kinda sounds familiar..."

Despite Yuigahama's discomfort, I began. "In middle school, he had a crush on a girl. She was in the school band, a cute girl who liked music. On her birthday, he screwed up his courage to give her a present. He had stayed up all night putting together a collection of his recommended anime songs for this girl, since she loved music. He had meticulously culled the best songs and even had the forethought to leave out anything too overtly romantic or *otaku*-ish."

"Hrrm. A spirit I can respect," said Zaimokuza.

"I can see where this is going, though...," commented Yukinoshita.

The next event was the crux of my tale. "She accepted the gift, and he was so happy, he cried. But the following day, tragedy struck. It happened during lunchtime, the period when one of the members of the broadcast committee would play tasteful music from the school-wide speakers. 'Okay,' she announced. 'The next song is a request from Hachiman *Ota*-gaya in Class 2-C! *Snrk.* It's a love song for Yamashita!'"

"That's enough! No more, Hachimaaan!" Zaimokuza latched onto me and clung tight in an effort to cut the story short.

"Ngh!" My tears spilled onto Zaimokuza's chest.

Yuigahama averted her gaze, avoiding the whole scene. "So it was about you after all."

"Jerk! It wasn't about me! It was Otagaya!" I protested, but not a single person believed me.

Yukinoshita in particular sported an expression that surpassed pity and approached fear. "I underestimated you, Hikigaya… To think you're even more wretched than I imagined…"

"Even after my brother graduated, people passed down stories of Otagaya," said Komachi. "Pretending it was some guy I'd never heard of was rough…"

"You're a legend, huh, Hachiman…?" commented Totsuka.

The somewhat gentle tenor of their remarks mingled with my sobs to create an even more miserable picture.

× × ×

"Well, thank you, guys! Really! This might have been my happiest birthday ever," Yuigahama said as she surveyed her mountain of presents.

Yukinoshita shrugged her shoulders. "That's an overstatement."

"No, it's true! I really am glad. I've always been happy with just the party my parents threw me, but…this year has been superspecial… Thank you, Yukinon."

"…I—I just did the obvious," Yukinoshita averted her gaze, as usual, and Yuigahama grinned broadly at her.

Indeed. Perhaps it was a good birthday. "But man," I said. "You sure seem close with your folks. For my birthday last year, my parents gave me ten thousand yen cash, and that was it. Plus, some of it was supposed to pay for a cake."

"Hrrm. 'Twas about the same for me," said Zaimokuza. "The most I receive aside from a cash present is takeout from KFC."

"Huh… R-really?" asked Totsuka. "My parents get me a cake and leave presents by my pillow for me to find the next morning."

"I think there's some other holiday tradition mixed in, there," I said. *I understand the desire to throw a birthday party for Totsuka, though. Good job, Mom, Dad.*

And then there's my family... Right as the thought reached my mind, Komachi ran her damn mouth. "But, like, my brother's the only one who gets treated like that, you know. On my birthday, we go buy presents together, go out to eat, and buy a cake on the way back."

"It sounds like your parents just don't love Hikigaya...," Yukinoshita remarked.

"What?! Don't be stupid!" I protested. "They superlove me! I'd sure be in trouble if they didn't, since I plan for them to support me for the next twenty years!"

"What an asshole son...," Yuigahama insulted, and I think she meant it. It sort of stung.

With a strained smile, Komachi attempted to smooth things over. "Well, our parents tend not to give a damn about a lot of things..."

"Our parents give so few damns, it's too much even for me," I added.

"Impressive..." Yukinoshita looked rather seriously disturbed, but it was nothing like that.

"They're the kind of people who would name me Hachiman because I was born on August eighth," I explained.

"They really *don't* give a damn!" cried Yuigahama.

I know, right? I think so, too.

However, Yukinoshita apparently disagreed. "Isn't that a fairly typical rationale for naming a child? It was about the same with me. My name was chosen just because it was snowing when I was born."

Oh my, so I'm not the only one. But I thought the name Yukino combined nicely with the surname Yukinoshita, so I didn't say anything.

Komachi seemed to have a similar opinion. "*Yukino* is a pretty name, though."

"Thank you," replied Yukinoshita. "I don't hate it, you know. In fact, I like it. And I think *Komachi* is a beautiful name that suits you well."

"Y-Yukino..."

"Hey. Stop that, Yukinoshita. Don't seduce someone else's *petite soeur*. The Virgin Mary is watching you." They might as well have had white lilies blooming in the background.

The one who ruined the mood was, of course, good old Zaimokuza. "Guh-heh. So all of you were named by your parents, huh?"

"What, and you weren't?" I asked.

Immediately, Zaimokuza pitched forward eagerly. "My name was handed down to me from the distant past… If I must name a godfather, then…yes, I suppose his name would be *fate*…"

"Uh-huh." *I really don't give a damn.*

"Hrrm. By the way, the kanji says *fate*, but the ruby reads *Grampa*."

"Why didn't you just say 'Grampa' in the first place…?"

But right as I thought I might die from how little I cared, Totsuka supplied a tidbit that I did indeed give a damn about. A juicy tidbit, so to speak.

"Ah-ha-ha, my name might be the most normal, then. My parents just wanted me to live a life full of color."

"It's like that old saying," I said. "'The name oft reflects the nature.' You sure add color to my life, Totsuka." I did my best to look cool.

"Geez, don't tease me like that!" he protested. "I'm gonna get mad, you know?"

I wish he would… My expression immediately shifted to a blissful smile.

Totsuka turned to Yuigahama as if he'd just thought of something. "Hey, so why were you named Yui, Yuigahama?"

"Huh? Me? Hmm…I've never asked," she said.

"It's your birthday, after all," said Yukinoshita, "so why don't you ask once you're home? It seems your parents love you very much, so I'm sure they have a wonderful story to tell you. And if you don't mind, you could share it with me sometime."

"Yukinon…"

"Watch out, Yukinoshita," I said. "This time, Buddha's watching you, too."

Now, I could see some mandala-like thing floating behind them. *That's not very romantic.*

"But man," said Yuigahama, "Hikki and Yukinon and Sai-chan and Snowflake, all of you have meaningful names…ah!"

"What is it?" I asked.

Gloom was clouding Yuighama's face. "W-well… I just noticed, but, like… I-I'm the only one who doesn't have a nickname."

"Uh, you forced those nicknames on us, though," I said. "I'm not happy at all about the one you gave me."

Yukinoshita chimed in. "I tried to make you stop, too, but you wouldn't drop it, so I capitulated…"

"Hrrm," added Zaimokuza. "I, too, am somewhat offended by the epithet 'Special Snowflake…'"

Complaint after complaint after complaint.

Yuigahama, however, was unmoved. "Huh? Why? I thought they were good nicknames…"

Totsuka attempted to mollify her. "Oh, I—I don't mind my nickname, though. I think the nickname 'Hikki' is cute and nice, too."

"I know, right? Right?!" Yuigahama cheered up.

"Well, I guess it's not as bad as the monikers I've had in the past," I said.

"In the past? So you've had others before?" Yukinoshita asked.

"Yup," I replied. "Time for *Top Three Things My Classmates Called Me That I Hated!*"

"This sounds random and depressing." Yuigahama seemed rather nonplussed by my announcement.

Komachi, on the other hand, was totally gung-ho. "And I'm his assistant, Komachi! Presenting number three!" She seized the role of announcer.

"Number three," I began the list.

"Da-dum!" Zaimokuza provided a drum roll, and I paused for effect.

"…*Hikigaya-in-first-year's older brother.*"

For a moment, Yukinoshita looked depressed. "It's quite an experience to hear that from your own classmates… It's denying your entire existence, isn't it…?"

"It's not my brother's fault!" Komachi protested. "I attract a little more attention than he does, and so tragedy struck!"

I held back my tears and declared the next one. "Number two."

"Da-dum!" Zaimokuza's drum roll reverberated through the room, and silence followed.

"That one over there."

"Hrrm. I, too, have had such an experience. They tend to employ demonstratives like *that* or *it*. Well, it can be an awesome and terrifying thing to have a name such as mine pass your lips, so I don't blame them!" Before I knew it, Zaimokuza had launched into his commentary.

Of course, Komachi again assumed the role of announcer. "And finally, the shocking number one!"

"N-number one...," I declared.

"Da-dum!"

Zaimokuza again thumped for dramatic effect.

"Gulp."

With a collective sound from their throats, everyone waited for me to continue.

"I—I don't want to say..." I really, *really* didn't want to say this one. My eyes spontaneously welled with tears.

Totsuka tenderly rubbed my back. "So it was that bad... H-Hachiman, you don't have to force yourself, okay?"

"Thanks, Totsuka..." A sob threatened to escape my throat.

"If this is just digging up trauma for you, you never should have brought it up in the first place...," Yuigahama quipped mercilessly.

"You shuddup! You just have this bizarre obsession with nicknames, so I wanted to shatter your illusions!"

"I think you're a unique case, Hikigaya...," quipped Yukinoshita.

I think this kind of thing is fairly ubiquitous, though. Seriously, nicknames are bad news.

Whether or not Komachi knew my feelings on the matter, she made a suggestion. "Well then, why don't we do this?" she said. "Let's all come up with a nice nickname for Yui."

"You're a good girl, Komachi!" said Yuigahama. "Okay, so starting now, you're Macchi."

"Whoa, Yui," replied Komachi. "You have *no* taste."

"Huh? No way... I thought that one was great."

Heedless of Yuigahama's mild shock, Totsuka pored over the matter. "Hmm...a nickname, huh? Yuihoho?"

"Oh, 'cause she's a ho, right?" I said. "I like how you think, Totsuka. Why not call her a plain ho, though?"

"Stop calling me a ho! Rejected!"

"Hmm, maybe it'd be worth a lot of Komachi points if I called you Big Sis?" Komachi suggested.

"Hey!" replied Yuigahama. "Manipulation is not allowed! Way too embarrassing! Rejected!"

"Ma-hmm…," Zaimokuza considered. "The Black Byakko."

"Uh, a nickname is not the same thing as a pen name," I said. "…And you do know Byakko is white, right? Pick a color!"

"Rejected! Obviously!" declared Yuigahama.

We were all vetoed one after another—Totsuka (or actually, me, I guess), Komachi, and then Zaimokuza. Then, Yukinoshita, who had been biding her time, took the stage. "Well…what about Yuinon?"

"Huh? It sounds weird…" Yuigahama instantly shot her down.

Yukinoshita's eyebrow twitched. "That's rich, considering your own choice of nicknames… In that case, why don't you simply create one yourself?" she said.

Yuigahama contemplated for a moment. "It's awkward to come up with a nickname for yourself…"

"You may not have noticed, but you're already awkward…," I said.

"Shut up! And, like, I'm not awkward at all. I'm supernormal."

Yukinoshita nodded vigorously. "Yes, you're exceedingly normal. Perfectly unexceptional."

"That's kind of a hurtful way to put it!" Yuigahama protested.

"Coming from Yukinoshita, that's a rare compliment," I said.

"She thinks that's a compliment?!"

"In her eyes, *not* calling you 'garbage' or 'scum' is high praise. Just think up a nickname, already."

"Hmm… But I can't just create one out of the blue…oh!" Yuigahama had a flash of insight.

Totsuka turned an expectant gaze toward her. "Did you think of something?"

"Yeah… I'm Yui Yuigahama, so…Y-Yuiyui, I guess?"

"Pft!" I broke into snickers. *Come on, for real? That's as embarrassing as you can get.*

"H-hey! Why are you laughing?" Yuigahama snapped at me.

Yukinoshita eyed the other girl with concern. "Giving yourself such an embarrassing nickname… Are you a masochist? If you have any issues, you can talk to me…"

"She's sincerely worried about me!" exclaimed Yuigahama, in shock.

Totsuka and Komachi, on the other hand, seemed to think her choice was passable. "I think it works, though," said Totsuka. "Don't you think it's cute?"

"Yeah, it's really Yui-ish," Komachi agreed.

That seemed to restore Yuigahama's confidence. "Y-yeah! I'm not awkward at all!"

"Oh, I think it's kinda weird to be saying that about yourself, though," I remarked.

"Now he's looking away with this little smile!" Yuigahama held her head in her hands and moaned.

Then, an unexpected party brought reinforcements. "Hrrm," said Zaimokuza. "'Tis true that at times, you get used to it the more you say it. I was uncomfortable with the title of Master Swordsman when first I inherited it, but after three days, the conviction that I was indeed such a man had grown within me."

"Well said, Snowflake!" replied Yuigahama. "But we're nothing alike."

"Hrrk, LOL." After tossing Yuigahama a rope, Zaimokuza was the one to drown.

Yuigahama turned back to Yukinoshita. "So, Yukinon, would you give it a go?"

"No way." Yukinoshita shut her down so firmly even Komachi flinched.

"Ack… No hesitation," Komachi commented.

Yuigahama leaned my way, looking chagrined. "Nghh… Th-then… w-will you try calling me that?"

"Wha…what? I don't wanna call you that fancy fairy-tale nickname." To be precise, it was too mortifying to say.

After I expressed my reluctance, Yuigahama met my eyes for a fleeting instant and immediately looked away. "Th-then…just Yui…would be okay." Perhaps Yuigahama found the nickname uncomfortable, too, as her fingers curled into the hem of her skirt, and she avoided eye contact, a faint blush on her cheeks.

"Hmm. Our definition of a nickname has loosened," commented Zaimokuza.

"Mr. Snowflake, they're having a moment," said Komachi, "so please be quiet."

"Y-yes'm!"

For a brief moment, tranquil stillness engulfed that silent room.

"Come on, Hikki..." Yuigahama's moist eyes slowly lifted, contemplating me earnestly.

"Y... Yu... Agh... If I have to give you a nickname, then...you know...can't I just get rid of the useless part and call you Gahama or something?"

"You'd go that far to avoid saying 'Yui'?!" Yuigahama was in shock.

"You're a loser, Bro...," scoffed Komachi.

Come on. I mean, it's embarrassing...

Regardless, we couldn't settle on a nickname, so Club Captain Yukinoshita brought the discussion to a close. "All right... Can we just call Yuigahama by her name?" she said.

"Whatever. Good enough...," muttered Yuigahama.

X X X

Totsuka clasped his glass between his hands and slurped noisily from his straw. "Ah. My drink is empty."

"Hmm? Oh, I'll go get more, then." I gently took his glass and my own, while I was at it, and stood.

Realizing my intention, Totsuka grinned and gave me his order. "Thanks. I'll have a coffee!"

"Roger. Anyone else want something?" I asked, scanning the others.

Yukinoshita quickly raised her cup. "Black tea, Hikigaya."

"Okay."

"I'll have cola, then!" added Komachi.

"All right. What about you, Gahama?" I asked Gahama next.

But her back was turned, and she made no move to reply. "...Hmph."

"Gahama?" I asked again.

"Urgh! ...Hmph!" This time, Gahama only glowered my way for an instant.

At a loss, I scratched my head. *Oh well. I suppose I have no choice but to call her* that. "Agh... Do you want something to drink...Yuiyui?"

"Oh, sorry. Let's not do that nickname after all..." Yuiyui pressed her hands together in a pleading gesture.

"Tell me whatever you want. What'll you have, Yuiyui?"

"Stop that, I said! Just give me what Komachi is having!"

"Okies. So is cola okay, Yui?"

"You're so stubbo—huh?" Yuigahama blinked at me.

Well, um, like. That was a verbal typo.

And last was Zaimokuza. "What do you want to drink, Zaimokuza? Curry?"

"Are you treating me like the fat character? I shall go with Ultra Divine Water."

"Cider. Got it."

"You understood that, huh...? You and Mr. Snowflake sure are close," remarked Komachi.

With all the orders in mind, I opened the door and left the room.

X X X

"Um...coffee, black tea, cola...and curry, right?" As I refilled the beverages at the drink bar, I heard music and voices belting at top volume. The source appeared to be the booth next to ours. "Whoa, the neighbors sure are partying it up. Well, I don't want them partying so hard they bang on the walls, though... Maybe I should go tell them to tone it down."

I've never regretted any reckless action more than the one I took at that moment. If I had never witnessed the harrowing scene that ensued, I've no doubts I would have been able to return home in peaceful bliss that day. But I never could have foreseen the tragedy I would discover...

I approached the neighboring room and rapped lightly on the door. But the music seemed to be drowning out the quiet knocks. "Hmm?

Can they not hear me? Well, I'll try peeking in." I gingerly turned the doorknob and peered in through the open sliver. "Ohh…is that… Miss…Hiratsuka? Yeah, she's by herself, so it's definitely her."

Miss Hiratsuka is almost always alone, so it was her for sure. She was clutching a mike and staring at the screen in an enervated stupor. "Heh… Love songs are nothing but fraud, deceit, and lies. I don't feel like singing… And to make matters worse, the people in the next room sound like they're having a blast, like they got married or something… You normies can go die in a fire…"

The moment I heard her voice, I panicked and closed the door, but I couldn't hold back the sobs that escaped. "Ngh…ghk… M-Miss Hiratsuka… Seriously, someone marry this woman already… Oh crap, she's coming." As she stirred beyond the door, I rushed back toward the drinks and assumed my best nonchalant facade.

Fatigued, Miss Hiratsuka approached the drink bar. "Agh… I'm thirsty… Hmm? Hikigaya? I'm surprised to see you here."

"H-Hello, Miss Hiratsuka. Wh-why are *you* here?" I asked.

She momentarily panicked, but she immediately adopted her usual comportment. "Me? I… W-well, I'm, uh, letting off stress. You're…oh, I see. Yuigahama's birthday party. Are you having fun?"

"Yeah, I guess."

A soft smile abruptly touched Miss Hiratsuka's lips. "…I see. Ah, pardon me. I'm going to have a smoke." After that comment, she pulled a cigarette out of her breast pocket, held it in her mouth, and lit it. The puff of smoke meandered around near the ceiling. "Maybe you've changed a little, lately. Before, you never would have come to something like a birthday party. But whatever brought you here, as your teacher, I'm glad to see these signs of growth."

"Miss Hiratsuka…"

"But despite that, Hikigaya, this is you we're talking about. You probably feel this kind of life is deceitful and fake. For now, that's fine. Those profound doubts of yours are proof that you deeply consider life, and it's good to do that. Things don't have to come to you right away… I hope that one day, you'll arrive at your own answers."

So Miss Hiratsuka sees me for who I am, huh? She doesn't reject the way I am now or affirm it. She's just trying to see me through the process. When I realized that, my heart warmed very slightly. "Miss Hiratsuka… since you're here, will you come say hi to everyone?"

"Hmm? I'm flattered by the invitation, but…earlier I told Yuigahama I was going to a party… If by any chance you kids find out I was kicked out of the matchmaking party… No, I'll pass. I'd feel bad for crashing your party."

"You wouldn't be crashing it. At the very least, we can clap along while you sing songs that none of us know because of the generation gap!"

Even though I was trying to be considerate, for some reason Miss Hiratsuka's hand slowly began to form a fist. "Hikigaya, clench your teeth… Shocking First Bullet!"

X X X

"They have a drink bar here, though." I heard Yukinoshita's voice. "I thought for sure those were only at family restaurants."

"Uh, I think most karaoke places have some kind of drink bar." Yuigahama's voice followed.

Komachi chimed in. "Now that you mention it, why did you decide on karaoke, Yui? If you wanted all-you-can-drink, we could just have gone to a family restaurant…"

"Maybe it was because…karaoke has private rooms?" suggested Totsuka.

"Ohh, I gotcha! But since we're here, anyway, I'd like to sing a bit," Komachi said in a subtle invitation.

I guess Yuigahama noticed, as she jumped on the idea. "Yeah! You know, I was getting the impression here that no one wanted to sing, so I just avoided it without thinking about it."

"The way you live seems exhausting, as always, Yuigahama…," said Yukinoshita. "You don't have to abstain from what you want. Besides, isn't it your birthday today? You're allowed to be a little self-interested."

"Yukinon… Oh, th-then…"

I heard snippets of their conversation through the door before I gave it a light *rap, rap*. "Heeey, open up!"

"Bro, you're back."

"I'll get the door, okay, Hachiman?" Totsuka trotted up and opened it for me.

"Thanks, Totsuka."

Maybe it was the slight sadness tinging my voice, but Totsuka peered up at me with worry. "H-Hachiman? What's wrong? Did something made you sad?"

"Oh, it's nothing. Nothing at all. No depressing sights whatsoever…" Indeed, nothing had happened. There had been no miserable single teacher… The punch had wiped out my memory of it. If it hadn't, I would have been a little upset.

When I set down the tray of glasses, I saw an offended Zaimokuza. "Hachiman! You took too long! Don't leave me all by my lonesome! I instinctively started playing games on my phone!"

"Cram it. In a situation like this, a loner avoids looks of pity by running all the errands."

"Whoa, what a horrible skill you've leveled up!" Komachi sure chose a weird thing to be impressed by.

My idea must have made sense to Zaimokuza, since he eventually slapped his knee after a bit of whining. "Nghhh. Next time, you are permitted to invite me when you go get drinks! I shall allow it!"

"No need to be so passive-aggressive. Here, Yukinoshita, your tea." I handed her the cup.

Yukinoshita accepted it without complaint and continued the conversation with Yuigahama. "Thank you. So, Yuigahama, what did you want to do?"

"Oh yeah. Yukinon, let's sing together. It's embarrassing by myself."

"Absolutely not." Once again, Yukinoshita immediately refused.

"Huh?! But just now, you said you'd do anything I asked!"

"No, I didn't."

"Give it up," I said. "You'll have to throw in the towel, Yuigahama. Yukinoshita just doesn't have confidence in her singing. Read between the lines here."

"Really?" Yuigahama asked, puzzled.

Yukinoshita puffed out her chest, softly put her hand over her heart, and struck a rather haughty pose. "Heh. I can't have you looking down your nose at me. Be it violin, piano, or Electone, music is something of a hobby of mine."

"Is there a point to doing both piano and Electone...?" Anyway, I suppose she was trying to convey that she was musically accomplished.

"I have no particular objections to singing," said Yukinoshita. "I only lack confidence in my ability to sing an entire song all the way through."

"That's a pretty hard-core lack of stamina, there...," I said. *Can you even stay alive like that?*

Yuigahama gave Yukinoshita's sleeve a few light tugs. "Yukinon, Yukinon. If we sing together, you'll expend half the energy, you know?"

"Under what mathematical system? Well, if you insist, I'll do just one song with you," Yukinoshita agreed.

"Yay!" Yuigahama bounced.

Komachi handed them the touchpad. "Okay, then maybe I'll sing one after you guys. What about you, Totsuka?"

While Yuigahama and Yukinoshita examined the selection of songs, Totsuka gently pointed at one of them. "Hmm...I'd like to sing this one..."

"That singer is a lady, though," said Komachi.

"Oh, I see... I wonder if I'll be able to sing it..." Totsuka looked a little discouraged.

"Oh, I don't think that'll be a problem...," Komachi replied. "If you're unsure, I'll help you out, 'kay?"

He beamed at her. "Really? Thanks. I was kinda embarrassed to do it alone."

"Urk... I—I...I get why he makes you lose your mind now, Bro."

Yup, yup, now you understand, too. Also, I haven't lost my mind.

"Hrrm. It seems everyone is pairing up to sing." For some reason, Zaimokuza was inching toward me.

"Huh? Hey, hey, hold on a second. Don't you think something funny's happening here? I thought our boy-girl ratio was even. Who even decided I have to pair up with Zaimokuza?!" I demanded, but nobody heeded me.

"Heh, my anime songs folder has been waiting for this day. So should we begin our assault with the late nineties?"

"Hey, I won't deny I like that stuff, too, but I don't wanna sing with you!"

"Hey, hey, it's too late to say that now," said Zaimokuza. "I don't wish to be the solo bard, either. I think it would make everyone feel awkward."

"So you do have some self-awareness...," I replied. "Forget it. Let's just sit quietly in the corner and pat our knees to the beat..."

"No! I can resist no longer! We shall sing! And when I do, raise your ultra orange glow sticks, please."

"Who cares about the color of the glow sticks?!" Besides, our turn would clearly be the downer piece of the evening, so something that obnoxiously bright wasn't even an option.

Meanwhile, the other pairs were steadily making their plans. "Ah, okay, then Yukinon and I will sing this one," said Yuigahama.

"Ah, I'm not familiar with that song, though. Hey, are you listening?"

Apparently, Yuigahama was not, as she immediately input the song. "Hmm...now, where's the Confirm button...?" she muttered.

"Right here, right here," chirped Komachi.

Beep-beep-beep, trilled the machine.

"Oh, ohhhh~! Dividing Driver!" Zaimokuza crooned. "Hrrm. It seems my throat is in good condition." He practiced his enunciation of *Ga-ga-ga!* in earnest.

"C-come on, hold on a minute, please! At least make it with Totsuka. Let me sing with Totsuka!" I protested.

An unfeeling synthetic voice interrupted Zaimokuza's vocal warm-ups. *"The song is about to begin."*

Yukinoshita let out a short sigh. "Aghh... Good grief."

"Yukinon, come on, come on! It's starting!"

"Yuigahama, the mike, please."

"Whoa, you're actually really into this!"

When I come to a birthday party, I don't really fit in. When I get a nickname, it just rubs salt in old wounds. And when I do karaoke, I end up in a duet with another guy... As I expected...my youth romantic comedy is wrong...

X X X

The automatic doors slid apart, and Yuigahama stepped outside, stretching. "Hnnng! What a great session! It's been so long since I last did karaoke. That was so fun. Let's come again sometime, Yukinon!"

"If I come with you, I imagine I'd be compelled to sing several songs in a row. I'd really rather not. I can't believe you forced me to sing five whole songs after that...," Yukinoshita said as she exited after Yuigahama, totally fed up.

"Huh?! But you were so good! Let's go again!" Yuigahama pleaded.

"Oh, me too, me too! I want to go, too!" Komachi leaped up to Yukinoshita's other side.

Trapped between the two girls, Yukinoshita flushed a little. "...Well, I don't mind coming with you on occasion."

"Yeah, thanks," said Yuigahama. "And thanks for today, too. I was so happy to have tons of different people come to my birthday party..."

"I'm not the one you should be thanking," replied Yukinoshita. "He's the one who gathered everyone together."

"Y-yeah... H-Hikki..."

I exited the karaoke parlor after the girls, and Yuigahama spun around to face me.

"What?" I asked.

"Um, thanks for... Huh?"

She started to speak, but then she glanced suspiciously at something behind me. Following her line of sight, I discovered a figure standing just behind the automatic doors. After a mechanical whirr, a single woman emerged. "Agh... I spent all that time by myself. Well, if I go home, I'll still be alone, anyway... Heh-heh," she chuckled scornfully.

Yuigahama spoke up, puzzled. "Miss Hiratsuka? Weren't you at a party?"

"Y-Yuigahama?! Y-you guys are still here?!" Miss Hiratsuka panicked as her eyes lit on each member of our group.

At the word *party*, I suddenly remembered something and blurted without thinking, "A party? Wait, do you mean like a marriage match-making party…?"

"…Did it not go well?" Yukinoshita asked, a note of pity coloring her voice.

Yuigahama attempted to comfort the teacher. "M-Miss Hiratsuka? You know, um…marriage isn't everything! You have your career, and you're strong, so I'm sure you'll be fine single. So cheer up, please!"

But the moment Miss Hiratsuka heard, tears welled up in her eyes. "W-waaaaaaaah! Someone told me the exact same thing once…," she mumbled. It was so heartbreaking, our spirits fell simply from hearing it. She promptly dashed off at top speed.

"Ah. She ran away," I said.

The Doppler effect distorted Miss Hiratsuka's cry as the distance widened between us, her lament reverberating through the night covering the city. "Agh… I want to get married…"

Twin Blades Cross: Metempsychosis of the Inverted World

P. iv **"...Shogun Ashikaga's line."** The Ashikaga family ruled Japan during the Muromachi period (1336–1573). Japan was ruled by a shogun and had a military government, and it was the era of the samurai.

P. iv **Yoshiteru Ashikaga** was the thirteenth shogun of the Ashikaga shogunate and ruled from 1546 to 1565.

P. iv **"You M-2 syndrome types really like your nullification powers."** M-2 syndrome refers to *chuunibyou*, literally, "second-year-of-middle-school disease," characterized by delusional behavior often exhibited by middle schoolers.

P. v **"Bright 'Swordian Master' Woodstock."** Zaimokuza is playing with the characters of his name. *Yoshiteru* contains the character for "shine/bright," and *Zaimokuza* has the characters for "tree/wood" and "forest."

Chapter 1 ... This is how **Shizuka Hiratsuka** kicks off a new competition.

P. 1 **"...Benkei Musashibou had his lord."** Benkei Musashibou (1155–1189) was a famous warrior monk. The story goes that he positioned himself on a bridge in Kyoto and disarmed every passing swordsman, eventually collecting 999 swords from his victories. The one thousandth swordsman to cross his path was Minamoto no Yoshitsune, who defeated him and accepted Benkei as his vassal. Eventually, Benkei would die protecting his lord.

P. 2 **"...a *suite pretty cure* for my morning hunger."** *Suite Pretty Cure* is the eighth series in the Pretty Cure franchise, a massively popular magical-girl series. While it's explicitly marketed to little girls, it also has a strong adult male *otaku* fanbase—the bronies of Japan, if you will.

P. 2 **"...one of those fake English words Japanese people made up!"** Komachi is referring to *wasei eigo*, Japanese words that sound like they came from English but were actually coined in Japanese.

P. 2 **Great Gitayuu** is the stage name for comedian/musician Masayuki Suzuki.

P. 2 **"...a basketball anime set in the near future would be dubbed *Baskish*."** Hikigaya is referring to the 2009 sci-fi sports anime *Basquash!* in which characters play basketball while riding mecha.

P. 6 **"...thanks to my class skill *Obfuscation*..."** The skill *Obfuscation*, or *Presence Concealment* in certain translations, is a skill of the Assassin class in the Fate media franchise.

P. 7 **"...But if AIC comes and recruits me by mistake, I'll be a good boy and make another *Tenchi Muyo!* OVA."** AIC, or Anime International Company, is the animation studio that did the *Tenchi Muyo!* OVAs.

P. 9 **"Hachiman Hikigaya withdraws coolly."** A reference to the character Speedwagon in the long-running manga *JoJo's Bizarre Adventure* by Hirohiko Araki. He often says out loud, "Speedwagon withdraws coolly."

P. 9 **"How cool am I, you ask? Enough to record everything I see with a cassette player."** This is a reference to the manga *Cool: Rental Bodyguard* by Takeshi Konomi. The main character, whose name is Cool, is always recording himself talking.

P. 13 **"It always ended with Komachi summoning my dad and draining my life points to zero."** Hikigaya is referencing the *Yu-Gi-Oh!* collectible card game.

P. 13 **Oda Nobunaga** was the most infamous warlord of Japanese history, known for his ruthlessness and brutality. He is famous for unifying Japan and ending the Sengoku (Warring States) period in the late sixteenth century.

P. 14 **"Like that thing you use to get the Masayuki Map."** The Masayuki Map is an item in *Dragon Quest IX* that you can get only through StreetPass functionality.

P. 15 **"All who come to him are refused, and all who leave him are free to go."** Hachiman is playing with the Japanese saying "All who come are welcome, all who leave are free to go."

P. 15 **"It's not time to give up just yet!"** This is from *Slam Dunk*, a basketball manga by Takehiko Inoue, published in *Weekly Shonen Jump* in the 1990s. This particular line has become something of an Internet meme among Japanese audiences.

P. 15 **"...Yukinoshita and I would have a Robattle Fight! (not that *Robopon* thing)..."** In Volume 1, Miss Hiratsuka referenced the battles of the anime *Medabots*, a relatively obscure series. *Robopon* is short for *Robot Ponkottsu*, a series of games from the Nintendo 64 and Game Boy Advance generation about capturing wild robots and having them fight each other. The gameplay style was highly derivative of the Pokémon franchise.

P. 16 **"You don't even see that movie on *Friday Roadshow* anymore."** *Friday Roadshow* is a movie programming show that's been on the air since 1985.

P. 16 **"...*Roadshow* does *Laputa* every year..."** *Laputa: Castle in the Sky* (1986) is a famous Studio Ghibli movie directed by Hayao Miyazaki.

P. 16 **"Do *Earthsea*, man—*Earthsea*."** *Tales from Earthsea* (2006) is a lesser-known Ghibli movie directed by Hayao Miyazaki's son, Goro Miyazaki, loosely based off Ursula K. Le Guin's Earthsea novels.

P. 16 **"Basically, it's like the Kaguya arc in *Yaiba*."** *Yaiba*, also known as *Legend of the Swordmaster Yaiba*, is a *shonen* manga series by Gosho Aoyama that began running in 1988. It's a lighthearted series about an adventuring samurai.

P. 18 **"You have so many orders for us. Is this all just leading up to us being eaten by a wildcat?"** Hikigaya is referring to the children's book by Kenji Miyazawa called *The Restaurant of Many Orders*. The story involves two men who come to a restaurant and are progressively asked to do more and more things, such as take off their belts and wash their faces, and finally, at the end, they find out that they are doing all of this so that *they* can be dinner for a wildcat. They are saved in the end, however.

P. 18 **"Who the hell does Miss Hiratsuka think she is, Princess Kaguya?"** In the legend of Kaguya-hime, Kaguya is a princess from the heavens raised by a woodcutter. She has many suitors, and she drives them away by giving them ridiculous, unreasonable demands to carry out if they want to marry her. In the end, her true family takes her back to heaven.

Chapter 2 ... **Saika Totsuka**'s youth romantic comedy is right, as I expected.

P. 22 **"Okay, I'll buy a hundred of his CDs! Then, once I get the ticket for a handshake, I'll sell them somewhere."** Hachiman is talking about the business model of the girl group AKB48. Special tickets for meet-and-greets are put into randomly selected hard-copy CDs. Hard-core fans will buy hundreds of CDs in order to get these tickets.

P. 24 **"...the park near Saize..."** *Saize* is short for Saizeriya, a cheap and ubiquitous Japanized-Italian food chain.

P. 25 **"...in a game of Shanghai and try to conquer the Great Wall of China..."** Shanghai is a game of solitaire played using mah-jongg pieces. "Conquering the Great Wall" is a reference to a video game called *Shanghai: The Great Wall*, where beating each stage allows you to conquer a part of the Great Wall of China.

P. 25 **"In a dilemma reminiscent of *Dotch Cooking Show*..."** *Dotch Cooking Show* (aired 1997–2005) was a cooking show akin to *Iron Chef*. It featured two competing cooks, and judges would try dishes prepared by both and pick out which they liked best.

P. 26 **"My perennial favorite, *Magic Academy*..."** Quiz Magic Academy is a series of arcade quiz games that test your *otaku* trivia knowledge. There is also a spinoff anime.

P. 28 **"Nay. He is an Arcanabro."** Arcana Heart is a series of 2D fighting games. All the playable characters are cute girls.

P. 30 **Koshien** is the stadium in Nishinomiya, Hyogo, that hosts the Japanese High School Baseball Championship.

P. 31 ***Purikura*** is short for "print club." They are photo booths equipped with various filters to make your skin whiter, eyes larger, legs longer, and add all sorts of digital effects before the photos are printed.

P. 31 **"...the area is only for girls and couples."** It is quite common for *purikura* sections of arcades to allow only girls and couples in. The rationale is generally that this rule prevents sexual harassment. Often girls will dress up or do cosplay, which can attract unwanted attention from the awkward male *otaku* like Zaimokuza, who frequently visit arcades. It's generally perceived and marketed as a girly hobby, so any guy who tries to get in alone is assumed to want to get in for creepy reasons rather than legitimately wanting to take photos.

P. 32 **"...*a world unknown to you.*"** *Anata no shiranai sekai* (*A World Unknown to You*) is a variety show that features viewer stories about supernatural experiences, ghost sightings, and stories about ESP and related phenomena.

P. 32 **"*Oh, so Tien Shinhan isn't the only one who can use Solar Flare.*"** The character Tien Shinhan in Akira Toriyama's *Dragon Ball* manga has an ability called Solar Flare, which causes an incredibly bright flash of light. Later, Goku learns it, too.

P. 34 **"Actually, I'm really more of a *Ribbon* kind of guy."** *Best Friends* (*Nakayoshi*) is the name of a *shoujo* manga magazine, and *Ribbon* (*Ribon*) is another *shoujo* manga magazine.

P. 35 **"Kodocha is particularly superb."** *Kodocha*, short for *Kodomo no Omocha* (*Child's Toy*) is a manga by Miho Obana about a child actress that ran in *Ribon* from 1994 to 1998. There is also an anime adaptation that diverges significantly from its source.

Chapter 3 ... Yukino Yukinoshita really does love cats.

P. 41 **"...like some kind of Super Saiyan bargain sale."** This line is a quote from Vegeta in Volume 36 of *Dragon Ball*, when he sees that his son, Trunks, has easily awakened to his powers as a Super Saiyan. It has since turned into something of an Internet meme among Japanese fans.

P. 41 **"*Kobo* was amazing today."** *Kobo-chan*, or *Kobo, the Li'l Rascal* in the English edition, is a comedy/slice-of-life manga by Masashi Ueda that began running in the *Yomiuri Shimbun* newspaper in 1982.

P. 41 **"U-Ra-Ra! Wait, that's Beetlebomb."** This is a reference to the characteristic roar of the character Beetlebomb (also known as Geronimo in the original Japanese) in Yudetamago's comedy manga *Ultimate Muscle*, or *Kinnikuman*.

P. 43 **"If a girl hits on you, she really just wants to make you buy paintings."** This is a kind of scam that is rumored to be common in Japan. A woman will approach a meek-looking man and invite him to come with her to a free gallery. When they arrive there, she pressures him to buy a painting for thousands or tens of thousands of dollars, and if he says he doesn't have the money, she tries to make him take out a loan and capitalize on his inability to say no.

P. 43 **"...like I was Masuo talking to his mother-in-law."** Masuo and Fune are characters from the long-running newspaper manga *Sazae-san* by Machiko Hasegawa that began in 1946. The anime adaptation of *Sazae-san* is the longest-running animated series in the world. Masuo is the titular character's husband, and Fune is Sazae's mother. Masuo and Fune's relationship is rather awkward.

P. 44 **Makuhari Messe** is a large convention center in Chiba and a site popular for big music shows, most notably the Tokyo Game Show.

P. 44 **Tokyo Big Sight** is a massive convention center in Tokyo, the site for large-scale events such as Comiket.

P. 46 **"...the Shinjuku subway station. And Umeda Station."** Shinjuku Station is a major train station in downtown Tokyo. It's the biggest transport hub in the world and extremely easy to get lost in. Umeda Station is the central train station in downtown Osaka. Like many Japanese train stations, it is combined with a vast underground and aboveground shopping center and has dozens of different exits in every direction.

P. 53 ***Jaja Uma Grooming Up*** by Masami Yuuki (more famous in the West for the *Patlabor* series) is a manga about horse racing that ran from 1994 to 2000. The main character lives on a ranch belonging to the Watarai family. A *jaja uma* means both a stubborn horse and a tomboy or unmanageable woman.

P. 53 **"Does Tsunayoshi have a hand in this, too?"** Tsunayoshi Tokugawa, the fifth shogun of the Edo period, was famous for being fond of animals, particularly dogs.

Chapter 4 ... **Komachi Hikigaya** is shrewdly scheming.

P. 60 ***World Great TV***, or *Sekai Marumie! Terebi Tokusoubu*, is a documentary/variety show that began running in 1990. The show is infamous for turning everything into a cliffhanger that will be revealed after the commercial break.

P. 64 **Lisa Lisa** is a character from Hirohiko Araki's manga *JoJo's Bizarre Adventure*. She is a master of the Ripple, a form of supernatural martial arts.

P. 68 **Rinko** is one of the girls in the Love Plus series of dating sims. She's a quiet loner and a member of the library committee.

P. 73 **"I don't think Yuigahama is looking for any bonus to defense in her clothes."** The plain clothes are typically the starting equipment in classic Dragon Quest games.

P. 74 **Puppet Muppet** is a comedian whose bit involves using a puppet on each hand (a cow and a frog), and a bag over his head to hide his face.

P. 74 **"*Oh man, this makes me want to laugh like* Ka-ka-ka-ka!"** The titular character of the cooking manga *Iron Wok Jan* by Shinji Saijo has this particular unique laugh.

P. 76 **"...a big 4D pocket in the middle."** In the children's anime *Doraemon,* the titular character has a large pocket on his tummy that has an infinite number of gadgets tucked away inside it. He calls it his 4D pocket.

P. 78 **Medal games** are ubiquitous at Japanese arcades. They are a sort of simulated gambling, since there are no casinos in Japan (gambling is illegal). You buy medals to play the game, and the game pays out in more medals. Unlike pachinko parlors, which are generally run by yakuza and will illicitly exchange your payout prizes for cash, arcades make an effort to appear clean and family oriented, so the majority will not award you cash, only cheap toys.

P. 79 **"I started wondering if I'd eaten some of Doraemon's weird translation jelly."** In the children's anime *Doraemon*, one of Doraemon's special items is called a *honyaku konnyaku*, or "translation jelly" in English. When eaten, it lets you understand any language. *Konnyaku* is a savory jellylike substance made from the bulb of the konjac plant. It tastes quite bland and has almost no calories.

P. 83 **"I *would* read a certain magical index, though."** Hikigaya is referring to the light-novel series *A Certain Magical Index* by Kazuma Kamachi. In this series, Index is a girl, not a book.

P. 86 **"Look, Chii is learning."** "Chii is learning" became an Internet meme due to how often the robot girl says that line in the CLAMP manga and anime series *Chobits*. It's something you say whenever you learn something new, especially new words.

P. 89 **"A fortified armor shell…or, no, maybe a mobile suit."** A "fortified armor shell" is the name of the mecha suit from the manga *Apocalypse Zero* by Takayuki Yamaguchi. It's small and fits the human body—about the size of an Iron Man suit. A mobile suit from the Gundam franchise is far larger—giant-robot sized.

P. 90 **"The Three Non-Connection Principles of the Foreveralone are carved into my soul…"** This is playing with the Three Non-Nuclear Principles of Japan: "Japan shall neither possess nor manufacture nuclear weapons, nor shall it permit their introduction into Japanese territory."

Chapter 5 … Despite it all, **Yoshiteru Zaimokuza** wails alone in the wasteland.

P. 96 **"I worried I might have honed that skill a little too well and unlocked my Stand power."** Stands are the superpowers in Hirohiko Araki's long-running manga *JoJo's Bizarre Adventure*. Particularly, in the third and most popular arc, *Stardust Crusaders*, the protagonist, Jotaro, has a Stand with the power to stop time. The main *JoJo* villain, Dio Brando, shares the same ability in this arc.

P. 99 ***"Is this the Hyperbolic Time Chamber?"*** The Hyperbolic Time Chamber is a special training room in Akira Toriyama's *Dragon Ball*, where time is slowed, gravity is stronger, and the air is denser.

P. 101 **"*Wahhhh!* Hachiemoooon!"** Zaimokuza is imitating Nobita, the protagonist of the children's anime *Doraemon*. Nobita often whines to his friend Doraemon, looking for help.

P. 101 **"Right, Gian?"** Gian is the bully character in *Doraemon*. He's often quite mean to Nobita.

P. 101 **"I can settle for 'Ninja Hachitori.'"** Zaimokuza is referencing another kids' anime, *Ninja Hattori-kun*.

P. 105 **"In your visage, I could see a quiver like a bow string's pulse."** Zaimokuza is referencing a line from the theme song of the Studio Ghibli film *Princess Mononoke*.

P. 107 **"What, are you Misawa?"** Jigoku no Misawa (Misawa from Hell) is a comedy manga artist whose humor tends to involve narcissistic and self-involved people saying annoying things.

P. 112 **"...perhaps a reflection of his sharp mind and sharp ideas."** Hachiman is quoting the Sharp Electronics slogan: *From sharp minds come sharp ideas.*

P. 112 **"...inspiring the next generation."** *Inspire the next* is Hitachi Electronics' slogan.

P. 113 **"...the regulars like the Guiltybros..."** Referring to the fighting game series Guilty Gear.

P. 118 **"Ha-ha-ha-ha! It's time to d-d-d-duel! Monster card!"** In the Japanese, Zaimokuza says, "It's always my turn!" This is a line spoken by Seto Kaiba in Kazuki Takahashi's *Yu-Gi-Oh!* manga, which has become an Internet meme among Japanese fans. This meme is referenced when a player pulls out a continuous series of moves in a game while often unfairly overpowered, not giving his or her opponent a chance to strike.

P. 119 **"I had tons of Miracle of the Zone...cards..."** *Daikaijuu Monogatari: Miracle of the Zone* (Giant Beast Story: Miracle of the Zone) is another collectable card game. There was also a GameBoy version at one point.

P. 135 **"The End of Genesis, T.M.R.evolution Type-D!"** The End of Genesis, T.M.R.evolution Type-D was the name of T.M.Revolution and Daisuke Asakura's one-time pop duo. Technically, it was Revolution Turbo Type-D. They likely changed this to avoid stepping on trademarks.

P. 137 **"In other words, since the opposite of opposition is approval..."** Hachiman is playing with a quote from Bakabon's father in the gag manga *Tensai Bakabon* (*Genius Bakabon*) by Fujio Akatsuka. He's always saying things like "The opposite of approval is disapproval" or "The opposite of approval! An approval of opposition!" It's all slightly nonsensical and generally just means "Whatever, that's fine."

P. 137 **"Zaimokuza doesn't have a Zetsuei, and I'm no Shell Bullet."** References to the 2001 *shonen* anime *S-CRY-ed*. Shell Bullet is the alias of the main character. Zetsuei is the name of his rival's Alter power.

P. 138 **"Are you the computer grandma or what...?"** "Computer Obaachan" ("Computer Grandma") is an NHK children's song from the 1980s. It's basically a song about how Computer Grandma can do anything and everything. It's part of a TV program called *Minna no Uta* (*Our Songs*) where they play children's songs with short animated videos repeatedly in between children's shows. Generally, the same songs will continue for months, so they're highly memorable.

P. 138 **"*Are you an Alter user?*"** In *S-CRY-ed*, Kanami, a young girl who lives with Kazuma, is also an Alter user with the power to read minds.

P. 140 **"Sagami's ejaculation of surprise resembled something out of Mitsuteru Yokoyama's *Romance of the Three Kingdoms*."** This particular manga is infamous for having a lot of distinctive shocked reaction faces.

P. 141 **"Whether or not your dreams come true is up to luck, as is victory and defeat. Source: *Tottemo! Luckyman*."** *Tottemo! Luckyman* is a superhero/comedy manga by Hiroshi Gamou about a boy who shares a body with an alien named Luckyman. When there is need, the boy transforms into Luckyman to defend the earth from invaders with the power of luck.

Bonus Track! "Like, This Sort of Birthday Song."

P. 155 **"As a wise man once said, never forget what it was to be new."** A quote from the Muromachi-era actor and playwright, Zeami Motokiyo. The quote is a caution to never forget the earnest feelings and humility of a beginner; the original context concerned Noh theater.

P. 157 ***Rurouni Kenshin*** is a manga from the 1990s by Nobuhiro Watsuki about a wandering swordsman, set in the Meiji period. The titular character, Kenshin, practices the Hiten Mitsurugi school of kendo. His technique is focused on Iai, the art of drawing a blade quickly from the sheath. One of the precepts of his school is that you should always be on guard and ready for a follow-up strike.

P. 160 ***"Come on, do you have heaven's memo pad or something?"*** A series of light novels, titled *Heaven's Memo Pad*, by Hikaru Sugii that also has an anime adaptation. It's a detective story that focuses on solving mysteries with limited resources via smarts and deduction.

P. 161 A ***yamato nadeshiko*** is the traditional ideal woman. She should always be quiet, be reserved, and walk three steps behind her husband. *Yamato* is an old word for ethnically Japanese people, and a *nadeshiko* is a flower generally called a "fringed pink" in English. In modern times, it's considered an old-fashioned ideal.

P. 168 **"...I dashed away as fast as a certain combat butler..."** This refers to the manga by Kenjiro Hata, *Hayate the Combat Butler*, which began in

2004. The main character, the "combat butler," is named Hayate, which means "wind." So in running as fast as him, Hachiman is running as fast as…the wind.

P. 173 ***Jooshy polly yey*** is a greeting coined by Chiaki Takahashi, a voice actor, singer, and gravure model. Meant to sound like "juicy party yay" and has no particular deep meaning.

P. 176 **"Are you blood type A, Yukinon?"** It's a popular belief in Japan that blood type determines personality. It's a sort of astrology, and almost everyone knows their blood type and the personality traits associated with it. Type A is the farmer: conservative, introverted, perfectionist. Type B is the hunter: creative, free-spirited, unpredictable. Type AB is the humanist: rational, organized, and empathetic. Type O is the warrior: outgoing, social, and a natural leader.

P. 177 **"Calm thyself, my right hand!"** This is most likely a reference to the manga *Parasyte* by Hitoshi Iwaaki, in which the main character has his hand possessed by an alien parasite.

P. 179 **"'Like how we both like celery, and we're both demanding.' Plus, we hate summer and are willing to compromise."** This exchange is a reference to the lyrics of the song "Celery" by the extremely popular, if aging, boy band SMAP. The beginning of the song goes: "We were raised in different environments, so it's inevitable we'd have different tastes / Like hating summer or liking celery / Not to mention that we're a man and a woman, so misunderstandings are bound to happen / We compromise and get demanding."

P. 185 **"They're the kind of people who would name me Hachiman because I was born on August eighth."** The *hachi* in Hachiman means "eight," and the word for "August" in Japanese literally means "eighth month."

P. 185 **"My name was chosen just because it was snowing when I was born."** The *yuki* in Yukino means "snow."

P. 185 **"Don't seduce someone else's *petite soeur*. The Virgin Mary is watching you."** Hachiman is referring to the girls' love light-novel series Maria-sama ga Miteiru (The Virgin Mary Is Watching) by Oyuki Konno, which was also adapted into a manga and anime. The story is set in a Catholic all-girls' school that has a system where an older girl, called the *grande soeur* (older sister), chooses a younger girl as her *petite soeur* (younger sister) to lead and guide her. Of course, it's a loaded relationship. *Yuri* means "white lily" and also girls' love.

P. 186 **"...the kanji says *fate*, but the ruby reads *Grampa*."** Kanji characters convey meaning, but it's difficult to know how to pronounce them unless you already know the word. Often in manga and light novels, especially for younger readers, tiny phonetic characters will be provided above the kanji. Pronunciation guides like this are called "ruby." Sometimes, instead of explaining pronunciation, ruby will be used for artistic effect. When Zaimokuza says "the kanji says *fate*, but the ruby reads *Grampa*," it's as if he is creating a new word that means "fate" but is pronounced "Grampa." Of course, this is something that works only in writing.

P. 186 **"My parents just wanted me to live a life full of color."** *Saika* means "add color."

P. 186 **"This time, Buddha's watching you, too."** Oshaka-sama mo Miteiru (Buddha Is Watching You, Too) is a spinoff novel series of Maria-sama ga Miteiru. Mandalas are a spiritual symbol in Buddhism.

P. 189 **Byakko**, the white tiger, is one of the four symbols of Chinese constellations, along with Seiryuu the dragon, Genbu the turtle, and Suzaku the phoenix.

P. 192 **Ultra Divine Water** is a special drink in *Dragon Ball* that will draw out the full potential of the drinker if they can survive its poisonous effects.

P. 194 **"Shocking First Bullet!"** This is a skill that is a special attack of Kazuma Torisuna, the main character in the *shonen* anime *S-CRY-ed.*

P. 197 **"Oh, ohhhh~! Dividing Driver!"** This is from the opening song of *The King of Braves GaoGaiGar*, a mecha anime from the late 1990s.